Marti

A Novel

Marti
A Novel

TONYA SNOW-COOK

AMETHYST
Publishing

Published by
Amethyst Publishing
info@amethystpublishing.com

LCCN: 2008900507
ISBN-10: 0-615-18803-6
ISBN-13: 978-0-6151-8803-4

For more information about the author and upcoming books, visit:
http://www.tonyasnowcook.com

First Printing January 2008
Printed in the United States of America
Fifth Edition

Contents

Prologue..1

Chapter 1 7

Chapter 2 17

Chapter 3 33

Chapter 4 45

Chapter 5 61

Chapter 6 67

Chapter 7 79

Chapter 8 83

Chapter 9 91

Chapter 10 95

Chapter 11 109

Chapter 12 123

Chapter 13 129

Chapter 14 143

Chapter 15 153

Chapter 16 159

Chapter 17 173

Chapter 18 181

Chapter 19 195

Chapter 20 205

Chapter 21 215

Chapter 22 223

Chapter 23 237

Chapter 24 243

Chapter 25 257

Chapter 26 269

Chapter 27 275

Chapter 28 287

Chapter 29 293

Chapter 30 303

Chapter 31 315

Chapter 32 325

Chapter 33 341

Chapter 34 347

Chapter 35 365

Chapter 36 379

Chapter 37 389

Chapter 38 399

Epilogue...409

Also by Tonya Snow-Cook 413

Prologue

The year was 1982. The month was May. The Johnson Family—George, Linda, Martin, and Donald—were renting a two-bedroom house in Baker, Louisiana, just outside the Baton Rouge city limit. Fourteen-year-old Martin shared a room with his younger brother Donald, who was turning eleven in three weeks; Martin's birthday wasn't until October 21st. He put aside some of his paper route money to get that set of Fleer baseball cards that his little brother had been hinting around for. Linda, their mother, was baking her famous three-layered lemon cake with chocolate icing—Donald's favorite. George, their father, probably wouldn't be around that day since he had been in and out for the past six months trying to keep his contracting business afloat. He'd just lost a contract to build a house in a growing community on the south side of town to a contractor who had under bid him.

These were tough times for anyone trying to wage against a U.S. economy in a post-war recession that would last sixteen months, and things weren't looking much better for Louisiana's state capital.

Besides, Martin thought it might be best that his daddy wouldn't be around. There needn't be anything going on to set George off. That last argument between his parents had alarmed the neighbors. Eight-thirty that night their block was set off by the flashing siren and several neighbors who had begun to collect outside to see what all of the disturbance was about. By the time the altercation had abated, his daddy had been warned to keep his shouting and door slamming to a minimum or face being booked for disturbing the peace.

Money. It was always about money. When they moved out of that apartment complex at the beginning of the year into the house, they thought they had finally moved up, even though they weren't paying a mortgage, just renting. And while it was no deluxe penthouse in the sky that came with a housekeeper and New York skyline, it was still a step up. Martin was especially glad about the move. Finally, they had their own backyard with a privacy fence. He and Donald would go out there and toss the baseball around sometimes, but they had to be careful not to throw the ball into their mama's clothesline or she'd beat them something terrible. She warned them one too many times about dirtying up her clean clothes with that filthy baseball. But, usually, she was pretty cool about stuff, except when it came to money. She and George argued about the bills piling up, how she was tired of getting calls from collectors, or how George was never around to take care of that stuff. He'd argue the fact that he was out there busting his hump trying to run the business and not have to lay off another one of his workers because he couldn't afford the overhead.

This last argument didn't seem to be much different than any of the others. Martin was in the bathroom tending to his afro getting ready for school. He had a thing for Marvella Williams, and somehow the word had circulated that she had a thing for him, too. So what they were doing in the other room was of the least concern to him.

"George, what's going on?"

"For the last time, woman, nothing's going on!"

"I'm surprised you're even here. You only come in for a clean shirt. Your sons don't even get to see you anymore."

"My sons? You talking like they babies."

"Donald's only ten."

"Oh, Linda, please. You know where I am—at the office. It gets so late that it's just easier for me to crash on the couch back in the back."

"Well, I'm the one who has to try to pacify all these bill collectors, telling them that the money's coming when I don't even know if it really is. We can't keep doing this."

"We? I'm the one who's out there working sixteen-hour days and, on top of that, trying to convince the white folks to hire us because we do good work. And you know who they choose—the white builder because they stick with they own. Meanwhile, our own people ain't

3

got no money for no new house, most of us can barely come up with rent because we're the ones affected most by this recession."

"Well, I don't know what you think I do all day, but I sure ain't sitting on my hands watching the sunset. No, I'm cooking and cleaning and washing your dirty shirts and making sure those sons of yours are taken care of."

"Listen, I told you that nothing's the matter. It's just slow right now. Things'll pick up, you'll see."

Martin had gone to school that day ready to woo Marvella. He wore his good plaid shirt and Levi jeans and put on an extra splash of Brut cologne. He had made up in his mind to make his move during lunch while she was goofing around with her girlfriends. He'd just walk up all cool, calm, and collected and ask her out.

"Hey, Marvella."

"Hey, Martin."

Martin rubbed his sweaty palms on the back pockets of his jeans. "I'm going to go see *Rocky III* at the movies this weekend. I was wondering if you'd like to go with me?"

Marvella's friends started giggling and whispering things in each other's ears. "I'd have to ask my mama if it's okay, but yeah, I'd love to go. I hear it's supposed to be real good, as good as the first two, and Mr. T is gonna be in it."

"Cool, how 'bout I pick you up around seven o'clock? My mama will drop us off."

"Okay."

"How 'bout I walk you to your bus this afternoon?"

"Okay then."

"Your locker is 118—" Suddenly, Martin heard his name being paged over the PA system. They wanted him down in the office immediately.

"I better go," he said, rushing off.

When Martin got to the main office, he walked back to the principal's office, where he found his mother crying hysterically. Principal Jacobson walked over and shut the door.

"Son," he said, "we've got some bad news to tell you. It's about your daddy."

"What's going on with daddy, mama?" Martin wanted her to tell him, but she was in no condition to offer up any explanation. He knew that it must be really bad for him to be seeing her this way.

Principal Jacobson, an older black man with a friendly face—all the kids liked him because he was fair—continued. "They found your daddy in his office today, son. He had shot himself. I'm sorry."

Martin could do nothing, but stand there with the soles of his shoes cemented to the floor, his body frozen from bewilderment. He couldn't believe it. That couldn't be right. His daddy wouldn't do something like that. That just couldn't be right.

Some twenty-odd years later nothing had changed, except everything…

Chapter 1

Vowing that he would not spend 2003 fixated on Leslie, the woman with whom he was in love, as he had done the previous year, Marti was filled with great anticipation, yet could hardly shake the nervousness in his stomach as he approached the LSU-Baton Rouge campus on his first day back in graduate school after more than four years. He had only eighteen hours of coursework remaining to complete his Master's degree in Education, a feat he had set out to accomplish four years earlier at LSU-Shreveport until a failing marriage left him unable to stay focused. After the divorce, he simply had no motivation to go back to school. Marti wanted nothing more than to get as far away from his ex-wife Carolyn as possible, and transferring to Baker High School in Baton Rouge, Louisiana, his hometown, to teach seemed ideal.

Earlier that day at work, Leslie tried to reassure him that it would be alright, that it was like riding a bike. Marti remembered thinking that he'd rather be riding a bike than feeling the way he was feeling, anxious and all. "Just remember, it's only six hours," Leslie offered. "It's not the full course load. You can handle this. Besides," she added, "your life is under far less strain and stress now. You can focus more energy on doing this. So just go in there tonight and learn something."

Even after remembering Leslie's pep talk as he sat on the first row waiting for class to begin, Marti still felt a bit of apprehension—that is until she walked into the doorframe. She must have been about twenty-five. Legs. Legs. And more legs. This girl was beyond beautiful. She was stunning, like she'd just stepped off a Caribbean Island and carried the sun's rays in her long, thick, black hair. She stood for a moment to map her seating options. He'd hoped that she'd find her way next to him. Then, it happened—what he had hoped. Her eyes zoomed in on the empty seat next to him. As she drew closer, he could smell her perfume. *Yes*, the voice inside his head whispered as Marti turned his head away to smile then back toward her to speak.

"Hi, I'm Marti…Johnson," he said, extending his hand.

She reached her hand out, smiled, and said, "I'm Sasha Clayborne." She then sat in the empty seat next to him. *My God*, he thought, *even her name is exotic. Sasha. Sasha.* She had to be interesting.

While he learned that she was from Denver, Colorado, during the brief introduction each pupil was asked to make at the beginning of class, they said nothing else to one another the rest of that evening, not even during break time. They merely exchanged smiles as they both rose from their seats at the end of class. And though they had exchanged nothing more than their names, Marti had already determined that Sasha was somebody he had to get to know better. Besides the fact that Marti thought she was one of the finest women he had ever seen, there was something seductive about her name, but his preoccupation with names had not stemmed from a fetish for beautiful women.

Marti Lumbard Johnson was a thirty-five-year-old schoolteacher from Baton Rouge, Louisiana, whose preoccupation with self-worth and image compelled him one day to change his birth name from Martin—his father's middle name—to Marti. With that adjustment came the sense of a huge burden lifted in one fell swoop, and only then did he feel like a new man.

Marti was easily six feet tall and possessed the physique of a committed athlete, a runner, ball player or just someone who religiously worked out with weights just so he could admire his bulging biceps in the mirror. Of fair complexion, he sported an always well-manicured mustache in contrast to his thick hair that always gave a casual look. When not wearing a low 'fro, he kept his hair trim cropped short. Meticulous about his appearance, he wore specs from time to time to add a bit of mystery to his persona, though a far stretch from being a model or corporate executive.

Perhaps he hadn't realized it early on, but he definitely believed this now that the most interesting people in the world had the most interesting names: Tiger Woods, Oprah Winfrey, Bill Gates, Donald Trump, Colin Powell, Condoleezza Rice, Halle Berry, Sylvester Stallone, Stocker Channing, Kenneth Chenault, Marti Lumbard Johnson. And Marti was interesting enough, not for what he did do, rather for what he didn't do.

Marti somehow managed normalcy after it all happened. His equanimity was a testament to those his age and older, who, in similar situations, tripped out on pot with the intent to see to it that their own lives were ended. He walked those high school corridors each day seemingly unaffected, and no one ever mentioned to him what they discussed and further pondered among themselves: *Why did his daddy do it?*

Marti entered college with a clean slate, leaving behind him the last four years. On "the yard" of Southern University, he sought increasingly to liberate himself from the weight of his past. In doing so, he managed to win the attention of his fellow collegians. Freshman year, Marti joined the debate team, instantly finding his place in an arena, which gave him liberty to vent after having closed himself up for so long—detached from that part of himself that wanted to...needed to grieve—to fill the shoes as the man of the house for his mother and be both brother and father to his younger brother, who consequently watched his every move. His rich opinions became so widely accepted that he soon thought that he had become the man that he wanted to be. By his junior year, convinced that he had learned and knew as much as any man twice his age, he changed his major to teaching so he could drop some of his knowledge on the young bucks of the world. He had a simple philosophy about education, but one about which he was quite passionate. In fact, when given the opportunity, he was subject to challenge any other philosophy about what constituted learning. In one of his most memorable debates, he argued that life and books are what make a man, not one over the other, not one without the other. "So you've lived, huh?" his female counterpart questioned. "Man, you do all this talking like you had *wisdom* for a mama." He shook his head and smiled. "Nope, and didn't have to," he said to her. "I've got a backyard. All the wisdom you need comes from there."

Later that year in one of his papers, he wrote that he wanted to teach kids a little bit about everything and a lot about nothing. There was something to *nothing*—definitely. *Nothing* wasn't just nothing. *Nothing* was something. A big something. It was the *nothing* that you should be concerned about when folks would say, "Aw, it's nothing" or "Nothing's the matter."

Something was always the matter. It was a life lesson he had learned years ago, one that shaped his attitude, his reasoning, his logic. When others didn't, he'd pay close attention to the silences that crept into conversation. He'd listen for the *nothings* that frequented casual exchange between friends, colleagues, girlfriends, or relatives.

Yes, *nothing* was never just nothing, and had he known this at fourteen, he would have stayed home, done things differently. When he overheard George and Linda arguing about money and bills that day, he kept right on raking over his afro in the bathroom mirror. It was one of a series of arguments they had had over the past six months. Martin's indifference wasn't even shaken when his daddy shouted at his mama that nothing was wrong. Truth is, he couldn't count how many times his daddy's contracting business was in a slump for some reason or another. That was the nature of the business, and the family had learned to live with the down times. "Things'll pick up, you'll see." It was the last thing he heard his daddy say before going to school that morning. But after he was paged over the intercom to come to the office, he soon learned that everything was wrong and that *nothing* was definitely something.

Nothing is what forced his daddy to drift into a state where he believed the other side would be much easier than the life he was living. His daddy never did go to church regularly; otherwise, he'd have known that suicide was a sure ticket into hell—so they said. How in God's name could that place be better than this? Marti often wondered that. How many times had his daddy thought about ending it? And what about the rest: wife, kids, house? Didn't they matter to him anymore? For the longest, Marti reasoned that the fear of losing it all must have been too great. After all, a man's ability to provide is his worth. If that is threatened, what more is left of a man, of a black man, especially? Still, Marti couldn't help thinking how much less of a man was his father for giving in to the voices in his head that told him to go ahead and do it, leaving him like that...and his mom...and his brother who later turned to theft to vent his frustrations. Maybe the ending to Donald story's would have been different had his father stuck around. Instead, he'd be spending the next twenty years in East Baton Rouge Parish Prison.

Now it was just Marti. His younger brother was locked up. His father was dead. And he hadn't spoken to his mother in over six years, not since the argument when he lost his head and blamed her for pushing his daddy over the edge. He had made the mistake of disclosing his problems with Carolyn to his mother, who like any maternal figure tried to give him counsel. Perhaps he just wasn't prepared to heed his mother's advice—or maybe it was as Leslie said, he blamed her—because by the time Marti processed his mother's words, it seemed as though she was siding with Carolyn.

"You've got to understand, son. She's just trying to help."

"What, by always trying to get into my head so she can tell me what she thinks is wrong with me? You call that helping? I don't know why I even bother coming to you, mama. You drove daddy crazy with your incessant complaining about bills and stuff, always on his back. He couldn't catch a break from you, not even to change his doggone shirt. That's probably why he killed himself."

13

Linda Johnson's heart sank; her countenance was fraught with disbelief. How could he say those things to her, making such a ludicrous insinuation? She hadn't deserved that. No, she hadn't deserved that. In a low voice, one filled with hurt, his mother returned, "Son, you can't possibly know what went on between me and your dad no more than I could know all that goes on between you and Carolyn, only what you tell me, but you had no right to say those things to me, no right, and I want you to get out of my house."

Dejected by the callousness of his mother's final statement, having remembered also the emptiness he felt as he backed out of her driveway, Marti later realized that he could not have been more wrong or out of line, but his mother took what he said to heart and had since refused every one of his phone calls and letters. What must have gone through her mind, hearing one of her sons, the one most disciplined and responsible, say those horrible things to her? She was absolutely crushed then bitter then unforgiving. He regretted that they were estranged, but he'd only say to his brother every prison visit that things had changed, that nothing could be better between him and their mom.

He used *nothing* without hesitation. He knew that most people, including his brother, wouldn't read between the lines. They wouldn't sense that there was something more to be said, that *nothing* was code for: *All hell has broken loose.* He had observed people long enough to know that they'd be far too preoccupied with their own issues and

14

problems and disappointments to even notice his. And even when people would sense that *nothing* was something, Marti would quickly pick up on their reluctance to involve themselves in anything that might be too complicated, so he'd quickly change the subject to avoid that uncomfortable moment of silence that was certain to follow.

The only person who did understand him, who could tell when he was hiding something, who was just like him in so many ways was her, Leslie Mitchell. She was his co-worker, a ninth grade English teacher, smart, witty, strong, successful, and beautiful. Yes, Leslie had a beauty that needn't be enhanced by makeup, and though the only cosmetic modification she regularly made was having her eyebrows arched, Marti liked it when she would opt to grow them out. Her thick brows and strong jaw line gave Leslie a masculine quality that Marti found attractive. Her flawless brown skin and toned neck, her deep brown eyes and short naturally wavy hair, her well-proportioned figure and the crinkle she'd get on her forehead whenever she was upset or perplexed or annoyed, all these attributes he'd randomly envision, as if putting a jigsaw of her together in his mind. She was his ideal woman, but she never once gave any indication that she was interested in pursuing anything with him outside of their friendship of nearly four years. Despite that discouraging notion, Marti found himself more and more attracted to her. She was the only person, since Carolyn, his ex, who he even considered on a serious level. Yet he had all these reservations about telling her how he felt, fearing rejection more than anything.

Chapter 2

At school the next day, Marti didn't bother to mention Sasha to Leslie. He felt strange telling her about this girl, although he had told her about all his other countless, but meaningless relationships. Things were different between them now that he realized he was in love with her. In fact, he hardly said anything to Leslie all day until she walked into the teacher's lounge, where he was sipping a cup of coffee.

"Quiet today, aren't we?" said Leslie, approaching the snack machine.

"Just busy."

"Busy?" she said, dropping her coins into the machine slot then pressing the key for the last pack of peanut butter crackers that came tumbling down into the storage compartment at the bottom of the vendor.

"Yeah," Marti returned.

"What's with the small talk? Did I do something wrong?" She retrieved the pack of crackers from the snack machine and sat on the couch.

"No, nothing."

"Okay, I see, you just don't want to tell me, Martin."

"It's Marti."

"I know what it is." Then there was silence for a few minutes—she, snacking on crackers; he, sipping his coffee. "This wouldn't have anything to do with your class last night, would it?"

"Of course not." Now he was lying to her. He wanted to do away with all this foolishness, forego the small talk. He was in love with this woman, but she wasn't in love with him.

"I've got to go," he said, rising.

"You still have fifteen minutes."

"Got some planning to do."

When he first met Leslie, the day he first saw her in the office at Baker High School, her hair was much longer then. It had been three and a half years ago, and she had changed in those years, or maybe it was he who had changed, at least how he saw her and what he felt for her—that had certainly changed. Then one day she upped and strutted into his classroom with it all chopped off. She didn't bother to tell him why and he didn't bother to ask. That was before they began

18

telling each other everything, which grew them even closer, but something was holding Leslie back and that made Marti even more cautious about tossing his heart out into the wind and hoping she would be there to catch it. He was certain she felt something for him, something deeper than friendship, but she hadn't sent and still wasn't sending any obvious signals. He often wanted to read something she did as a signal, a kiss on the cheek, a long embrace, a gaze she'd sometimes give him, but the fact remained that Leslie was awfully good at disguising and undermining these gestures with sarcasm or witticism that often preceded or followed. She was driving him crazy. His "only friends" cap was getting a bit too tight for his head and cutting off circulation to that side of his brain that housed logic and reason. Frankly, it was getting harder for him to be around her and frustrating because he really wanted to be with this woman, but still couldn't bring himself to tell her.

What is it that women wanted—an open, honest man, someone who was sensitive and willing to communicate and listen? All that required lots of work, especially since men were terrible at expressing themselves without saying something wrong, so they usually wouldn't open up at all. Once they finally did open up, they'd often be misunderstood or worse—rejected. And Marti knew all too well from his first marriage what it was like to step out into the deep and sink.

Maybe he should never have married Carolyn, not so soon after college anyway, not with the misconception that he had become the man that he always wanted to be, and certainly not still having unresolved feelings about his father's suicide. But he was young then and in love with her, and there was nothing that anyone could have said that would have dissuaded him from marrying her.

Junior year of college, while Carolyn and Marti lived on campus, sparked their romantic interlude. In school on grant money, Marti had just started work study three days a week over at the Office of Student Affairs, where he first saw Carolyn, Carolyn St. James. Her name sounded so official, so Catholic, although she was Baptist. Marti was smitten with the young woman, who wore glasses and always put her hair back in a ponytail for easy management. A tomboy to the core, she'd drape herself in oversized shirts and jeans or anything baggy that swallowed her up, including the extra large shorts she'd sport in the summertime.

Enticed by the thrill of the chase, Marti hustled to work study to play their game of cat and mouse. And, to his surprise, Carolyn sometimes did the chasing. When she thought he wasn't looking, she would surreptitiously glance over at Marti, who never hesitated to flash his pearly whites when he caught her spying. A leer here, a smile there, they were on their way to something special if ever one of them remembered that they were no longer in high school, that it was okay to initiate a move, to go in for the score. Finally, Carolyn executed her move, and it had only taken her a month to approach him, to Marti's astonishment, no less.

"How long are you and I going to play this game?" she said, taking a seat at the worktable where Marti was alphabetizing a box of forms.

"Is that what we've been doing these last few weeks because I didn't know if you were interested or not?"

"I'm here, ain't I? I know you've been checking me out," she said arrogantly.

"Tsss, I know you've been checking me out, too. You ain't slick, you just think you are."

Rolling her eyes, she cynically returned, "Whatever, you know you want me, so let's stop with this nonsense and just go out. You got a problem with that?"

"How about we catch a movie on Saturday?" proposed Marti.

"Fine, I'll drive," she said, returning to her work study duties. Was she upset? Maybe she didn't like the fact that he had called her on her failed attempt at spying. *Whatever.*

It was not long before Marti had fallen for Carolyn, who loved sitting in as his audience while he rehearsed his debate topics. Her constructive criticism was a source for his improvement, and she never wavered to give him praise when he said something intriguing. Junior year for Marti was shaping up to be something pretty special, especially now that his time with Carolyn had included weekend getaways.

With the top dropped on Carolyn's candy apple red '69 Volkswagen beetle, the two of them drove all over Baton Rouge on the weekends, making an appearance at their favorite spot on the LSU campus—The Silver Moon Café—before returning to their side of town. The Silver Moon Café, where they could get the "best soul food in town," was one of many hot spots located on Chimes Street, a playground for eccentric college students, who wore army garb and dog tags that they'd bought from the army surplus. More student variety came in the form of those donned entirely in black, sitting curbside with a 400-page novel in one hand and a cigarette in the other. On a really busy weekend, the tables and chairs set outside local shops were the gathering place for several chess matches. A musician would find himself a comfortable spot on the ground and play his guitar as passers-by dropped spare change into his guitar case. It was a different world here, and for those like Marti and Carolyn who wanted to break from the monotony of campus living and going to class all week, the strip was a welcomed change of scenery.

But if Marti had to choose a defining moment for their relationship, it would be the night that Carolyn invited him into her world of poetry, introducing him to the language of abstract expression. On "the yard," there seemed to be a reading going on in the Fine Arts building every week. Carolyn insisted that Marti come to the reading that they were having that particular night because she was going to read something she had written and hoped he liked it since he had inspired it. When she got up to the podium to do her reading, she gave a brief introduction about how she'd been dabbling around with the genre since she was in grade school, which Marti was interested to learn, but had not ever thought that people would want to hear her thoughts, and how this type of vibe was good for people like herself because she now knew that she was among fellow poets. Marti, of course, was no poet—in fact, he never believed he could be that creative—but he was eager to hear her words. And it was also here—the night of the reading—when he really fell in love with Carolyn. She paused only to adjust her papers on the podium then began to read:

As Beauty Speaks

Before there was you,

I was afraid of the hour and of the hour's end,

Afraid of the dust, afraid of the wind,

Afraid of the trees, afraid of the ocean,

Afraid of the sky, afraid of the evening,

Afraid of the sunset and of the sun's rising.

Then beauty revealed to me

That which it whispered to the poet

And to the poet's lover and to the lover's keeper.

No longer do I toil with fear.

No longer do I reject my predecessors.

T'is written, "Better to have loved and lost..."

At last, I know love.

Perhaps I haven't the most profound words to describe you.

Somehow I've misplaced my genius,

But this I know:

Whenever my eyes are filled with your image,

My heart abandons its restless state.

I remember our first encounter, how beauty spoke to me.

The heat in that café was torrid, the windows opened to chaos.

I sat at breakfast, sipping my tea, watching the fading images.

When you rustled in from the busy streets and scourging sun,

Your body carried that familiar smell of outside

And a warm feeling came over me.

I was reminded of a long-forgotten childhood,

Playing in the swaying wheat field,

Stealing melons from the neighbor's patch.

Our eyes met and I knew.

Before there was you, there was another.

Someone whose love was a wretched thing.

Oh, how easily the heart is blinded

And the mind is fooled.

Yes, that encounter left me empty, so empty

I shut out the trees and saw only a gray sky,

I saw no beauty in the sunset, no promise in the sun's rising.

I longed for the evening, and even more for evening's end.

Then self-pity grew into anger and anger into fear.

I was afraid to trust and afraid to want,

Afraid to feel and afraid to not,

Afraid to live and afraid to die,

Afraid to shut down and afraid to cry.

Afraid of the hour and of the hour's end,

Afraid of the dust, afraid of the wind,

Afraid of the trees, afraid of the ocean,

Afraid of the sky, afraid of the evening,

Afraid of the sunset and of the sun's rising.

Afraid of nothing and afraid of everything.

Then I saw you and beauty spoke to me.

When Carolyn stepped from behind the podium to the applause of her fellow poets and took her seat next to Marti, he leaned over into her left ear and whispered, "I love you."

Right after college, Marti and Carolyn moved to Shreveport, Louisiana, her hometown. Four months later, they exchanged their wedding vows during a quaint ceremony at the Rose Garden before about fifty to a hundred relatives and closest friends, some of which having driven in from as close as Marshall, Texas, and as far as Orlando, Florida, for the event. Yellow jackets serenaded rose blooms, day lilies, and daffodils while the funky improvisations of a live six-piece Jazz combo kicked off their garden-side reception. The buffet-style spread of Swedish meatballs, mini quiche, catfish bites, fruit salad doused in mango juice, chicken salad, shrimp cocktail and sauce, Buffalo wings, stuffed mushroom caps, grilled vegetables, and cheese platter satiated their appetites until many of the guests were so replete that they could not themselves partake, yet only anticipate the first dance of the newlyweds. As they glided across the floor in each other's arms, Marti and Carolyn imagined only a lifetime of bliss.

Bliss, however, was soon overshadowed by the consequence of living his pre-adolescent years with a father whose idea of communication came in the form of yelling and arguing. Resentment and bitterness toward his father drove Marti to spend much of his eight-year marriage to Carolyn trying to be nothing like George Johnson. He overcompensated for everything he saw lacking in his father's marriage to his mother. With Carolyn, he desperately sought to talk about everything, yet communicating with her often proved pointless because she was quick to treat him as if she was in session with a therapy patient whenever he made an attempt to share something with her. But Carolyn was not only to blame for their failing marriage. Marti's obsession to correct the wrongs of his family and provide the two of them with financial stability stirred him away from his wife's longings of motherhood to pursue his career further through graduate coursework, which he never completed. In the end, lies and betrayal dissolved any hopes of reconciliation, and divorce was inevitable.

A childhood daunted by his father's belligerence coupled with the failure of his marriage made it that much more difficult for Marti to open up in the way in which he knew women wanted, but, more importantly, in the way in which he believed Leslie deserved if he was to have even the slightest chance with her. Not even Carolyn evoked in him the desire to change, to acknowledge his mistakes, to deal with his father's death, to try to repair his relationship with his mother, although Carolyn made several attempts. Leslie did. Her amazing ability to dissect him had been proven the day their casual conversation over the phone took a turn for something far more serious and she read him like a book.

Marti was not prepared to hear Leslie say that the reason he had said those harsh words to his mother was because he had never really dealt with his father's death. Still, he sat there on the other end of the phone listening as she told him that he needed some sort of justification—something that justified why his father killed himself— that he needed to blame someone, so he blamed his mother. She said that while he must have spent years trying to understand his father's reasons and accept what his father had done, he spent those same years despising his mother, blaming her until he just could not hold it in any longer.

He also remembered lashing out at Leslie, saying that if he wanted a shrink, he would have gotten one. He never asked for her two-bit analysis. She obviously didn't know who she was talking to, telling him about his life and what he needed to do and how he shouldn't have done what he did, judging him like she was so perfect. He just wasn't going to take that from any woman, not even her. Later that day, after he had time to cool down and think about the things she said, he called and apologized. What made him so upset about her that day is what he grew to love and appreciate most about her. He came to rely on her honesty and value her opinions. He needed her. She made him a better man. He had to tell her, just not yet.

He'd sometimes play the scene in his head, the two of them at dinner and then him going into this spiel about how great she was and how she was all he could ever think about. He'd imagine the look of surprise on her face, thinking it was just Leslie putting him on because she already knew he was in love with her. His fantasy would go as far as her becoming his wife, and would end abruptly when he would imagine them having a discussion about starting a family. Marti knew she wanted to have children someday, but he wasn't so sure he wanted any. Somehow he managed to use his career as an excuse for not having them with Carolyn. The truth—he really didn't think he was emotionally equipped to be a good father. His only example of a father had bailed on him and his mom and brother. And the one thing Marti had learned from his first try at marriage was that his father's shortcomings had crippled him as a husband and were certain to affect his parenting as well. He wanted only to teach kids about books and life then send them home to their parents who could give them the emotional guidance he felt he couldn't. He found himself considering the possibility only with Leslie, but she wasn't throwing out any romantic gestures, and Sasha could prove to be fairer game.

"What was that about earlier today?" asked Leslie as she drew closer to Marti, who was sitting at his desk jotting down grades. School had only been out five minutes.

"What?" replied Marti.

"You know, why did you rush out of the teacher's lounge like that? What happened last night during class?"

Marti leaned back in his chair and folded his arms. "I met a bunch of new people and a cool teacher, nothing more than that." Marti convinced himself there was really nothing to tell anyway since he had just met Sasha. He hadn't proposed to the woman or anything.

"You know I can tell when you're keeping something from me, and you are definitely keeping something from me."

"Whatever," replied Marti, returning his attention to his grade recording.

"You've been acting funny since last December," she said.

Marti sat there thinking back, remembering that this was around the time when he realized that he was in love with her. It was a few days after Christmas when she'd gotten sick for a week. And while she kept insisting that it was unnecessary that he stop by everyday because it was just a bad cold, he did anyway. He wanted to do it. He liked doing it and imagined himself doing that always, taking care of her, making sure she was safe, making sure she was okay.

"Then why do you put up with me?" asked Marti.

"I'm not. I'm leaving. If I hurry, I can catch *Oprah*. Maybe she can shed some light on you men and your mood swings."

"Again, I repeat, whatever."

Chapter 3

Four weeks into grad school, Marti and Sasha had finally gotten around to their first date. He wanted to take Sasha somewhere different, somewhere he could reveal to her his passions and interests. He'd never done this with the others. He'd never invested anything into those relationships that would turn into something sticky. With Sasha, it was just different somehow. He liked that she was beautiful, but not hung up on that. He liked that she was putting herself through school and not depending on a man—God knows she could have had any—to pay her way. And she seemed genuinely interested in what he had to say whenever they'd have conversation during break time.

Marti decided to take her to one of his favorite spots, M's Café, a cozy little downtown Jazz club. As soon as he seated her at a front table, he made his entrance onto stage with the rest of the combo, flashing one of his million-dollar smiles at Sasha before slipping comfortably behind the drums. With psychedelic lighting beaming down on him, Marti began to play to Sasha's eclectic ear. He knew she loved music, all kinds, and it made it easier for him to play to someone who could appreciate his love of Jazz. It's the only thing his father ever listened to. And when Marti was seven or eight, his daddy gave him a pair of drumsticks and taught him to play, leaving Marti with one of the few good memories he had of his dad—teaching him how to put the "d" in drum.

The day Marti walked into the garage and saw the used set of drums he remembered thinking that he'd never gotten anything so great ever before. Marti would watch attentively while his father accompanied on the drums the musical stylings of Jazz legends Miles Davis and Dizzy Gillespie and J.J. Johnson playing on the turntable. There was no other time in his life that he wanted to be like his father as much as he did then. He wanted to know what his father knew and do what his father did and learn to play as well as his dad. "First thing you gotta learn to do, son, is stay in the pocket," he instructed Marti, "until you learn 'em and make 'em your own, and when they start talking to you, you talk back, play what you feel, just play what you feel." In that respect, his father was a great man, a great musician. Marti always thought that his father was good enough to have toured the world playing Jazz with some of the greats, but his father made different choices and did what most people, Marti included, do—fell in love and got married.

Taking the one good thing that he'd picked up from his father, Marti impressed Sasha with his drum playing. And while they played, she remained loyal to him, watching him, studying him, admiring him as if no one else was up there. Every man wanted this, to look out into a crowd and find that one woman who was into him. Why couldn't that woman be Leslie?

"I see you enjoyed us," he said, taking a seat, his clothing damp with perspiration.

"I enjoyed *you*."

"Trying to make me blush, woman?"

"Maybe."

For several minutes they sat there flirting like teenagers, saying very little between the teases and gazing and hand holding. "How about something to drink?"

"Sure, as long as it's virgin."

"Not a drinker, huh?"

Suddenly, she pulled her hands away from his. "Nope, I watched my grandfather drink himself to death," snapped Sasha.

"Hey, Sasha, I'm sorry. I didn't mean—"

"I know you didn't."

"For what it's worth, neither am I. I tried that stuff back in college, wasn't for me."

"Can we talk about something else?"

"Yeah, sure, but first let me go get a Sprite?"

Sasha nodded.

"I'll be right back," Marti said, rising from the table. "Don't go anywhere."

With that, he had won a smile from her.

Returning with the beverages a few minutes later, Marti sat back down. "I brought you some cherry grenadine in case you wanted to make a Shirley Temple," he said.

"Thanks," said Sasha before taking a sip of her Sprite.

"You know, I still can't get over the fact that you're from Denver," said Marti, initiating typical first-date conversation.

Sasha snickered. "What, you think all Denver has is snow, no black people?"

"That's not it. I just don't meet too many black folks from there."

"We're there," she said, adding some grenadine to her beverage. "But let me ask you something."

"What's that?" said Marti.

"Well, I know you have a brother, but you never did tell me much about him during class. What's he like?" she asked. "Are you two close?"

"Not as much as we could be. He chose a different life, didn't have to be that way. I try not to think about it."

"Kinda like my sister and me," she said.

Marti ears were pricked now. "What, you two don't exactly see eye-to-eye?"

"Something like that. I mean I love her, but she can be overbearing. She's older and married and always trying to advise me on my love life or my choices in life because she thinks she knows best. Most times we end up on opposite sides of the fence. And that bothers me at times because sometimes I just need a big sis and not another mother."

"Sometimes I think that maybe if I had been a bit more overbearing, my brother might not be sitting in jail right now," he said, "but the truth is, there really wasn't much I could do. I was busy trying to make my marriage work, which, obviously, didn't. I had my career to think about. I really didn't have time to play babysitter to Donald."

"Am I my brother's keeper?" responded Sasha in an empathetic tone. Her sister Ylana insisted on being her keeper, but she wished Ylana would just take Marti's position and leave her to sort out her own life.

Marti nodded as he replied, "Exactly!"

"Still, that must have been a pretty tough year when your brother got into trouble, especially with you trying to make your marriage work and all," she said.

"No, that wasn't a good year for me; neither was the following year—that's when Carolyn and I split up."

"How long were you two together?"

"Eight years," said Marti.

"I'm surprise you don't have any kids. Didn't you want any?"

"She did."

Finding Marti's past more and more intriguing, Sasha then asked, "Is that why you two divorced?"

"Part of it."

"Ylana says she'll never divorce. She hypes up her marriage to be the greatest thing since electricity and that's fine, but give it a rest, you know. Some of us are still weeding out the toads."

"No offense," he said, "but I think people like your sister rather pretend than confront the harsh reality of their lives. I should know. Carolyn was like that."

"How so?"

"Don't get me wrong, Carolyn had a pretty good life, and maybe that's why she couldn't believe that not everybody had the kind of life she had growing up. One of the things that attracted me to her when we first met was that she listened to me. I later learned while we were married that she was simply making a list in her head. I guess she was sort of formulating how she was going to help me become a better man."

"You're kidding?"

"No, I'm not. I tried to tell her that everything couldn't be solved over one long conversation. Some things just ran deeper than that, you know. Then we split for awhile, but I finally came back. And that *was not* the right move."

Sasha leaned forward, placing the elbows of her folded arms on the table before saying, "So what happened? Why didn't it work?"

"Carolyn thought a baby might fix things. She just couldn't get it in her head that quick fixes were no match for things that couldn't be repaired like our marriage. Anyway, she tried to have a kid without my consent, and, frankly, that was the last straw for me. By the time the divorce went through, we had stopped communicating altogether."

"That must have been hard, you know, not being able to go to your wife about stuff."

"Not really," answered Marti. "I think we men are built that way. My father was the same way and so was his dad, but I swore to myself that I wasn't gonna be that way in my marriage. It didn't work that way, though. In the end, I had lain beside a woman for eight years and never really let her inside my head."

"So what changed?" asked Sasha. "I mean, I imagine that you're telling me things now that you never even told Carolyn."

"I'm older," surmised Marti. He stopped himself short of mentioning Leslie's name. In all honesty, she was the reason for his change. She was the reason he was more open, more expressive. Yet expressing to Leslie his feelings for her remained his quandary.

"You know sometimes you talk like you're middle-aged. You're only thirty-five."

"Sometimes I feel like I'm much older than I am," he said.

"It's just a number, you know."

"Try telling my body that. That's why I work out as much as I do. Too many brothas just let themselves go, especially after they get married. They blame it on their wives' cooking."

"Well, I like the fact that you work out. I've always been attracted to men with nice physiques, but not too big. That's scary."

"Yeah, I've got a buddy who body builds. He's pretty big, but that's because he competes on the amateur level."

"Still scary," said Sasha.

"You're just saying that because you don't have a healthy knowledge base of bodybuilding and people who do it."

"I'm not basing this on any knowledge or lack of," she contested. "I know what I like to see, and I don't like to see men built like comic book characters."

"Don't you think that comparison is a bit exaggerated?"

"Maybe," she said.

"So what aren't you telling me?" asked Marti.

She gave him a long look, as if contemplating whether or not she would confide in him. "I've just had bad memories on the subject."

"What memories? What happened?"

"It was an ex-boyfriend. It started out innocent enough with him. He'd go and lift weights." Sasha stopped to chuckle. "I was beginning to like what I was seeing, how his body was developing. But then he got crazy with it...spending most of his time trying to get bigger. Why? Why was he trying to get like that?" She paused. The look on her face suggested that she was wrestling still with that question, still wondering what pushed her ex over the edge. And though he was anxious for her to continue, Marti didn't push. He gave her time to collect herself, hoping after a few minutes she'd find her way back to the present. Instead, she just sat there peering off. He wondered what thoughts must have been racing through her head. Finally, he could wait no longer.

"Hey, talk to me," encouraged Marti.

"I didn't even want to think those thoughts, you know? It was too ridiculous. I mean why would anybody want to get mixed up with that stuff?" Sasha digressed. "It's a funny thing…the stuff we obsess over, the things that turn us into addicts. Mama says after her oldest brother died of cancer that that's when pops became an alcoholic. She said his taste for the stuff would be so great he'd stash bottles inside the toilet or places nobody would think to look. But for the life of me, I still don't know what happened with Leonard, my ex. I just know that whatever he was seeing in the mirror wasn't enough for him because he started injecting steroids like it was syrup." Sasha stopped.

"So what happened?"

"He-um…" Sasha's voice was low and shaky. She was obviously fighting back tears, which soon began to stream down despite her efforts. "I'm sorry," she said, wiping her eyes. "This still gets to me because I was the one who found him."

Marti felt bad for her. He knew what she was feeling—losing someone close like that. It was a kind of pain that wouldn't go away—pain that was haunting. "No, no, don't apologize. How about we just get out of here, okay?"

The ride to Sasha's apartment was quiet. She sat on the passenger side staring out the window. He wanted to say something, but what? Normally, ending a good date came easy for Marti. His date would invite him in and he'd accept. Tonight was different. Their date had gotten heavy toward the end, and Sasha's vibe suggested that she just wanted to be left alone, which was fine by Marti because he wasn't so sure he would accept an invitation into this woman's home. He *dug* her enough, and she was gorgeous and smart and sensitive and interesting. She was everything and then some, but she was no Leslie. She was no Leslie.

Marti pulled up into Sasha's complex and parked the car. "I had a great time," he said, leaning over in the car to kiss her on the cheek.

"Me, too."

"I'd like to do it again, you know, since you can appreciate Jazz," said Marti. "Some women can't get into it. I'm glad you can. It's good we have that in common."

"Is there something you're not telling me?" asked Sasha.

"Why do you say that?"

"Well, you seem to be stalling or talking around something. Do you want me to ask you in? Is that it because I *never* invite a man in on the first date? Nothing personal."

Marti released a boyish snicker. "Actually, I'm relieved. I don't want to rush anything."

"Neither do I," she said.

"So I guess I'll see you in class on Monday?"

"Yeah…yeah," said Sasha.

Marti then unlocked her door from the control panel on his side of the car. "I guess this is goodnight then," he said.

Sasha opened the car door, got out, shut the door then bent down into the window to address him one last time. "You really did play great. You're so good, you know. And, uh, thanks for listening."

He watched as she approached her front door and entered. He didn't want to hurt this girl, but he didn't want to stop seeing her either. One thing he did know, he had some decisions to make: forget about Sasha and tell Leslie how he felt or pursue Sasha and never tell Leslie? If he were to put both these women's names through his "interesting name = interesting life" theory to solve his dilemma, then he'd remain at a crossroads. While Sasha's name was exotic and mysterious and dangerous, Leslie's name was unisex, which could easily be interpreted to mean and what Marti knew to be true that she had a combination of feminine and masculine aspects about her that he found equally as interesting and attractive. No, his theory would not come into play on this. And perhaps if he had used the name game on Carolyn rather than listened to his hormones, he'd have left her alone altogether, a truth that became more and more apparent to him not long after he and his mother had their fall out.

Chapter 4

(Six Years Earlier)

The wound was still fresh with his mother, even though it had been seven months since the incident. This became quite clear to Marti as he tossed on the coffee table the unopened letter with the words "Return to Sender" written across the front. One more to add to the collection of rejected letters he had stashed away in a box at the top of his closet. Carolyn insisted he keep them because she was certain his mother would come around soon enough, and when she did, he could give them to her. Marti knew differently. Carolyn wasn't there that day. She didn't see the look in Marti's mother's face or how her head sank and her lips parted as if to surrender what fight she had left. A dead husband. A son in prison. Marti was the one good and stable thing she had remaining until he upper cut her with his sharp tongue. He meant those words to sting and sting they did. No, Carolyn didn't understand. She had a good relationship with her folks.

The first time he met her parents was not just awkward for obvious reasons, but grew more uncomfortable as the conversation got around to his family history. They wanted to know what his father and his mother were like and whether or not he had any brothers and sisters. He knew this was a mistake, but Carolyn insisted her folks were open-minded. Still, Marti realized that while you might be able to convince your folks to be open-minded about you quitting your high-pressure, but good-paying job to start a basket weaving company, he just couldn't expect complete strangers to be so objective about or unprejudiced toward the *dysfunction* he called his family. So he played the safe card and excused himself from the dinner table, claiming that something he had eaten wasn't agreeing with him. He'd much rather offend Carolyn's mother's cooking than divulge all his dirty secrets.

He tried to explain to Carolyn in the car on the way there that she was being naïve, that nobody was that open, not even her parents. He should have realized then from that very incident that it would never work with her. Sure Carolyn was different from the other girls he'd dated. She used to listen to him, especially when they first started dating. That's what drew him to her. She made him feel good, but he soon learned that that wasn't enough to hold a marriage together.

He regretted marrying a woman he really didn't know, a woman who thought she had the answers to all of life's questions. Eventually, he just stopped talking to her about anything of real importance to him because she never heard what he was saying over her own voice. God knows he made an effort to be nothing like his father. He wanted there to be some kind of civilized exchanged between him and Carolyn. And often that's all it was—civilized because "whatever" or "it doesn't matter" usually ended a conversation.

Even when Carolyn persisted, Marti would insist that *nothing* was on his mind to keep a sticky conversation from brewing. "But that's not what that look on your face is saying," she'd argue. Sometimes he felt she was trying to get an honorary degree in "driving him mad" with all her psychobabble. Oh how she annoyed him with the way she poked and prodded him and then went about explaining to him why she thought he was so closed off with his feelings. So many times he wanted to stop her mid-sentence before she started off on some tangent and upper cut her like he did his mother. How easy it was for him to spew out acrimony and argue his antagonist into submission. He was good at debate and even better at saying things that were unforgivable. This he had inherited from his father, a man whose bark was as fierce as his bite. And he wanted to be nothing like his father, so Marti would simply dismiss Carolyn. "Whatever," he'd return cynically, thinking to himself that this was about as much therapy as he could take for one day and that the sports section of the local newspaper had far more interest.

Today, however, Marti just didn't feel like pacifying her anymore. Maybe getting that letter back had set him off or maybe he had just gotten fed up with Carolyn's babble.

"Hey, you'll just try again next week. Here, give me that one. I'll put it in the box."

"No. I'm not doing this again. It's a waste of time."

"You don't know that. The next time cou—"

"Why don't you listen to me?" Marti interrupted. "I ain't some head case. You don't L I S T E N! All you do is talk and talk and talk and nothing comes out of your mouth. I tell ya that I don't want to meet your folks and you yack and yack until I say squash it. Then these stupid letters I've been writing for months now because of you—she's never gonna read them. I was the one thing she could count on, the one thing, and I said those stupid, stupid things. This is ridiculous. Why am I even here? What's the point?"

"What are you doing?" Carolyn asked with concern in her voice. Marti stormed into his closet, grabbed the box of letters and tossed them to the floor. He grabbed his suitcase and garment bag from the closet then tossed them on the bed.

"What does it look like I'm doing?"

Carolyn didn't know what to do. She was afraid to try to stop him physically, fearing that this would only heighten things. She thought he'd cool down if she just stood by the dresser and watched and maybe talked him through this. "Can't we just talk about this? I mean, you know—listen, leaving won't solve anything."

"They teach you that in school or did you learn that off television?" he replied sharply, throwing socks and shirts in the suitcase.

"Okay, I'm sorry, okay. Just forget the letters. You don't want to write them anymore—then fine. I won't push it."

"You won't push it?"

Carolyn shook her head then walked over and sat on the bed. Marti kept packing. "I said I'd let it go. Why are you still packing?"

"I think we need some space."

"I don't need any space, Marti."

"Okay, then, I need some space."

"Why?"

Marti stopped what he was doing and looked her in the eyes. "This is not just about those letters. We...we don't fit together. What we got," he said, shaking his head, "it doesn't work. I can't even talk to you, not even about little stuff because you're busy talking at me. Most times it feels like you're insulting my intelligence. I just need to get out of here. Clear my head."

Marti zipped up his suitcase and garment bag and left their bedroom heading for the door. By the time Carolyn walked into the front room, he was getting ready to open the front door.

"So that's it?"

Marti opened the front door then turned back toward her briefly. "I'll call in a few days I guess. Maybe we can talk about this then," he said before leaving.

A few days turned into a month separation. The phone calls between the two of them mounted, but Marti and Carolyn talked about everything from what went wrong—starting with the first time he met her folks—to having laughs about some of their funnier moments. And for the first time since they dated, he felt she was actually listening to him. He couldn't, however, be sure that going back wouldn't ruin things again. Maybe they were only good together apart.

From Carolyn's vantage point, they were ready to give it another try. She now knew what he was feeling and believed things were really going to work between the two of them. She wanted him back.

"It doesn't make sense for you to spend anymore time at the motel, Marti. Why don't you move back?"

"Is that what you want?"

"You know I do. I never wanted you to leave, that was your decision."

"And I don't regret it either. We were a train wreck ready to happen. We had been going in different directions for years—it was just a matter of time before we collided."

"I didn't know. You never told me you were feeling that way. On the surface, we seemed fine. I thought you were happy."

"And that was my mistake for giving you that impression. I guess I was expecting you to read my mind, and that's not your job."

"So what now? Will you come home? Will you be with me?"

Marti gave more thought to what she was asking before answering. He wanted to be sure he was making the right decision. He just couldn't go back to the way it was. "I don't want you to misunderstand," he said. "My coming back doesn't mean that we've resolved everything. That's gonna take time. There are things that we still need to talk about, but I love you, and I want to try to make this work."

"I love you, too, and I want to try to make this work."

"Then I'll check out today. I'm coming home."

A year passed before Marti learned why Carolyn wanted to try to make things work, and it had little to do with her having already invested six and half years into their marriage. When Marti found the new pregnancy test stuffed in her underwear drawer, her motives were clear, and there was nothing that she could say in her defense that would pacify Marti. There wasn't going to be one of those "let's sit down and talk about starting a family" talks because they had had several of those talks early on in their marriage, and not once had Marti changed his position on the matter. Still, Marti had to prove his suspicions by going to the source—her prescription of birth control pills. He searched all over the apartment for those pills, the medicine cabinet, her other drawers, her closet. He found nothing, but he knew where she had her prescription filled since sometimes she'd send him to have it filled for her. As he had suspected, calling her pharmacist up with some bogus story about how he accidentally tossed out his wife's pills and wanted to have them replaced had gotten him what he needed to hear. The pharmacist was more than happy to accommodate Marti's request, casually disclosing to him the date of Carolyn's last prescription fill. Two months ago was the last time she had stopped by the pharmacy, he told Marti. Two months.

Marti could hardly wait for Carolyn to get home before he tore into her. As far as he was concerned, there was nothing she could say to justify what she tried to do. It was the ultimate betrayal—his wife trying to trap him in their marriage with some kid he didn't even want, thinking that once she got pregnant he'd change his mind. This was definitely the straw that broke the camel's back. And now it was over. He was through with her. He wanted *out*!

Since they had nothing, this was not going be one of those messy divorces that led to a lengthy custody battle and arduous fight over property. There was no question about who would get what. They were still living in an apartment. He'd retain ownership of his car and she'd drive away from their eight-year marriage in the car her parents had given her for college graduation. And he really didn't care anything about the furniture. She could have that. He just wanted out.

Marti heard the front door open as he stood there in the bathroom staring down at the pregnancy test. He waited for Carolyn to find him there and she did.

The look on Carolyn's face said it all. For a good minute or two nothing was exchanged, except silence. Still, Marti couldn't wait to hear what she had to say…what kind of babble she planned to use to convince him that having a baby without his consent was in their best interest. *Right,* he sarcastically thought to himself.

"So?" said Marti, holding out the pregnancy test.

"What do you want me to say, Marti? I told you I wanted a baby."

"And I told you I didn't. So, in other words, you've decided that how I feel about this doesn't even matter—as long as you're happy," he said, stressing that last part.

"I just—I just figured you'd—"

Marti interrupted. "You just figured I'd do the noble thing after I found out you were pregnant and stay with you and the kid. So this is your way of trapping me in this marriage when we both know this thing isn't working. And ain't no kid gonna fix it."

"Trap you? Is that what you think? I'm not trying to trap anybody. You knew before we got married that I wanted children. I never hid that from you." Carolyn paused for a second. "I just don't understand why you don't want any kids?"

"I just don't."

"But how can you not want kids and be a teacher to them everyday?" Carolyn shook her head in confusion then added, "It doesn't make any sense."

"I have my reasons."

"Well, I'm your wife. Don't you think you need to tell me so I can understand why?"

"Listen, Carolyn, we've had this conversation a million times already, and I'm not changing the way I feel about this. I don't want to have children."

"So what am I supposed to do—go out and make a baby with somebody else? Well, that's not gonna happen. You're my husband. I want your baby."

"You watch too much television. This ain't a drama you can twist and manipulate. This is my life you're screwing with. But let me tell you something," he added, walking over to his closet, "it ends here. I'm moving out and filing for a divorce. Besides, you don't need me.

You like making all the decisions anyway, except let me help you with just this one—we're through."

***

Wasting no time to leave behind the last eight years that he had spent with Carolyn, Marti made the four and a half hour drive from Shreveport, Louisiana, to Baton Rouge, Louisiana, in a record three and a half. Still, Marti never would have thought that at thirty-one he'd be divorced from her and back in Baton Rouge, where it all began.

By the time the new school term rolled around two months later, Marti was much too preoccupied with making a good impression to focus on his split from Carolyn. Strolling into the school office with the confidence of a CEO, wearing a pair of charcoal gray slacks and light gray dress shirt with coordinating satin tie, Marti flashed his killer smile. He approached the office counter and signed his name in the teacher's check-in log. What the external veiled, his insides certainly did not. Nervousness gushed around the pit of his stomach like a tsunami. This was his first teaching day at Baker High School, and he only knew a handful of people, mostly teachers who had taught him when he attended there some thirteen years ago. Marti had given the secretary a wink and was headed to the teacher's lounge to check his mail slot when Leslie walked in. She was breathtaking, he thought to himself after turning back to look when he heard the jingle of the office door. She had shoulder-length black hair and flawless

55

caramel skin. Her eyes were deep brown sultry orbs that gleamed from her face. Her lips were full and her smile, hypnotic. She stood at least five foot seven, give or take an inch, which Marti thought perfect for her gorgeous body that she managed to conceal under a black pin-striped business suit. All professional, she was. He already liked what he saw.

Marti proceeded to the teacher's lounge, hoping he'd get the opportunity to exchange conversation with her. He was obviously intrigued by her looks, but what about her personality? While shuffling through a stack of material that he had found in his box, Leslie slipped through the door. Again, Marti smiled and said, "Hi, I'm Marti Johnson, the new ninth-grade Geography teacher. And you are?"

Leslie walked up to her own mail slot that was only four down from his. "I'm Leslie, Leslie Mitchell. I teach ninth-grade English. I heard that there was a new teacher in town."

"Yep, that's me," he said, smiling.

"So where are you coming from?"

"I'm originally from here, but I moved to Shreveport when I got married. I transferred from Captain Shreve up there."

"So what does your wife do?"

"I'm recently divorced. That's why I'm back, you know, to get away from that madness."

Leslie face grew grim. "Yeah, I know how that can be. Well, it was nice to meet you. Maybe we'll bump into each other later. The bell's going to be ringing in ten."

"Yeah, you're right. I better get to class myself. It's always an ordeal when it's your first day."

"Tell me about it," she said, smiling. "My first day came three years ago, glad it's over. Later."

"Later."

With one hand clasping his mail and a briefcase gripped tightly in the other, Marti headed for his classroom.

By the time break rolled around, Marti had decided to sit it in his classroom to work on some lesson plans for next week. Five minutes later, Leslie peeped her head through his door.

"So how was it?" she asked while walking in then taking a seat in one of the student chairs.

Marti grinned. "Piece of cake, but I think I'd better tone it down a bit on my aftershave. I'm afraid I have a few cases of young female adoration."

"Yeah, they are well past that age when they start digging older men, especially those who are accomplished and as tall as you." *Tall?* Was that all he had going for him? Was that all she found appealing about such a fine brotha as himself? He had to work on that.

"Well, I don't want any trouble. I just want to do my job and get paid."

"Geography, huh? What made you choose that field?"

Placing his pen down, Marti answered, "Well, I always wanted to travel around the world. Unfortunately, we could never afford exotic vacations. I even thought about going into the Marines to get international exposure, but after my father killed himself, I pretty much put all that out of my mind so I could take care of my moms and younger brother. I don't know, I guess studying Geography gave me a way to see the world right from the pages of a book. Don't get me wrong, I still plan to travel someday. I don't ever think that's something I'll be able to relinquish until I actually do it."

"I'm sorry to hear about your dad."

"Yeah, it was long time ago. I try not to think about it, but sometimes it just hits me, you know?"

Leslie gave an empathetic nod.

"So what about you, why English?"

"It's simple, I love to read and I love to show kids how our language can spawn so much creativity—the formation of words and worlds..."

There was an excitement in her voice that Marti found most appealing. As she explained her love for teaching, his heart began to pump hot blood through his body at a rate much more rapidly than usual, but he resolved not to show his attraction for her on his face, letting his mind wander to settle his urges. It was much too soon. He'd just met her and certainly didn't want to come off as a womanizer.

"Listen, I'm going to let you get back to your planning," said Leslie, rising from the chair. "I just wanted to check in on you, see how you were doing. Remember, I'm just a few doors down if you need anything."

Marti nodded his head as Leslie vanished through the door to her classroom, thinking to himself that coming to work everyday to that portrait of perfection was going to be worth being back in Baton Rouge. Now, having been a teacher at Baker High for three and a half years, Marti still felt the same way he did that very first time he met Leslie.

Marti

Chapter 5

Marti and Sasha had been dating a little over a month and had already developed a Friday-night routine when Sasha would cook. Marti loved her cooking. Girl could throw down in the kitchen. He loved watching her because she'd be coaching herself through her culinary masterpieces: *add more salt, yeah, yeah, just right, oh yeah, the rice, can't forget the rice.* He wondered what linguini lingo he'd hear coming from her kitchen this night. She was making pasta.

Marti was sitting at her bar when he offered to help. He knew a thing or two about cooking; he even impressed himself with what he knew. He made a mean pound cake and the best grilled sirloin ever.

"No, baby, I got it," replied Sasha. "You just relax. I know school's been a real drag."

"That's cool. I like watching you anyway."

"No, you like seeing me talk to myself—that's all."

Smiling, he said, "That, too."

Marti got up and went over and put his arms around Sasha and kissed the back of her neck. "Smells good."

"That's the garlic."

"I was talking about you."

"Okay, okay, go sit down, lover boy, you're distracting me. Go on. I'm almost through. Hope you like it."

"You needn't even say that. You know I love anything you make," he said, walking over to the cabinet to get plates."

"You wanna know why I fixed pasta tonight?"

"Sure."

"It was your name."

Marti placed the plates on the dining table along with silverware and glasses. "My name?"

"Yeah," she said, approaching him with a large bowl of steaming pasta. "Here, would you give me a hand and grab the garlic bread out of the oven? Thanks."

"No prob, but I still want you to finish telling me about the connection between my name and this dinner."

"I will. Don't worry."

As soon as they were both seated at the table, Marti wasted no time picking up their conversation. "So?" he said with great expectancy.

"Well, I've wondered since we first met how you got your name. Only Marti's I know are Italian and work for the mob, at least that's what I see on TV."

Marti laughed out. "So, Marti reminds you of something Italian and that gave you the inspiration to fix pasta tonight."

"Hey, laugh all you want, but seriously, where did Marti come from?"

Over dinner, Marti proceeded to explain to Sasha with some reluctance how he blamed his mother for his father's suicide, and expressed that he wished his father alive long enough to tell him how much of a coward he thought he was. Feeling rejected by his father, Marti decided that he would denounce him and anything associated with him, he explained to Sasha, recalling the day he took that bold step to change the course of his own life forever when he turned eighteen. He hadn't even told his mama his plans to legally drop the "n" from his name when he drove down to the courthouse to get all the necessary paperwork. It would be a tedious process of filing forms with the court clerk, getting a docket number, and waiting for a judge to review his petition and then either grant or reject it, but, for Marti, it was well worth the filing fee it had cost him, especially since it would grant him a new identity and relinquish him of his father's mark. Still, even that wasn't enough to rid himself completely of George Johnson, he later realized.

"What are you thinking?" he said.

"How much I miss pops."

"Want to tell me about that?"

Sasha released a long sigh. Marti watched while she fidgeted with her fork as she began to speak about her grandfather. "I'd just completed my junior year of undergrad. I always went home for the summer, loaded all my stuff in my car and headed for my grandparents' house. I was gonna store most of my things there, just wasn't enough extra space at my parents' place, not even in my room. I was about an hour from home when I got the call on my cell phone. An accident, they said. Mom was hysterical. I knew it wasn't good. Told me to rush home. I put on my hazards and sped the entire way. 'Be okay, be okay,' I kept saying and praying. 'Just be okay.' By the time I got home, he was already gone. Internal bleeding." She paused briefly. "I loved that old man, but I hated to see him drink. I always thought he was better than that, you know?"

"Hey, hey, come here." Sasha got up from her seat at the dinner table, went and sat in his lap, and put her arms around his neck. Marti then embraced her.

"Want me to stay tonight? I'll sleep on the couch."

"Yeah," she said, nodding her head. "Thanks, but you don't have to sleep on the couch."

"Hey, we don't have to talk about that right now, try not to think about anything else, but how good this feels."

Chapter 6

When Marti woke about seven-thirty that next morning, Sasha was already up and in the kitchen fidgeting. She was just across the hall, so he could hear nearly everything going on in there.

"Good morning," he called out.

"Sorry, baby, did I wake you?"

"Naw, I usually get up around this time on the weekends. I'm so used to getting up early for work that I can't seem to break myself from it even on my off days.

"I couldn't really sleep," she returned, with the sound of her voice growing closer. Sasha was now standing in the doorframe of the living room where Marti was still reclined on the sofa. Her standing there took Marti back to the moment he first saw her. He was completely mesmerized by her beauty.

"Bad dream?" asked Marti.

"Yeah, it was about me and you."

"What about us?"

"We broke up," she said, still standing there.

"Broke up, why?"

"You were in love with someone else."

Marti raised himself up on the couch. "Say what?"

"Yeah, you heard me."

"Hey, hey, what are you thinking? I didn't like your tone," said Marti, "I'm with you, okay, and I want to be here."

"I woke up this morning and came to see if you were still on the couch. That dream made me realize how much I care about you. I would have been crushed if you weren't there."

"But I am here and it was just a dream, Sasha. You know that, don't ya?"

"Yeah, I know, but—"

"No *buts*, alright. Let's, uh, let's do something today. I don't know…whatever you want to do."

Marti had to remind himself that this girl was just twenty-five, so while he was settling into his age—five years short of forty—she was just getting started in hers. When he said they would do whatever she wanted, he didn't know she was going to ask him to throw on a pair of blades and drag him out on a frozen floor. She, on the other hand, was a natural ice skater. And rather than compete for everybody's snickers while he fumbled on the ice, Marti simply elected to watch her.

He sat there on the bleacher watching her float on ice as if she had not a care to weight her down. She was so full of life, flawlessly gliding about. He imagined how it would feel to be as free as she seemed. Far too long he had carried the burdens of his dysfunctional family. Far too long his life had been impeded by his father's mistakes and eventual suicide. Far too long he had wondered about the safety of his imprisoned brother. Far too long he had gone without speaking to his mother, hearing the calm of her voice, seeing the sweetness of her face, for she was quite beautiful. There were photos all over their house of his mother as a young woman: her wedding picture, one of her with her siblings, even her high school graduation picture. In deed, he thought she was stunning, one of the most beautiful women he'd ever seen, and he took pride in having a mother with such attributes.

The day of the funeral, even then she was flawless, though it was apparent from the redness of eyes that she had been crying. Whatever troubles she and Marti's father had, there was no question she loved her husband. She had stuck by him through it all. Helped him get his business off the ground in '79, filling in as his personal secretary, taking his messages, advertising the company to friends, neighbors, strangers, anybody she could think of who might one day need a builder. And even though the business had survived the next two years, times had gotten extremely difficult for the Johnson family by 1982 because of the recession, one of the longest the economy had seen since 1975. They tried, but couldn't seem to catch any breaks, so Marti's parents argued constantly about the money. What he could not understand then, but now knew, was that both his parents were under a great deal of stress and strain. While his father, no doubt, questioned his ability to provide for his family, which, if he could not, made him less a man, his mother worried about losing the house, feeding the kids, making ends meet. Back then Marti could only think about how much she nagged his father and how that would drive any man crazy. But he was wrong about his mother, and that greatly saddened him because his misjudging her had been the cause of their estrangement. Though he could not see clear to admit this seven years ago, he missed her, missed her face and could no longer shake the overwhelming feeling of loneliness.

Laden with regret, Marti desperately wanted to convey to his mother how much he wished he had refrained himself from saying those things to her. While they never had the closest relationship, he loved her because she was his mother and respected her because she always tried to be there for him and his younger brother, though she never fully understood either of them. It astonished her so that Donald could begin stealing, especially since she had taught him better, but Marti understood what was happening with his brother. He knew what had caused him to change. He, on the other hand, could not bring himself to do the same. Changing his name better suited him. They were both trying to escape their lives, and Donald's desperate need to escape his life much sooner is what landed him behind bars.

Marti remembered having to sit there listening to his brother plead guilty to several counts of theft and the one robbery that ended with the death of a sales clerk. It was all so pointless, he thought. Donald never walked away with more than a few hundred dollars from any of those robberies, but now he was spending a good portion of his life behind bars because he took it too far and killed someone. Donald once told him during a visit that it was easier being in prison than it was living in the free world because he didn't have to deal with the responsibilities and pressures and disappointments and ugliness of the world. For an instance, Marti was envious, but only for an instance. Still, he could understand his brother's logic given everything the two of them had gone through.

In some ways, Marti, too, was in prison. He certainly had no steel bars to confine him, but he felt locked up, trapped, unable to break free from the past. He'd spent the last ten years trying to escape, trying to do things differently than what he saw and experienced as a young boy, and he had failed much of the time. He did, however, seem to find some solace in his relationship with Sasha.

Marti returned his attention to Sasha who had taken herself a partner, a little boy who seemed to have developed an instant crush, a harmless crush similar to one the young boy likely had on his teacher or any other pretty female with whom he had come in contact. It was humorous to watch the little boy, with the widest grin on his face, every now and then sneak glimpses of Sasha as they skated. Sasha must have known his motive, though innocent, for wanting to pair with her, Marti thought. She was obviously flattered. Even in their youth, the male species would fall over themselves behind a beautiful woman. And the young boy had served as prime example that there was little a man wouldn't do to be near an attractive woman. Somehow a man having a beautiful woman on his arm made him feel better about himself; it validated him, stroked his ego, boosted his manhood. Her intellect, quite honestly, usually almost always ran a distant second to her physical attributes. Men, and Marti was no exception, were creatures of sight. If what they saw was extremely pleasing, it drove their sexual impulses through the roof. Given that well-known truth, it was a wonder that Marti had not yet made any sexual advances toward Sasha. Here, again, Marti refrained himself and curbed his impulses, thinking he would undermine his feelings for Leslie if he slept with Sasha. He reasoned with himself that if he were to give in to those impulses, he would not be making love to Sasha; it would only be sex because, while he cared for her, he did not love her. For once in his life, that mattered. He had already gone through a series of physical relationships after his divorce, none of which amounted to anything special, not even close. He was not going to travel that path with Sasha.

Sasha circled the rink one last time with the boy before joining Marti on the bleacher.

"Should I be jealous?" asked Marti, smiling.

"No, that's just my buddy, T.J. He's a good little skater, couldn't you tell?"

"Well, it wasn't your skating he was studying."

"Quit playing, he's just a kid."

"Yeah, he's a kid with male impulses just like the rest of us. We know a pretty lady when we see one."

Sasha leaned over and gave Marti a kiss. "You're not so bad yourself. So, ready to go?" She began unlacing her skates.

"Yeah, where to next?"

"How about we get some food? I'm starving," she said.

"You? Man, I could eat a horse right now."

At Ruby Tuesdays, Marti and Sasha were seated in a cozy little booth. For a Saturday evening, the place was scarce. After only a few minutes of wait, the waiter had taken both their orders and served their first round of beverages.

"I thought you said you were starving," said Marti.

"I am."

"All you ordered was a salad. You can't be that hungry. I hope you're not worried about your weight. If so, don't be."

"I always get their salads when I come here," she said. "What's wrong with that?"

"Whatever. I'm a man's man. Give me some meat."

"I guess that explains the whole slab of ribs you got coming," she quipped.

They both exchanged a laugh. "You know I'm digging this, you and me," Marti said, initiating new conversation. "We have a good time together."

"You sure about that?" questioned Sasha.

"What do you mean?"

Sasha answered, "We've been going out for a month now, and we've never been together. I even offered last night, but you shot me down. Is there something you're not telling me?"

"Like what?" Marti said, raising his brow.

"Is there someone else?"

"No," he insisted.

"You answered that too quickly. There is someone else. Who is she, Marti?"

"She's nobody. Listen, I've been hurt before, and I've been in too many relationships since my divorce that were nothing, but physical. I wanted something different with you. I hope you can hang with that."

"It's a first for me," said Sasha. "I don't know any guy who doesn't want sex unless either he's gay or getting it from somebody else."

"Well, neither of those applies to me," Marti assured her.

"I hope not, but you are attracted to me, right? I mean you've thought about it?"

"Sasha, you just don't know the half of it. Man, the way you look in those short skirts and fitted tops. Woman, you fine, too fine for your own good. Yeah, I think about it."

"Hey, I won't tell if you won't," hinted Sasha, before reaching across the table to place her hand on top of his, seductively groping it. "So what's stopping you?"

Marti started smiling. "Are you trying to seduce me?"

"Yes," replied Sasha, running her hand slowly up his forearm. Her touch felt good, and she was starting to turn him on.

"I don't suppose that you're still hungry then?" asked Marti, realizing full well where this was leading.

"Not for food," Sasha answered.

Marti beckoned their waiter, who immediately approached. "Yes, sir, did you need something?"

"Yeah, man, there's been a slight change of plans, we'd like to get that food to go," said Marti.

"Not a problem, sir. We'll have that right out to you soon."

"I appreciate that."

Having made several seductive glances over at him while he was driving, Marti knew that Sasha was definitely game for whatever. Her flirtatious body language was screaming out to his testosterone cravings. Yet by the time he had parked in front of her apartment, he was having second thoughts about tossing out all that logic and reason about betraying Leslie just to satisfy his sexual urges.

The two of them got as far as her front door when Marti changed his mind. "Hey, maybe I shouldn't."

"Why not," she said, kissing his lips. "You know you want to."

"I do, but—"

Before he could finish his sentence, Sasha began to plant soft kisses on his neck then on his lips. Leaving him with a long wet one to whet his appetite and send his heart racing, she turned to open the front door and took a few steps inside before turning back to say in a tone that was every bit the markings of the seductress, "Are you coming?"

Marti

Chapter 7

When Marti rolled over in the bed the next morning, he found himself staring at Sasha whose face was partially obscured by the bed covers. What had he done? Stealthily, he pulled back his side of the covers and got out of the bed. He had made a huge mistake, forgiving himself momentarily for not being able to resist her feminine persuasion or her body. She was looking so good last night at the restaurant, in the car, even on the ice while she skated. He told himself that he'd just kiss her goodnight and leave. That scenario got blown out the water somewhere between the kiss at the front door and him trailing her into the bedroom.

Marti had slipped on his jeans and was putting on his other tennis shoe when Sasha woke. "You're leaving?" she asked, wiping the sleep from her eyes.

"Yeah, I better go."

"Don't go," she said, smiling at him as if she wanted to pick up where they'd left off.

"I have to," he said, now pulling his polo over his head.

"Hey, last night was great," she said, holding the covers over her mouth, hoping to spare Marti the stench of her morning breath. "You know you talk in your sleep? Who's Leslie?"

Marti stopped in his tracks. He couldn't believe he had done that. "Who?"

"Leslie? You kept saying her name. She's somebody you know?"

"Naw, I better go."

Sasha raised herself and rested her back against the headboard. "You can't leave it like that," she said. "You're rushing out of here like I did something wrong."

"I think we should just cool it for awhile," said Marti, looking her dead in the eyes.

"Why? I thought things were good. You wanted last night to happen, right?"

"Yeah, let's just cool it for awhile," he said. "We'll talk later. I've got some stuff I've got to sort out." And with that, Marti exited Sasha's bedroom, leaving his beautiful seductress bewildered by his overnight mood change.

After jiggling the key in the lock a few times, the door unlatched and Marti walked inside, tossing his keys on the coffee table before crashing on his black leather couch. What in the world had he just done, his mind wondered behind closed lids? He lay there trying to piece together his life as if some enigma, realizing there was something not right about it. There was still something missing, and in his thirty-five years on earth, he still had not found what that was or how he could get it. And he wouldn't be satisfied until he figured that out.

Now reminiscing through his string of flings over the past four and half years, he knew it wasn't a question of who was missing, even though he now loved only one woman. It was more than that. It had to be. He'd just spent the night with Sasha. Yes, Sasha, who was beautiful and smart and witty and young and exciting, yet he felt unfulfilled. Worse than that was how he just ran out of Sasha's apartment like a thief. Now she would be wondering what she had done wrong and it wasn't even about her. This was about him. There were too many unresolved issues in his life. A relationship would only complicate things more.

Marti grappled a bit on the sofa before jumping up, grabbing his keys, and heading toward his car. An hour later he found himself parked outside his mama's house, edged up enough for him to see into the backyard where she was tending to her garden. Part of him wanted to approach her, but the other part of him, the part that remembered all the unopened, returned letters, kept him inside his car until he eventually started the ignition and drove off.

Driving on the freeway, Marti noticed the huge billboard for TV Land Network, which showcased the blast from the past faces of Archie and Edith Bunker, and it transported him back to a time when he and Donald were just boys. It was one of the rare occasions that his father was in a good mood. The television was blaring *All in the Family*. Archie had grumpily muttered an insult to Edith, and his father burst into laughter, a hardy rumble with his legs flailing in the air. Their mother, in the kitchen preparing dinner at the time, stopped what she was doing and came sat on the arm of their father's favorite chair and laughed with her husband. While Donald remained stretched across the floor glued to the set, his head propped up by his arms, seeing what was happening between his mom and dad garnered Marti's full attention. They were actually having a good time. Whatever happened to that, Marti wondered as he pulled onto the exit ramp? Whatever happened to that?

Chapter 8

Next day, Monday, the start of another school week, Marti called in sick, something he hadn't ever done since he'd been working at Baker High. It was out of character for him, and Leslie would no doubt wonder about his absence, he might even get a call from her later. Having taken hiatus from a workday, he also contemplated missing his evening class, knowing that what awaited him was the awkwardness of having to confront Sasha after having bailed on her the day before. She would have a lot of questions, would want to know what was going on with him, something he didn't even know himself.

When he walked inside the Education building, headed in the direction of his class, Sasha was already standing in the hallway in front of the classroom.

Approaching her, he gave a faint smile before saying, "Hey." Marti knew he couldn't avoid her forever and anticipated her response.

"Hey," she replied. "Listen, I don't understand what yesterday was all about, Marti. Why did you leave like that? I know you said that I didn't do anything wrong, but I can't help thinking that I did," she said, shifting her book satchel from one shoulder to the other.

Marti took Sasha by the elbow and guided her to the bench in the hallway, just a few feet from their classroom. "I'm sorry about that, you know. I shouldn't have just left like that, but..." he said, pausing.

"But what? You can tell me," she said, reassuring him.

"I don't know what's going on with me, and I promise you that it's not about you, Sasha. You are wonderful. I love being with you, I do. I just think maybe we should cool it for awhile until I figure some stuff out in my head."

"So the other night did complicate things for you, didn't it? Tell me something. Is there somebody else, Marti?" That she said looking him dead in his eyes, expecting no less than the truth from him.

"Listen, we better get inside. Class will be starting in a minute."

The entire time in class Sasha kept glancing over at Marti, who'd return only a blank stare. He knew what she wanted...yes, an answer to her question. Was there somebody else? And there was, but this wasn't even about Leslie.

Marti leaned in toward Sasha, "Listen, I know you want to pick up where we left off before class, but I just need some time, and I really don't want this to be awkward for us the next time we see each other in class."

"Are you breaking up with me?"

"No, no, that's not it. Listen, I can't do this right now, okay? We'll talk. I just need time," said Marti, rising from his desk then leaving Sasha behind to watch as he vanished through the door.

When he got home, Leslie had left him a voicemail, wanting to know if everything was alright. How could he tell her that his life was falling apart, that he was confused about everything that he thought he knew? Not tonight, he told himself, not tonight. I'll talk to her tomorrow.

***

Marti managed to avoid talking to Leslie the next day at work until he ran into her in the teacher's lounge, which he knew that he would, and she wasted little time beginning the inquisition.

"So, ya wanna tell me what happened to you yesterday?"

"Not really," answered Marti, grabbing the paper from the table to skim through the sports section.

"You've never missed a day since you've been here."

Marti stopped reading and thought about that statement for a minute before responding. "You ever been tapped out?"

"What to do you mean 'tapped out?'"

"You know like you're just tired of doing stuff because you don't feel fulfilled anymore."

Leslie now looked confused or perplexed by what he could mean. "You mean teaching? But you love—"

"I mean everything. Face it, Les, my life is a mess."

"What is it, Marti, what aren't you telling me?"

Let's see, he thought to himself. *Well, I'm in love with you, and oh, by the way, I've met somebody, and we spent the night together. Now she's all confused because I've left things between us unsettled. Basically, I skipped out on her*. Marti, of course, would say nothing of the kind to Leslie, only think such things. Instead, he'd make it seem as though his family troubles were the culprit.

"I drove by my mama's house the other day," he answered.

"And?"

"And she was out in the backyard working."

"What did you do?"

"Sat there and watched her for awhile then drove off."

"Why didn't you go talk to her?"

"Leslie, you know why."

"Listen, Marti, you've got to make her understand. Sometimes a letter won't do what looking directly into her son's face will. Or maybe it's you who's afraid."

Marti jerked as if baffled by that last remark, "Afraid? What do I have to be afraid about?"

"All this time," she said, "you've been able to hide behind the excuse that you'd tried to mend things with your mom through the letters. Yes, you put forth an effort with those letters and she rejected them, but sending a letter doesn't take much courage. Showing up on her front step, knowing how hurt she's felt for years—now that takes courage."

"I-I don't know what you're talking about."

"Yes, you do," she said, rising from the sofa and walking over to him. "I've gotta go, but we'll talk later, okay," said Leslie, placing her hand on his before leaving.

"Yeah, later." *What the heck does she know?* he thought. *Afraid? Whatever.*

Later came as soon as the three o'clock school bell rang. Leslie did her famous "peeping head in the door" routine then walked in and sat on a nearby counter. "So do you wanna keep making this hard, or will you tell me what's really going on because you were talking in code earlier? I'm an English teacher, remember, that's the language I best communicate in. Spill it, buster."

"There's nothing to spill. I'm just trying to figure some things out in my head."

"Then maybe I can help."

"I wish you could, but ya see, you're…" Marti caught himself before saying that she was part of the problem.

"I'm what?"

"Nothing, it's just that I'm sure you have your own issues to deal with, don't need me weighting you down with my baggage."

"Is that what you think of our friendship?" Oh, my God! She said it, the dreaded "F" word—friendship. Now he was convinced that she felt nothing for him romantically. "Do you honestly think that you are weighting me down or that you don't give me as much as I give you? Please say it ain't so. You're talking nonsense, Marti."

"Am I? C'mon, Leslie, you've always been there for me. You listen and advise me and you've got my back. I trust you completely. And I've grown to depend on that. I've come to respect that about you. I need that."

"I still don't understand how you think that you're weighting me down if that's what you've grown to need from me."

"Never mind, you're right, it was silly of me to say, so I retract that statement."

Leslie just looked at him incredulously. "I suppose now you just want me to drop this entire conversation, even though I still think you're holding out on me?"

"Honestly, yes, I do," replied Marti. "For once, I'm asking you to trust me when I tell ya that I have to go at this one alone."

"Alright, fine, do whatever you want. Just know that I'm here if you need me."

"Yeah, I know, Les. Thanks."

"Guess I'm out then. How late do you plan to stay up here?"

"I'll probably be here another half hour and then I'm going to go workout or something."

"Well, I'll see ya tomorrow then."

"You bet."

Chapter 9

It wasn't until Saturday night that Marti finally decided to call Sasha and try to patch things between them. He'd gone almost a week without talking to her and the truth of the matter was he missed her company. Maybe a relationship didn't have to complicate things. Maybe she was as good for him as she made him feel.

No, Marti was not in love with Sasha, but he did have strong feelings for her—he cared about her, cared about what happened to her, cared what she thought of him. He was really feeling this girl. It just made sense that he'd fight to keep Sasha, to try to mend things with her? They were great together, and not just that, but she was good to him, she made him feel...yes, something other than rejected. At this point, he didn't see anything wrong with pursuing her, even though deep down he was still reserving his heart for Leslie. In time, maybe Sasha would...no, Marti couldn't think of it. He'd just see where it all would lead, providing she'd give him another chance to make things right between them. Besides, it was senseless to pine after someone, blocking any potential of something great and lasting with someone else, especially if you didn't think you had a chance with the object of your affections anyway. With Sasha, at least he believed he had a real shot at something good. Maybe he was going about this all wrong. Admittedly, he was old enough to have been around the block and learned some things about relationships, but he was no Moses. Marti was still figuring things out, and the one thing he knew for sure was that it was important that he try to win back Sasha.

"Hey, Sasha, it's me. I wasn't sure I would catch you."

"Yeah, I'm just sitting here watching television, although I'm a little surprised to hear from you. I thought maybe the next time that we'd talk would be in class on Monday. You said you needed time."

"I know, but I missed you, and I was stupid for running out like that. I was trippin' and I'm sorry."

"Why did you freak out like that?"

"I don't know. I've got all this stuff in my head. I just didn't want this between you and me to be like my past encounters with women. I really want to take things slow. I don't want to make a wrong move with you. Am I making any sense at all?"

"I think so. Listen, we can slow things down even more if you like. It's not like we rushed into anything, though. We've been dating a little over a month, but I don't want to pressure you, Marti. Gosh, that sounded like such a guy thing to say."

Marti could hear Sasha giggle on the other end of the line. "I just don't want to lose you, not now. I do care about you and I want to try to make this work. I do."

"Then we'll just take it one day at a time," she assured him. "It'll be fine; just don't scare me like that again. If you have a problem or you get freaked out, then talk to me. I am a good listener."

This time Marti laughed into the phone. "Among other things," he replied naughtily.

"Oh, you mean the other night?"

"Uh-huh," said Marti.

"Yeah, I had a really good time, too."

"Not bad for an old man, am I?"

"Let's get one thing straight, you are many things, but old sure ain't one of them." On that note, they both laughed.

"You do realize that spring break is coming up a week from Monday?"

"That's right," said Sasha, "it is the last week of March for us."

"How about we do something that week?"

"Like what? I'd just assume we stay around here and spend time together."

"Well, if that's what you want, but I promise I'll paint you a Baton Rouge that you've never seen on canvas before."

"Wow, quite the poet," Sasha teased.

Marti smiled inside his mind, thinking that maybe some of Carolyn's creative instincts had rubbed off on him. "I'm no poet, but you do make me feel like one sometimes."

"Well then, Lord Byron, what shall we do?

"You'll find out soon enough."

"You're assuming I like surprises."

"Don't you?" asked Marti.

"Of course I do."

"That's what I thought. Now don't be trying to figure out what I'm planning, you'll ruin it."

"Well, I can't wait."

"Like I said, you'll find out soon enough."

Chapter 10

"Have I got a treat for you."

Sasha eyes grew with curiosity. "What is it?"

"You'll see," said Marti, cranking up the car.

When Marti drove into the TGIF parking lot, he motioned for Sasha to wait in the car. He'd be right back he said to her smiling. A few minutes later, he returned with a plastic bag inside of which were two takeout boxes.

"What's this?" asked Sasha, smirking.

"Open it."

Sasha eagerly opened the lid of one of the takeout boxes. "Oh, my God, tell me this isn't—"

Before she could get it out, Marti finished her sentence. "Uh-huh, French vanilla bean cheesecake with a whipped cream top layer and white chocolate shavings sprinkled on top. They get their cheesecake special order from the Cheesecake Factory. I did good, huh?"

"You sure did, baby," she said, leaning in for a kiss. "Wow, this is soooo bad. I really don't need to eat this, and it's still cold, too. Soooo bad."

"What's life without a little impulse? Hey, but wait, that's not all. We can't tear into that now, not until we reach our destination."

"Destination?"

"Just hold tight. I promised you a good time during this spring break and a good time is what I plan to deliver. I just need to stop by my place first. I forgot something." What Marti wasn't telling Sasha was that the little detour to his apartment was all part of his surprise, that what awaited her back at his place was a bouquet of a dozen red roses, a bottle of wine, and whatever else the evening would bring.

Back at his place, Marti insisted Sasha come inside for a second and not wait in the car because he had to search for whatever he had claimed to have forgotten. "You sure, Marti, because I can just wait here in the car?"

"Naw, baby, come on in."

"Alright then," said Sasha, still not realizing what any of this was all about.

Marti swung the front door of his townhouse open, where the vase of roses was set on his coffee table. Sasha's eyes gleamed in amazement, not nearly as brightly as the huge smile on her face.

"Like I said," said Marti, "I wanted this to be a spring break to remember, and it's kinda sorta a peace offering for tearing out of your apartment like I did that day. I shouldn't have handled things like I did."

"Oh, my God, Marti, they're absolutely gorgeous!" exclaimed Sasha, raising the vase to her nose, taking in a whiff of the botanical fragrance. "I love them."

Their romantic evening, while just starting, was then momentarily interrupted by a ringing phone. To his despair, it was a call from the hospital informing Marti that his mother had been rushed to emergency when one of her neighbors stopped over for their usual afternoon tea, but got no answer. The neighbor immediately called 911, who found his mother lying unresponsive on the kitchen floor. Apparently, she had slipped from a step ladder trying to reach something off the top shelf in her kitchen cabinet and hit her head on the tile floor, knocking her unconscious.

"What's wrong? What's the matter?"

Marti grabbed his keys and headed for the door. "It's my mother. She's in the hospital. I've gotta go. I'm sorry about this, but I've gotta go."

"Yeah, of course. I'm coming, too."

Marti stood over the hospital bed staring down at his mother for several minutes before leaning down to embrace the frail motionless figure. The last time he had ever held his mother that intensely was the moment just before they read off Donald's verdict. When the foreman uttered the word "Guilty," Marti latched on to his mother's hand, not once letting go as they escorted Donald away in handcuffs. The steady pulsation of her heart reassured him that though she lay there unconscious, she was still with him and that he still had a chance to make things right between them.

"I can't believe this has happened," he said to Sasha, who stood on the opposite side of the bed from Marti.

"I'm sorry," she replied, shaking her head. "I'm so sorry."

Marti never looked up at Sasha. He remained fixated on his mother, who lay there peacefully, her long locks fallen to the sides of her face, the corners of her mouth defined by the age lines. Marti could never bring himself to think they were laugh lines, sadly telling himself that his mother must have had very little laughter fill her days since their estrangement.

"I should take you home, Sasha."

"No, I can just take a taxi; you should stay here with your mother."

"No, no, I'll drop you off. I need to talk to you about something. Seeing my mother like this has made things clear to me now."

"What does that mean? What are you saying, Marti?"

Marti walked over to Sasha and gently escorted her into the hallway. "Listen, I think I need to just focus on my mama right now."

"Are you saying that you want to end this with me?"

Marti shook his head and proceeded to explain to Sasha just what he meant, that he just couldn't think about his relationship with her right now, that he had to be there for his mother because she needed him. "When she comes out of this," he assured Sasha, "I'll be able to focus on us again. I'm sorry it has to be this way, but I don't know any other way to do it. There's just so much going on, and I tried to tell you this before, Sasha, that my life was complicated, that I had all these issues to resolve; making things right with my mama was one of them. Now fate… no, this is forcing my hand."

"I understand you needing to be there for your mother, Marti, but what am I supposed to think when it sounds to me like you are using this as an excuse to break up?"

"I'm not," he told her. "I'm just putting us on hold for now."

"But is that really necessary?" she questioned. "Why are you doing this if I'm important to you and you want to be with me?"

"I do want to be with you," said Marti. "It's just that I've gotta do right by my mother. It's too important to me. Don't you understand that?"

"I'm trying to. I'm trying really hard. I just thought that it was times like these that you would need someone to be there for you, too. You shouldn't go through this alone. Let me be here for you." Marti's thoughts went to Leslie and the fact that he would not be alone. He still had Leslie; she knew exactly how he felt, she understood him completely. She'd be there to console him like a true friend should.

Sasha then argued that sometimes he treated her as if she was too young to understand him or what he was going through, and she reminded him that she had had her share of tragedy and loss in her life; she knew exactly what he was feeling right now, and admonished him not to shut her out.

"I should drop you home," reiterated Marti. Sasha said nothing more on the matter, not even in the car ride to her place, only stared out the window still perplexed by his actions. He didn't need to do this, she thought. The silence was broken only after Marti pulled into Sasha's apartment complex and parked the car.

"So that's it?" she said, facing him in the car. "I can't say anything more to convince you to think about this?"

"I'm not ending it. I just can't do this right now."

"And what am I supposed to say to you in class on next Monday?"

"No reason why we still can't be—"

Sasha halted Marti with a hand gesture. "Don't say it, just don't say it," she said.

"She needs me, Sasha."

"I need you, too."

"How can you say that? You're not in love with me. You don't even know me."

"Okay, I've heard about enough. If this is what you want, if you want to throw us away like this, fine go ahead, but don't expect me to come running when you realize how foolish you're being about this. You don't have to choose between us. I think you should be there for your mother. I just don't understand why you think you have to put us on hold."

"I just do, okay. I'll call you when I can."

"Yeah," Sasha said, opening his car door then facing him one last time before getting out, "you do that. Besides, we'll still see each other in class."

The scene was familiar, Marti watching Sasha from his car as she disappeared into her apartment. Only now it felt like a split, like this was the conclusion to a brief, but torrid affair. *Nonsense*, Marti thought to himself. He'd make things between them right again, but he had more pressing matters. His mother needed him.

A few cups of coffee and several drafts later, Marti had written a letter making sure this time that the apathetic tone in which he had written all the others—most of which she had returned unopened—had been blunted by his sincerity. Though he'd only heard that the comatose patient could hear the voices of loved ones, Marti hoped that the earnestness with which he had written the letter would be enough to reach his mother. Marti sat at his mother's bedside and began to read:

Mom, it's me, Marti. I know I've tried to fix things between us before, only to walk away with things still remaining unresolved. Maybe you could still sense the resentment, resentment I obviously wasn't hiding very well. Maybe not, but before I was different, too. I judged your part in all this. When daddy killed himself, I held that against you because you were his wife. You were supposed to know what he was thinking, what he was feeling, what he was getting ready to do or not do. I now realize that I had no right to make that judgment. I know now that you didn't always know what was going on with daddy because he didn't always tell you. And you didn't make daddy pull that trigger no more than I did. It wasn't your fault, but I blamed you and for that, I'm so sorry. I'm sorry for disrespecting you and questioning your love and loyalty to dad when I couldn't possibly have known everything that was going on. I'm sorry that I let you down perhaps when you needed me most. Mostly, mama, I'm sorry that he's gone because he took a big part of you with him. And I just hope that when you come out of this you can forgive me. I hope that you can find it in your heart to give me another chance. I love you, mama.

Marti folded the letter and placed it on the nightstand beside his mother's hospital bed. He gently clasped her hand in his own and watched her as she lay. He could feel the tears swelling in his eyes and the lump forming in his throat. He didn't want to lose his mother, not like this, not with so much unsaid. He needed her to wake up. "Just wake up," he repeated to himself, but she hadn't moved once, not a flinch, nothing. He was sorry that these circumstances were what forced him finally to come see her. He was sorry for all the pain he'd caused her over the years. He was sorry he had said those things. He wanted her forgiveness. He needed her forgiveness. There were so many thoughts racing through his mind. Everything was running together. Yet he managed to say everything that he needed to say to his mother as she lay there, and hoped that she could hear him.

***

Marti's mother's state stretched a week, each day of which Marti sat bedside talking to her, telling her about the things in his life that she had missed over the past several years; he'd even told her about Leslie, and on this visit, he brought his co-worker with him.

"Leslie, this here is my mother, Linda," said Marti, placing his hand on his mother's and tenderly stroking it. "I wish these were better circum—"

"Don't worry about it," Leslie said, stopping him just short of finishing his sentence. "She's a beautiful woman. She looks peaceful."

"I know, she does, and that worries me sometimes."

"Why?"

"Because what if she doesn't want to come back? What if where she is right now is more peaceful? I could lose my mama."

"Don't think like that," said Leslie. "She's gonna pull out of this and when she does, you've got to cherish her."

"Trust me, I will. I think what's making this hard, too, is that I have to tell Donald. I don't want to have to make that trip to tell him either."

"Yeah, but he has to know."

"I was hoping I didn't have to tell him at all."

"She's his mother, too. He deserves to know," insisted Leslie.

"Well, I'm heading that way this afternoon. You're right, he has to know. This has been one lousy spring break, I'll tell ya."

Leslie offered sympathetically, "But she's a fighter and so are you. You'll get through this. I promise you that." He may not have said it aloud or showed it in a gesture or a facial expression, but Marti trusted those words because they had come from Leslie.

Donald extended his hand toward his approaching older brother. "I'm surprised to see you here, man. What, I just saw you a couple of weeks ago. What brings you this way?"

Marti grimaced. "I've got something to tell ya, Donald."

"Yeah, what?"

"I guess I might as well tell ya that mama and I have been on the outs for about as long as you've been in this joint. And I didn't want to say anything about it because I don't really like to talk about it. Plus, I didn't want you worrying about it. You've got enough to think about up in here."

"Yeah, I figured as much."

"How's that?"

"Well, every time I got around to the subject of mama, you got real short, and it was always the same thing: 'Mama's fine.' So what happened? What's going on with you and mama?"

Marti scowled. "I don't want to get into that right now, man, and that's not why I came to see you. Mama's in the hospital. She fell and hit her head on the floor. She's in a coma, man."

Donald stood there speechless, peering at his brother, staggered by the news.

"Man, you alright?" asked Marti. "Say something."

"When, man, when did it happen?"

"It happened last week. I'm sorry I didn't tell you sooner, but I was hoping that she would have pulled out of it by now and that I wouldn't have to tell you anything at all." "Hey, man, just because I'm locked up in here doesn't mean you've gotta keep trying to protect me. I messed up alright, but I don't need you keeping stuff like that from me. I can handle it."

"I'm sorry, Donald, you're right. I should have told you then. It's just that I'm trying to come to terms with all this myself. I hadn't spoken to mama in over six years and then I get a phone call saying she's in the hospital."

"Then you'll keep me posted?"

"You know it, man," said Marti, patting his brother on the shoulder. "I've gotta run, gotta get back up to the hospital. Are you gonna be alright?"

"Yeah, man, I'm straight. Thanks for coming."

"Hey, I had to come; she's the only mama we've got."

Chapter 11

A week and a half passed before Linda Johnson finally opened her eyes and recognized the face glaring back at her as Marti.

"Mama, mama, you awake?"

Her voice was low and shaky. "Where am I?"

"Don't try to say anything else, mama. You're gonna be alright now." His mother slowly drifted back to sleep. Marti waited patiently by her side until she woke again a few hours later. She squeezed his hand before her eyes actually opened.

"Marti, that you?"

"Yes, ma'am. You remember what happened?"

She shook her head.

"You fell in the kitchen over a week ago. You're in the hospital, mama. You've been in a coma."

Slowly, she attempted to raise herself on the bed. Marti aided. "A coma? What are you doing here?"

"The hospital had to phone your next of kin, mama."

"Well, you don't need to stay here anymore, I'm alright now."

"No, mama, this has gone on long enough. I'm not gonna run from you anymore. I'm not leaving your side ever again. Don't try to talk anymore, mama. I want you to rest. I'm going to go get the doctor. I'll be right back."

Marti returned a few minutes later with the doctor, who proceeded to examine his mother. "Well, Mrs. Johnson, everything looks fine. I'd suspect that the swelling in your brain from the fall has completely healed and that's why you are back with us right now. I'd like to keep you here a few more days so that we can monitor you and run a couple of more tests. All in all, I'd say we have a modern miracle."

"I'd say you're right about that doctor. The good Lord saw me through this one," she replied.

Marti saw the doctor to the door of his mother's hospital room. "Thanks again for everything you've done for my mama."

The doctor then frankly replied, "Honestly, it was nothing that I did. I'd say that your mother had her some guardian angels working overtime for her."

Marti returned to his mother's bedside, thinking about the doctor's last comment. It was outlandish to think that some angel, or even God, had had anything to do with his mother's recovery. It was what the doctor had initially offered as an explanation; her brain swelling had just gone down. Yes, that was it.

"You alright, son?"

"Yeah, mama, I'm fine. I'm just fine."

When Marti got home later that evening, he immediately called Leslie.

"So I didn't get a chance to talk to you before you left the school headed to see your mama. Any change in her status?" asked Leslie.

Marti released a sigh of relief. "That's why I'm calling. Mama came to this afternoon around 4:30. The doctor said that her swelling must have gone down in her brain, and then he said the oddest thing."

"What was that?" she asked.

"He suggested that mama's waking was the work of God, 'a modern miracle' were his exact words."

"That's not so odd, Marti. Not all doctors subscribe to scientific principles only. Many actually do believe in God, and have suggested that modern medicine alone cannot explain some phenomenal occurrences."

"Well, what do you think?" asked Marti

"You know I don't talk about God much, but what if the doctor has a point? What if it was more to it than just her brain healing itself?"

"That's just nonsense, Les, and you know it. When has God ever done anything good for me?" replied Marti, slamming the magazine that he was flipping through onto his coffee table. "All I know is that I have my mama back and I'll leave it at that."

"And that's another thing, when are you gonna take me to see her again now that she's awake?"

"It ain't like I'm trying to keep you from her. You can come with me after work tomorrow if you like. They want to keep her up there a few more days to monitor her."

"Yeah, I do want to come," said Leslie.

"Then it's settled. Tomorrow I'll take you to see mama."

***

Leslie was already patiently standing on the passenger's side of Marti's car when he approached nearly ten minutes after school was let out. They had agreed that she'd carpool with him today since they would be going to the hospital to see his mother after work and would grab a bite to eat afterward before he dropped her off at her place.

"Yeah, I stuck my head in your classroom, but I see you're already out here," said Marti, walking over to unlock the car door for Leslie.

"What kept you?" asked Leslie, slipping into the hot car. With a heat index of ninety-nine degrees, it was a wonder the interior of the car never caught ablaze.

"Man, it's like a heat box up in here," said Marti, quickly starting the ignition to get the refrigerated air coming from the car vents circulating. "And I was checking some papers; that's what kept me."

"Well, let's go see your mama," she said. Leslie then took a CD from Marti's case and popped it into the CD player. A sultry Jill Scott oozed from his Kenwood door speakers and rear subwoofers. "Man, I love this woman's voice."

That was another thing Marti loved about Leslie. She was so cool to be around. And she didn't care about making fun of herself. She was not much of a singer, and she'd be the first to admit that she got passed over on that talent, but that never stopped her from doing a sing-alone to her favorite music. Marti only shook his head and smiled as Leslie crooned, no, belted the lyrics to "Gettin' In The Way."

"What, are you making fun of me?" snarled Leslie. "Why don't you just keep your eyes on the road, buster!"

An amused Marti answered, "I didn't say anything."

"I know I can't sing. I don't care. I love my girl Jill."

Stopped at a traffic light, Marti cut his eyes over at Leslie. "Then why don't we just listen to Jill for awhile, you know, just Jill?" He could hardly get the quip out of his mouth when Leslie took a jab at his arm.

"Negro, I'll have you know that I used to sing in my church choir along time ago," Leslie countered.

"Man, I'm surprised you didn't do anything with that talent of yours," retorted Marti while accelerating. They were just a few lights from the hospital now.

"You know what, forget you. Just drive." And just like that Leslie put an end to the verbal bout.

"I'm driving, I'm driving, geez."

When they walked into his mother's room, she was being attended to by the nurse. "Ahhh, just in time, guys. I'm just finishing up here with Mrs. Johnson," said the nurse, removing the blood pressure cuff from Linda Johnson's arm. "Your pressure is normal, Mrs. Johnson. I'll check in with you later, okay?" The nurse then took her exit, leaving Marti and Leslie to visit.

Marti leaned in to kiss his mother's cheek. "Hey, mama, I brought Leslie with me today. Remember, I told you about her? She's my best friend."

"I remember, I remember," his mother said, getting a good look at Leslie. "So nice to meet you, baby."

Leslie latched on to the older woman's hand. "You, too, Mrs. Johnson," she said, smiling. "I'm happy that you're okay. Marti tells me the doctor says you can come home in a few days."

Linda Johnson nodded. "That's what they say. 'Bout time, too. I bet my garden looks a mess."

Marti interjected, "Mama, we've already talked about this. You're coming home with me for awhile."

Mrs. Johnson sighed, as if to say, *Need I be reminded of that?* "Yes, yes, I know. You talked about it…I never agreed, though."

"Mama—"

"Hush up, Marti, we'll discuss that later. Let me just enjoy your friend here," sniped his mother. She was now pulling rank on her son, something that was obviously in the mother's handbook. "Well, don't just stand there, baby, have a seat. Marti, pull one of those chairs close to the bed for Leslie."

"Sure, mama," replied Marti, following his mother's orders. It was like being back in their house in Baker when he was a kid and she'd give him commands. Had nothing changed in all those years, or would it always be this way between parents and children, no matter the age? Did parents ever stop being parents? Likely, the answer was "no."

"That's right, baby, sit your pretty little self on down next to me. My son tells me that you're a teacher up at the school with him."

"Yes ma'am," Leslie politely replied. "I teach ninth-grade English, and I love it."

"Well, look at that. It seems like you and Marti have a lot in common."

What was this? Marti's mother, though wise beyond her years, had not even committed Leslie's last name to memory and was already trying to insinuate that there was something between the two of them, both of whom sat there shifting glances at one another while trying to fight back the embarrassment.

"Mama, I told you already that Leslie and I are best friends," Marti reinforced.

"Hush up, son. I didn't mean anything by it," said his mother, winking at Leslie who returned a warm smile.

"So how are you feeling, mama? At least your pressure is regular, and you're looking pretty good."

"God willing, son, I've got a few more good years in me."

"Nonsense, mama, you're gonna be around here a long time, long time. Shucks, you're gonna see your grandkids grow up."

"And about that, son…when are you gonna start on that?"

"I'm working on it, mama, I'm working on it," he said.

Leslie cut her eyes over at Marti. What did he mean he was working on? What did that supposed to mean? Or was he just saying that to pacify his mother?

Feeling the steadiness of Leslie's eyes on him, Marti peered back and shook his head, as if to say to her in that silent language the two of them seemed to have mastered, *It's nothing; don't worry about it. I didn't mean anything by that. You understand, right? It's my mama. I had to tell her something.* With that single, but illusive gesture from Marti, Leslie relaxed and returned her attention to his ailing mother. She did understand.

"Mama, I think we better go."

"Go? You just got here, son."

"I know, mama, but I think you should get your rest and I need to get Leslie home. We do have work tomorrow."

"Well, you don't have to rush off," she said, grabbing her son's hand and pulling him toward her for a kiss on the cheek.

"Yes, ma'am, I know. I'll be up here tomorrow, okay?"

"Well, alright. Leslie, dear," she said, now pulling her into an embrace, "it was so good to meet you. You keep my son in line, ya hear me?"

"Yes ma'am, I will. And you take care, Mrs. Johnson. I'm sure I'll see you again, though."

Leslie and Marti headed toward the door. With his hand pressed at the small of her back, the two of them looked like the perfect couple. "Bye, mama."

"Bye, son."

"Your mama is a trip. You know that, don't ya?" said Leslie to Marti as they exited the hospital, headed to his parked car. "She had me rolling."

"I saw that. I felt like I was back in grade school again," hissed Marti. "So what do you want to eat, whatcha got a taste for?"

"I don't care, food!" she said jokingly.

"We'll pass Rosie's. Up for Mexican?"

"So I can be up all night in the bathroom?" replied Leslie. "Don't think so."

"Okay, how about Tony Roma's?" suggested Marti. "I could eat ribs."

"That's cool."

Marti pulled into Leslie's complex. "Thanks for treating me tonight. I owe you one," she said.

"You just need to hope I can make it to my place. I think I overdid it on the ribs."

"Who you telling," said Leslie, grabbing her purse from Marti's backseat. "You know you can always crash here for awhile until your food settles. I can pop in a flick and we can chill. We haven't done that in awhile. You know, just hang out."

Marti thought about that prospect for a split second. "Ah, man, Les, I would, but I've got some papers to grade. I promised the kids I'd get them back to them tomorrow. How about a rain check?"

"Yeah, sure. I'll catch ya when I catch ya," she said, opening the car door to make her exit.

Marti grabbed her arm before she had a chance to remove herself from the car. "You're upset."

"I don't know how else you expect me to be," she said in a steely tone.

"I'd thought you'd understand. It's work."

"No, what I don't understand is why you aren't being upfront with me, and you know how much I loathe that from anybody, especially from you, Marti."

"I swear, Leslie, I really do have papers to grade. Otherwise, you know I'd come hang with ya."

"It's all good. Maybe it's just me," she conceded. "Maybe I'm just reading too much into this."

"I just don't want you to be mad at me."

"I'm not."

"You sure we're cool? I don't wanna pull away from here knowing that you're still bothered by this."

"Yeah, Marti, go home and handle your business," she said, shutting the car door. "I'll see you tomorrow at school. It's no big deal. There'll be other times."

Marti peered into Leslie face before she turned away. She made the attempt to pacify him with her words, but her discontent was ever resonant in every line, every facial curve, even in her tone. He knew she was unsettled by the way things were between them; her offering to hang out was her way of trying to regain something they had obviously lost. And he felt it, too. *Some other time*, thought Marti as he drove off. *We'll confront this some other time.*

Tonya Snow-Cook

Marti

Chapter 12

A few days later, once the doctor had signed off on his mother's release, Marti finally convinced Linda to come stay with him for awhile, at least until she fully recovered and had gotten her strength back. Like he anticipated, she fought him all the way at first, and despite her protest, a relentless Marti won the battle.

Marti pulled up to his townhouse. "Okay, mama, we're here. Just sit tight and I'll come over and help you out of the car."

"I'm okay, son. I just got a bump on my head, I ain't paralyzed," she remarked.

"Mama, you just woke from more than a week-long coma a few days ago. I'd say that qualifies as more than a bruise on the head. Now, don't argue with me, just sit tight." His mother shook her head, as if to suggest that all this ado over her was not in the least bit necessary.

He helped his mother into the living room and put her things into his extra bedroom that served as his home office. There was a day bed in that same room. Marti never knew when he might be entertaining a guest, so he figured a day bed would be a good idea. Honestly, had he his way, his mother would be taking his wonderful king-sized bed upstairs, but he didn't want her having to bother with stairs everyday. For that, he apologized relentlessly for his accommodations. And again, Linda scorned him for making such a fuss over nothing.

"Can I get you something, mama, something to drink, something to eat?" asked Marti while standing in the doorframe of his office.

"I'm fine, son," she said. Then patting the sofa seat cushion, she added, "Come sit down beside me."

"Yes, ma'am," said Marti dutifully. He then joined his mother on the sofa.

"I know you never understood why I kept going to see your father's grave, bringing those flowers. But let me tell ya, son, it's hard to remove someone completely from your life when you've been tied to them for so long. You remember the good times. You remember what it was about them that you fell in love with, that's what keeps you coming back."

"You're right, mama, I never understood how you could go see him like that."

"I think that going there to visit him made me able to find peace and forgive him."

"I know I need to do that, mama. I know that I need to try to forgive him. I've made too many mistakes already because of what he did to us...with you...with Carolyn."

"I know, son, but it's the only way you'll ever find any peace. You've got to confront your demons."

"Maybe some day I will, mama, just not now. I'm just glad I have you back."

"Son, you know I really do appreciate you letting me stay here, but I think maybe I should be back at my own place. I don't want to be a burden, and I have my work at the nursing home as well."

"Mama, you just got here, and you won't be a burden. I want you here. Let me take care of you. And you don't have to work anymore. I'll help you out."

"You will do no such thing and, frankly, I don't mind working. It keeps me busy, keeps my mind strong. Besides, I'm sure having your mama around is not the best thing when you want to entertain your lady friends."

"What lady friends, mama?"

"Well, son, I don't mean to pry, but what's going between you and Leslie?"

"There's nothing going on between us. Like I told you, she's my best friend."

"Friend, huh? Well, that's not how you were looking at her that day you brought her up to the hospital. I think there's something more there and she seemed very fond of you as well."

Marti began to glare pensively in the direction of the blank television screen.

"What are you thinking, son?"

"Actually, I was thinking about someone I was seeing before. Well, doesn't matter now. She probably doesn't want to hear from me."

"Why do you say that, son?" asked his mother.

"Well, I broke it off with her when you had your accident."

"And you did that because?"

"Because I wanted to be there for you. I didn't think it was fair to be distracted by anything else."

"A distraction? Is that what you think of this young lady—?"

"Sasha, her name is Sasha," said Marti, picking up his mother's cue for a name. "And no ma'am, I don't think of her as a distraction. I care about Sasha."

"I see. Well, I think you better fix things between you and her. That's if you're sure she's the one you really want."

"What do you mean by that, mama?"

She looked him dead in the eyes like she would always do when he and Donald were boys. And just as it did then, that unyielding stare of yesteryear now also demanded his complete honesty, not an attempt to deceive her with some pretense that he was oblivious, just the truth. "You know exactly what I mean. That Leslie friend of yours is important to you, too."

"Yeah, mama, she is. You know, mama, I-uh-I better go grab us something to eat for dinner. Some chicken, right?" said Marti, evading the subject of Leslie and his apparent feelings for her.

"Yes, son, chicken will be fine."

Chapter 13

She lasted two weeks before she approached Marti with the dreaded subject of going back to her house, and this time he would not refuse his mother's wishes. She'd done as he'd asked and let him take care of her for awhile. She'd actually stayed with him longer than he anticipated she'd even agree to. For that he was grateful. The time gave him the chance to get to know his mother all over again, and she her son and leave with him her sound, maternal advice. She, too, believed that he had been foolish to break things off with Sasha and presumed that his attempt to win her back would be no small task. Marti promised his mother that he'd try. Seeing where things with Sasha would lead was just that important to him.

Except for their brief exchange of civilities during class, Marti hadn't said much to Sasha in nearly four weeks. He was well aware that he'd need a thoughtful, but unique approach to even have a chance, so he seized a night after class to try to win back her affection.

Marti escorted Sasha outside of the Education Building, where they found a spot to sit on the steps. It was dark out, but well lit by campus lighting.

"Seeing anybody?" he asked her.

"Up until about a month ago."

"What happened?" asked Marti. He hoped she'd play along with his little game, relying on his charm to gain him her cooperation.

Sasha cut her eyes at Marti, displaying her disdain for what he'd done. "He dumped me."

"What idiot would be foolish enough to do such a thing?"

"No, I'm wrong, he didn't call it a breakup," she said, correcting herself. "He said he was putting things on hold." Marti could hear the condescension in her voice.

"I take it from your tone that you didn't agree?"

"I thought it was unnecessary, yes," Sasha replied.

"Well, let me ask you something," said Marti, removing from her face the wayward strand of hair tossed about by a gentle night breeze.

"Okay."

"What if this dude realized that he made a mistake? You think he could get you back?"

"Depends," said Sasha.

"Depends on what?"

"How do I know that you're not gonna run every time you can't handle stuff in your life or you get scared? I need to know..." She stopped mid-sentence then resumed a few seconds later. "I need to know that you're committed to seeing this relationship through."

"I'm here, Sasha. If I didn't want to see where this thing leads, I wouldn't be having this conversation with you right now. I wouldn't be wasting either one of our time."

"I don't know, Marti."

Marti grabbed Sasha's hand. "Listen, I'm sorry that I left you hanging like that. I made a mistake. You were right, I should have included you in this and I didn't. I won't try to promise that I'll never make anymore mistakes, but I won't just decide things for the both of us. Carolyn did that in our marriage and I hated that. It was unfair of me to do that with you, and I apologize." Marti brought her hand up to his lips and kissed it. "I want another chance."

With the moon casting reflected light into her beautiful brown orbs, making them pools of wonderment, she said to him earnestly, "I really want to say "yes" to you, but just let me think about it, okay? I don't want to get hurt again."

"Yeah, sure, take your time," Marti replied in an understanding tone while feeling somewhat dejected by her reservations, which she had every right to have.

***

Marti had just about given up on any chance he may have had with Sasha when the phone rang a week and a half later and it was her on the other end.

"Hey," she said.

"Hey."

"So I've thought a lot about everything you said to me that night after class, and I think…I think we should try again. You know part of me wanted to forget about you and just move on, but you got under my skin, Marti. There's just something about you."

"You know you couldn't have called me at a better time," said Marti.

"Why do you say that?"

"Don't you have a birthday coming up in a couple of days?"

"Yeah."

"Thought so. Anyway, I told my mother all about you after she was released from the hospital, and she's wanted to meet you ever since. I think maybe we should have a nice little dinner at my mama's to celebrate your day. So what do you say?"

"I'm a little surprised you remembered," answered Sasha.

Marti chuckled. "I sorta cheated. I've got May 12th circled in my day planner with your name scribbled underneath. I was flipping through it the other day and ran across that date."

"Still, I'm impressed."

"So does this mean you'll go, you know, to my mother's?"

"Yeah," she answered. "Yeah, I'll go."

***

"Are you nervous about meeting my mom?"

"Of course I am. I'm afraid she may think I'm too young for you."

"You're a grown woman, Sasha. Twenty-six is not too young for me."

"Still, I know how mothers tend to be about their sons—no one's ever too good for them."

"Well, mama's not like that. She knows full well I can make my own decisions when it comes to women. Besides, she's not the interfering type, at least not anymore."

"What do you mean by that—'not anymore?'"

"Nothing, I prefer not to revisit the past."

"If you say so," said Sasha, pressing the powered window switch upward. Her blowing locks were obstructing her vision.

"Trust me, she's gonna love you," said Marti, smiling.

133

By the time Marti pulled into the driveway of his mother's house, it was pitch black out. A single source of light came peeping through the kitchen window. She must have been slaving away in there over that old gas cooktop. He told her not to go to any trouble to prepare anything fancy, but he knew his mother. She loved to cook, especially for her son. And the closer they reached the front door, stronger was the aroma of whatever it was that she had prepared. Yet the enticing savor—though perhaps the cause—could not blot out Marti's growling stomach.

Sasha laughed out.

"You heard that, huh?"

"The entire neighborhood heard your stomach."

"Well, you ready?" asked Marti, reaching for the doorbell.

"Ready as I'll ever be," she said, leaning toward him to straighten out his collar. "That's better."

When the door flung open, his mother was wearing an apron and a huge smile. Immediately, her eyes fixed themselves on Sasha, and her smile grew even wider. Her eyes gleamed like that of a young child, and her countenance was warm and inviting. Sasha could see traces of Marti in her features, and seeing him in her made her less anxious. "Well, come on in," she said, pulling her son into an embrace. And Sasha was not to be forgotten. She must have held her even longer than she did Marti. "I'm so glad you could make it, sugah. I've prepared something special for your birthday."

"Oh, I'll be sure to get the recipes then. I love to cook, too," said Sasha, following Mrs. Johnson into the kitchen.

"You two have a seat. I'm just about finished with everything."

"Mama, you sure you don't need any help?"

"No, no. You just sit there and keep Sasha entertained. You know I don't like anybody messing around in my kitchen, but me."

"Yes, ma'am."

Mrs. Johnson lifted the lid on the huge cast iron pot and began stirring.

"That smells like stew," said Marti, licking his chops.

"It is, son."

"You ever cook stew before, Sasha?"

"No, ma'am, I haven't."

"Then you mustn't leave here without getting this recipe. It belonged to my grandmother. She was a cook on a cruise ship."

"Mama, I never knew that." Marti's interest was piqued.

"Yeah, baby, that's where your great grandfather and great grandmother met. Grandpa Lester worked in the boiler room."

"Oh yeah?"

"He sure was, son. Mama Mildred—that's what we used to call your great grandmother—used to tell us all kinds of stories about how she and Grandpa Lester would sneak off during their break and listen to music on an old gramophone they found in one of the ship cabins. Nobody was supposed to be in there, especially no colored folks and most especially not the hired help. One time they almost got caught. Someone was standing just outside the door where they were because they could hear the person's voice, and they just knew that was it for them, but soon the voice went away, so Grandpa Lester peeped his head out and no one was there. You can imagine how eager they were to get out before they really were caught. Needless to say, they stopped sneaking in and out of that cabin to have a listen. But they fell in love on that cruise ship and married a few months later.

"Well, don't that beat all?" Marti said, baffled. "And I thought you and daddy had some interesting stories about your courtship."

Sasha glanced over at Marti and smiled then returned her attention to Mrs. Johnson over at the stove. "So do you have any old photos of them that I can see?"

Mrs. Johnson stopped what she was doing long enough to turn around and address Sasha's inquiry. "As a matter of fact, I do, baby. Marti go look in the top of my closet and you'll find an old round hat box. It's the only one I got up there. Bring it here. My, my, Marti, I don't think you've even seen some of them pictures in over eight or nine years."

"I probably haven't," he said, rising to go fetch the box of photos.

"I'm sure handsome runs in the family," Sasha added once Marti had vanished into the other portion of the house.

Marti's mother chuckled. "Yes, my son is quite handsome, isn't he? But I'm sure he doesn't need me to tell him that. He's always found plenty of beautiful young women like you to ensure that his confidence is never lacking."

Marti re-entered with the hat box. "Okay, what's going on? Both of you have huge grins on your faces, so you must have been talking about me."

"Quit being so nosy, Marti. We were just having a little girl talk," said Sasha.

"Which means I was the topic of conversation."

"Well, if you really must know, we were simply saying how handsome the men in your family are and that quality certainly didn't pass you over."

Marti blushed. "Oh, well then carry on. Don't let me stop you."

"Shut up."

"Okay, kids, grab you a bowl from the cupboard. This stew is hot and ready. We'll have a look at those photos after supper, but save room for the birthday cake."

During dinner, little conversation was exchanged across the dinner table, as they were all busy having their fill of Mrs. Johnson's beef stew of carrots, celery, beef sirloin chunks, tomatoes, herbs and spices, onion, and potatoes. After finishing off the last spoonful of stew, Marti pushed back from the table a bit and rested both hands comfortably on his stomach, bringing to Mrs. Johnson's mind her late husband, who had the same mannerism.

"I don't know, mama," said Marti, rubbing his midsection, "I may not have room for that cake."

"Nonsense, son, I've never known you to turn down any kind of sweet."

"Well, mama, I don't eat them like I used to. In fact, I rarely eat sweets at all. Ask Sasha, she'll tell ya."

"Mrs. Johnson, your son has become somewhat of a health nut, which is good. He's doing the gym thing and watching what he eats. I, on the other hand, can't seem to keep up with him because I love hearty foods. I love to cook them and I love to eat them. If it weren't for my fast metabolism, I'd be in some serious trouble."

"Well, it's good to see a young person enjoy cooking. The kitchen has always been the meeting place for the family, at least back in my time. I'd like to believe that cooking and having family dinner have been a way for us to share a bit of ourselves. Trace your roots and you'll find that you come from a long line of folks who loved to eat and loved to cook. I don't think you'll find a black person who can't appreciate good old-fashioned home cooking—soul food is what they call it. And they are right. Eat a plate of soul food around a table of family and friends, and life, for that moment, doesn't seem so harsh or toiling. But the world has changed; people have changed. It's going at a pace that you need day planners to keep up and clocks for your clocks. I won't sit here and tell ya that technology ain't good, but I work around a lot of old people, and it seems to me, although they are nearing the end of their lives, that they just have more peace and contentment then some of you young people. You're spending your lives chasing things, and sometimes I wonder if you ever find what you're looking for. I wonder if it's even worth it. You'll have to ask yourself these questions someday. And maybe you ought to ask them sooner rather than later."

Her impartation of maternal wisdom left them both reflective to the point that they each began to wonder if they had ever really stopped to think about such things. Like so many, they were party to the rat race, chasing dreams they'd likely spend their lives trying to obtain. Perhaps the real point Marti's mother was trying to make was not the notion of the chase, but the effect it had on so many people; what the chase brought out in people; how it compromised quality of life in some ways. People weren't happy as they should be. People were too busy to stop, to appreciate...even as mundane an occasion as Sunday dinner. The world was evolving, but somehow, in Mrs. Johnson's mind, people weren't able to keep up in a way that they were unaffected.

"Well, don't just sit there. We'll have cake in the other room while we look through these here photos. Marti, escort your lady friend into the living room. I'll be in in a minute with the cake. Here, grab that hat box, too."

Marti and Sasha spent the better of two hours visiting with Mrs. Johnson. And sorting through those old photos proved quite entertaining. Marti couldn't believe he had ever given that much attention to a super 'fro that he wouldn't dare sport today. Or the striped Izod polo shirts and tight Levi jeans—*my God*, he thought, *whose idea was it to turn those articles of clothing into fashion statements?* Some twenty years later, just about every stripe or plaid or bold color or big hairdo that they proudly modeled in that scrapbook was a fashion faux pa. These were certainly different times.

And more than just entertaining pieces of still life, those photographs were links to his past—before the struggling family business; before his father took the .45 caliber pistol and placed it up to his own temple; before Donald's home away from home was a barred cement cell, twin bed, and leaky faucet; before nearly eight years of estrangement from his mother; before his life became too distorted and troubled. Marti couldn't have asked for a better visit, and from the way Sasha raved incessantly about his mother on the drive back to the city, she could not have either.

Chapter 14

The last day of class—the day teachers spent packing up their things and closing up their classrooms for awhile, a day educators throughout the country could exhale and thank God for surviving one more year—was here. Unlike many of his colleagues who'd be spending their summer vacationing in Hawaii, HGTVing their homes, or doing whatever it took to steer their minds clear of the hustle and bustle of teaching, Marti would still find himself in the classroom, only now looking from the opposite side of the teacher's desk. He registered early for summer classes, grateful that he had found the two courses that he lacked being offered in the summer sessions. With only the six hours for his thesis project to contend with in the fall, he hoped to walk by December with a Master's degree.

His only regret was that he had spent very little time with Leslie since he had started dating Sasha again. And the demands of juggling summer school and his relationship with Sasha and starting the preliminaries of his thesis project meant that he would be spending even less time with her over the summer vacation. His best opportunity to speak with Leslie before they went their separate ways for two months was now.

Marti stuck his head in her door. "Hey, got a sec?"

"For you, always," she said, packing some school materials in a box. "What's up?"

Marti approached her and started helping her pack. "Oh, nothing, just wanted to know your plans for the summer. Going anywhere special this year?"

Leslie said nothing in return only stared at him.

"Why are you looking at me like that? It's freaking me out," said Marti.

Leslie raised her left brow, something she'd often do when the wheels in her head were turning. "You seem different."

"Different, different how?"

"Maybe different is the wrong word. More like distant. Where are you these days?"

"What you are talking about, Les? I'm right here, standing next to you."

"Oh yeah, Marti, you're here in body, but you're a million miles away emotionally."

Marti sat on one of the student desks and folded his arms. "What makes you say that? I speak to you everyday at work. We do lunch break together."

"Exactly my point, the job doesn't give you much leeway to avoid me, but when was the last time we went somewhere on the weekend or did something fun together? And going to the hospital to visit your mother last month doesn't count. While I didn't mind at all, there was nothing fun about that. How is she, by the way?"

"Mama's fine. And don't try to snowball me, Leslie. I want to know what you're talking about."

"Oh, now you're gonna pretend like you don't know what I'm talking about. You've been avoiding me, Marti, admit it, and I want to know why."

What was she—telepathic? How in God's name was she inside his head like that? He so did *not* want to do this right now, but it served him right for falling for such an amazing woman, one who could read him like a good mystery novel. "Is that seriously what you think, that I've been avoiding you? Tell me, why would I do that?"

"That's what I'm asking you, Marti. Are you seeing somebody and just don't want to tell me?"

"I've gotta go," Marti returned, jumping up.

"That's it, isn't it? You've got a woman."

"Dang, Leslie, if you only knew how much I love you, but sometimes…" he said, trailing off. Marti couldn't finish his thought; he could only shake his head in amazement of her perceptiveness.

The expectant look on Leslie's face quickly shifted to surprise. "What?!"

"Naw, Naw, c'mon, I didn't mean it like that."

"Then how did you *mean it*?"

"Hey, you're my girl. You know you're my ace, my partner in crime."

"Oh, because for a minute there I thought you were getting sappy on me. I thought you were going there. I really did."

"Naw, Les, you know I care about you. I've got love for you. You're my best friend, right? Can't have love for my best friend?" Marti wanted to take one of those books she was packing and whack himself over the head, first for his slip of the tongue then for his inability to recover effectively since the dubious look on Leslie's face had him convinced that she wasn't buying any of what he was saying anyway. It was a good thing they were getting a break from one another. "Anyway, I've got to get back to my room and finish up. You know where to reach me if you need anything. If I'm not in, just leave a message. I'm gonna be busy with school, but never too busy for you. Okay, well, have a good one, Leslie."

"You, too."

***

When Marti turned over in his bed, the clock read eight-thirty. He'd spent the better part of last night thinking about his conversation earlier that day with Leslie. He was so affected by it that he called off his date with Sasha, claiming that he really had a bad headache and wouldn't be much company or fun. Truth is, Leslie had gotten under his skin. He must have been really transparent when he thought he was doing a good job of hiding the fact that he was seeing Sasha. No, that wasn't it at all. Leslie just knew him, and that was another difference between her and Sasha. With some probing, Sasha would eventually figure out that something was wrong with him, but wouldn't push him to confide in her. Leslie always knew when things weren't right in his world, and often times pinpointed why something was awry. She always, always prodded him to talk it out with her, which most times he would—just not this time because it directly involved her. He still didn't know what to do about these feelings he had for her or even how to tell her about Sasha.

Suddenly, Marti's comparison of the two women was interrupted by something of a more mundane nature. It was May 29th. Donald had a birthday today. His younger brother was due another visit anyway, even though Donald was no longer that eleven-year-old kid who welcomed the fuss over him and loved the party favors and presents, especially those baseball cards Marti had gotten him that year. Donald wouldn't want to hear of it because it only reminded him that it was another year that he'd spent locked up in a correctional facility with little prospects of getting out on good behavior. So Marti wouldn't make a fuss or give him a card, none of that. That's the way Donald wanted it.

It was noon by the time Marti arrived at the East Baton Rouge Parish Prison in Scotlandville, Louisiana, and signed the visitor's log. A despondent Donald stood glaring out the window when Marti approached him for a hug.

"Hey, man, I know, you don't want to be reminded, but Happy Birthday," said Marti, embracing his brother.

Donald mustered a half-hearted smile as he pulled away from his brother's embrace. "That's alright, man. I appreciate it."

"Hey, what's wrong? You seem down. What's going on?"

They sat across from each other at a nearby table. "Same ole, same ole. Just a little depressed."

"So talk to me."

"Sometimes I think I'm never getting out of this place."

"I know it's tough, Donald, but you've gotta hang in there."

"I get pissed off every time I think about how stupid I was. I had no business in that store that day or with that gun. Just stupid."

"And you're serving your time, man. You can't beat yourself up."

"Listen, Marti, you've never killed anybody. You don't know what it's like to live with that everyday of your life, knowing that somebody is dead because of your foolishness. I don't think I'll ever be able to get past this."

"You have to, man, or it will eat you up inside."

"It already is, has been since I've been in this place. And it doesn't seem to get any better. I don't know what to do."

"I'm sorry, Donald, you're right. I don't know what that feels like. I don't have to live with that, but I live with so much other stuff everyday, and I tell ya, man, sometimes I feel like I'm losing it."

"You're talking about the old man?"

Marti ran his hand over the back of his head. "Yeah."

"And what about things between you and mama?"

"Mama and I are doing okay. I hate that it took her going to the hospital for me to do right by her, but we're working things out. She even came and stayed with me for a few weeks after she came out of the coma. I wanted her to stay longer, but you know mama. She's proud and head strong, and well, you know, when she sets something in her mind, you just can't talk her out of it."

"I'm glad, man, I'm glad you and mama are working things out."

"So am I," said Marti.

"And what about the love life?" asked Donald, hoping to live vicariously through his older brother's current escapades.

"Well, there's this woman I'm seeing, Sasha. Man, the woman is gorgeous and funny and smart and she makes me want to be younger, but I'm in love with somebody else and I don't know how to tell her."

"What do you mean 'you don't know how?' Just tell her, man."

"You think it's that easy, don't ya?"

Donald shrugged his shoulders before answering, "Frankly, man, I don't see why it's gotta be hard. You dig a woman, you tell her. Pretty cut and dry to me."

"Well, what if you don't know if she feels the same way about you? You're telling me I should just profess my love for her and risk being rejected? I don't think so."

"Yeah, I see your point," said Donald, chuckling. "That ain't cool."

"Exactly."

"So what are you gonna do?"

"I'm gonna keep seeing Sasha."

"What about—"

"Leslie?" interrupted Marti.

"Yeah, Leslie."

"I don't know," said Marti, rising from the table. "Listen, man, I better get out of here. It was good seeing ya."

"Yeah, and listen, Marti, things will work out…with your lady friends."

"I hope so." Marti extended his hand for a brotherly grip. "You take it easy, man, and Happy Birthday."

"Thanks. Later."

"Later."

Chapter 15

With only three weeks of summer school behind him, Marti was ready to concede to the travail of cramming a regular semester's worth of studying into five weeks. His first summer session class was arduous at best, especially since he'd rather spend his time on some golf course. No matter, the end was near, and he had Sasha to fill his nights and weekends.

A kiss on the forehead stirred Sasha from her sleep around eight that Saturday morning. The two of them had an alternate arrangement in place for the weekends, and this time she was staying over at his townhouse. Of course, Sasha would have much rather slept in all day, but Marti was an early riser and would not give her the pleasure of remaining snuggled underneath the covers. The sun was shining too brightly through the partially opened blinds causing the dawn of a perfect morning to bounce off her face. She was absolutely gorgeous even just waking up.

"What time did you get to bed last night?" asked Sasha with her mouth still covered by the sheet.

"Around twelve-thirty. I had to knock out some studying for that test I'm having Monday."

"I must have been really tired then because I didn't even hear you when you got into bed, and you know how light a sleeper I am."

"I know because I was playing around with your hair and kissing on you and rubbing on your thigh and you didn't budge. You were completely spent."

"Guess I'm in wind-down mode. Last year I was pounding the summer school pavement, so happy I finally get a break from school."

"Wish I could say the same," said Marti, grabbing a t-shirt out of his chester drawer. "You want something, some eggs, how about an omelet? I think I got some stuff for a bacon and cheese omelet?"

"Naw, baby, I think I'll just have some chicken soup. I'm feeling a little queasy this morning."

Marti walked over to Sasha's side of the bed and sat down on the edge next to her and placed his hand on her forehead. "You don't have a fever or anything. How about you just lay here and I'll get everything for you? Can't have my baby sick."

Smiling, Sasha replied, "You're so sweet."

"Hey, don't let that get out."

Marti went into the kitchen and stirred around a bit, retrieved a can of chicken soup from the pantry, and opened it then heated it on the

154

stove to a nice simmer. Ten minutes later he had returned to the bedroom carrying a tray of breakfast. Sasha had her eyes closed when he approached her side once again.

"Hey, Sash, you really don't look too good. Maybe we need to go to the clinic up the street."

"Tell ya the truth I feel even worse," she said before throwing her hand over her mouth and leaping from the bed and scurrying to the bathroom.

"Okay, that's it, we're going," insisted Marti, rushing in behind her. "You're not just nauseated, you're sick." Sasha was bent over the toilet vomiting. "Oh, man, this ain't good."

Several minutes later Sasha was able to pull herself away from the toilet long enough for Marti to help her throw on something decent and make it to the car. With his hazards blinking, Marti sped down the highway. Yet half way to the clinic, which was only twenty minutes from Marti's place, a doubled over Sasha showed signs of getting worse.

"You need me to pull over?" asked Marti, concerned that Sasha wouldn't make it to the clinic before having to regurgitate again.

"No, I'm...I'm okay. Just keep driving." The words of assurance had come from her mouth, but she certainly didn't look good at all.

"I don't know, Sash, you don't look too hot. I'm pulling over." And no sooner than Marti had pulled the car over onto the shoulder did Sasha throw the car door open and vomit.

Slowly, Sasha raised herself. Her eyes were glazed over, and she looked even more squeamish than before. Marti leaned over to the glove compartment and retrieved a napkin from it then proceeded to wipe the corners of her mouth. "Feel better now?" he asked, to which Sasha could only nod. "Good, just hold on, baby, I'll have you at the clinic soon enough," he said turning the ignition. "We'll be there in a few minutes."

It was a good thing Sasha's nausea had settled by the time they arrived at the clinic because she had a fifteen-minute wait before she could be seen by the doctor, a tall, slender white man, whose graying hair gave him a distinguished quality.

Fairly certain of the diagnosis after initially speaking with Sasha, the doctor responded, "Well, Ms. Clayborne, based on your symptoms, sounds like you may have a virus, but I'll just give you an examination to rule out anything else."

Marti had waited patiently in the waiting room for twenty minutes reading a magazine when the physician appeared and asked him to come back to the examination room. Sasha was sitting up on the table looking exhausted.

"Okay, what we've got here," said the doctor, shutting the door, "is Viral Gastroenteritis or stomach flu. You really needn't be alarmed because you have a mild case; however, there have been several cases this time of the year because it's highly contagious. The virus usually resolves itself over time, within a few days, I would say. You should take it easy and rest, drink plenty of fluids to prevent dehydration, and eat easy-to-digest foods. That's it, Sasha. If your case worsens—the vomiting and nausea, or you develop an acute case of diarrhea—then don't hesitate to come see me again."

Marti extended his hand, "Thank you, doc."

Smiling, the doctor replied, "Just make sure she gets plenty of fluids and rest. And you shouldn't eat or drink after one another until she's no longer infected."

"Will do."

Chapter 16

Another Independence Day had rolled around. And this year's festivities would be a celebrated change from the melancholic events of the previous year. During this time last year, Marti found himself up at the prison with Donald, the two of them wishing they had something far better to which to look forward, especially Donald since the irony of it all was that he'd foolishly thrown away his personal liberties. Leslie had gone home to Dallas, and the truth was Marti had nowhere else to go.

Today, however, would be nothing like that. Preparation for the big gathering at Marti's mother's house began yesterday evening with Sasha in the kitchen whipping up her famous potato salad and broccoli cheese casserole. Marti had fired up the pit on the patio to grill beef ribs, sausage links, and chicken quarters—enough to feed a herd, an overstatement perhaps, but at least enough for all the local Johnson clan who would be at the gathering. For Marti, it would feel much like a family reunion since he had not seen some of his family in years. He was especially excited and thrilled that he would get a chance to show off Sasha.

Of all those who he wanted to see, spending some time with Uncle Kyle, his mother's oldest brother, would be one of the highlights of the day. Uncle Kyle told some of the most fascinating stories in the world. He was a complete riot. Sitting back in the recliner with a stogy in one hand, he'd spew embellishments about his adolescent years of living with outdoor plumbing and having only one Sunday outfit, of how pork and beans with wieners was a delicacy and a pair of Converse sneakers was all the rave back then.

It was the cookouts and family gatherings like these that made days like July 4th so important, important enough for Marti to pull up in front of his mother's house two hours early, only to be met by her indignation.

After the second ring of the doorbell, Linda Johnson opened the front door with a stern look on her face. "Y'all, come on in," she said, her face now softening a bit at the sight of them. "Bring that food into the kitchen," she added before turning away and heading in that direction.

Marti followed her into the kitchen, feeling somewhat slighted by her lack of affection. He couldn't take it personal, though, because he was sure her mood had nothing to do with him. "Mama, what's wrong?" he asked while placing the potato salad into the refrigerator. Sasha sat quietly at the eating table watching the two of them.

His mother pointed in the direction of her backyard. "Look out there and see what those dogs did to my trash," she replied in an angry tone.

Marti opened the backdoor to a yard covered with garbage—tin cans and food wrappings and bottles and paper. The yard was a complete mess. It was a good thing he and Sasha had arrived early. "Whose dogs were they, mama?"

"Probably some strays."

"Well, how'd they get back here?" he asked. "You have a privacy fence."

"They dug a big hole under that back fence. Darn rascals."

"Okay, mama, let me get those two pans of meat out of the car then I'll take care of it. I'll refill that hole and clean up that mess in the yard."

Marti left for the car, leaving the two women in the house momentarily to socialize.

"Mrs. Johnson, do you need any help?" Sasha asked.

"Naw, baby, you just sit there and rest yourself. I'm sure glad y'all came over here so early. I've got too much to do still. One of these days, those dogs are gonna trespass on the wrong person's property."

"I just hope y'all enjoy my potato salad and casserole."

And, for the first time since they had arrived, Linda Johnson had a smile on her face. "Well, this family loves to eat, so I don't think you'll find anyone complaining."

Marti soon rejoined them carrying the first huge pan of grilled meat.

"Mama, where do you want this?"

Linda was putting the last of the icing on a lemon cake she'd baked when she replied, "Just set it in the oven. It's not on...we'll heat it up when folks start arriving."

"Okay, one more pan then I'll clean up that yard."

By three o'clock, the Johnson house buzzed with laughter, chatter, and the occasional gossip. The younger set could be found huddled in the backyard, viewing music videos on their iPods or playing pocket-sized PlayStation games, things that kids tended to do. Fascination with these techno gadgets was shared by some of the older set as well. Marti and Sasha, however, were in the living room finding much amusement in Uncle Kyle's glory days.

"So what happened next, Unc," Marti asked, playing narrator to his uncle's embellishments.

The older gentlemen, gray on top, with narrowed eyes, a thick mustache, and fair skin, took a sip of his beverage before continuing. For sixty-one, Uncle Kyle looked exceptionally well; his youthfulness could likely be attributed to his daily neighborhood walks. "Well, you see," he said, clearing his throat, "I wasn't much of a fighter back then. I was more of a Casanova. And this one young lady, Barbara Levine, had eyes for me. What I didn't realize at the time was that she also had the same pair of eyes for Melvin Davidson. Actually, they were an item. And—"

Uncle Kyle was cut short of his climatic end when Linda Johnson entered the room with her hands on her hips. "Marti, after you finish listening to my brother lie," she stated cynically, "some of the kids want you to come out and watch them pop firecrackers."

"Yes, ma'am, I'll be out in a minute," he said, smiling over a Sasha.

Uncle Kyle dished out a retort, "Linda, you just ain't happy unless you're raining on somebody's parade. Why don't you go back into the other room and leave us grown folks alone."

"Oh, hush!" she returned to her brother before disappearing into the other room to tend to other family.

"Now where was I?" Marti's uncle asked.

Sasha, now as eager to hear the ending as Marti, answered, "I think you were about to get to the part where you get pummeled by the boyfriend." Laughter in the small room erupted.

"Oh, so you heard this story before, I see," Uncle Kyle said, grinning. "No, actually, it didn't go down like that. Now, Melvin did want to rearrange my face and he'd gotten plenty of practice doing that on the wrestling team and blocking cats on the football field, but did I also mention that I was a smart cat as well? There was no way I was going to trade in my good looks for something you see on an impressionist painting. Uh-uh."

"Well, how did you avoid that whippin', Unc?" said Marti.

"I told him that it probably wouldn't be a good idea to go toe-to-toe with me because I had a rare disease that was contagious through bloodshed."

"Man, c'mon, Unc, no way he believed that," Marti said incredulously.

"Let's just say that he wasn't the sharpest tool in the shed, son. Besides, I was a scrawny thing back then. I probably looked sick to him compared to his huge stature."

"Unc, you're crazy, man."

"That may be, but I'll tell ya one thing—I didn't have anymore problems out of those two after that."

"Unc, listen, we better get outside and pop some firecrackers," Marti said.

"Uncle Kyle," said Sasha, raising and walking over to give him a kiss on the check, "it was a pleasure talking with you. I hope I get a chance to do this again."

"Marti, this one here is a keeper," said Uncle Kyle, admiring Sasha, no doubt wishing he was still in his prime. He'd likely give Marti a run for his money.

Marti replied with a smile, "I'm working on it."

The streetlights had come on by the time the last car, save for that belonging to her son, pulled out of Linda Johnson's driveway. A day that began with utter frustration fostered a gradual mood change in Marti's mother. With her countenance now bearing signs of satisfaction, Linda Johnson saw the last of her remaining two guests off.

"I'm so glad you two got a chance to come," she said to her son while pulling him into her for a motherly embrace. "I know the family was happy to see you, son."

"Yes, ma'am. We had a good time. And if you need anything, mama, anything at all, just let me know."

"I will, son. And Sasha, you keep that son of mine in line and I hope to see you again real soon."

Sasha gave his mother a warm hug. "Thanks for having me. You have a wonderful family," she said to the motherly figure standing the doorway, still wearing her apron.

Marti's mother stood waving in the door until the two of them drove off.

***

The next morning, Sasha walked into the kitchen to find Marti twirling a pair of his drum sticks smiling as she approached.

"What's that look for?" she asked, grabbing the orange juice from the fridge.

"Oh, I don't know, I just feel inspired."

Sasha motioned at the drum sticks. "To do what, play?"

"Something like that. Outside of doing our regular club gig on Thursday nights, I don't have an opportunity to play as much. I hate that, too, because playing takes the edge off."

Sasha looked a little confused perhaps because he didn't have a practice set at his apartment, which made sense—those things could produce a lot of noise, and he had neighbors.

And Marti read her well enough to discontinue the wondering. "I know, you're thinking where am I gonna practice? Right, I'll get to that in a minute, but first, I got this call from one of my frats. He wants me to work on this project with him. He's a base player and recording an album with a Neo-Soul type vibe. He's got a band, but his drummer just got this hot gig in Atlanta with some popular artist. My boy needs me to lay some tracks in the studio for him. It's a couple of weekend's worth of work. Anyway, I'm headed to the studio in a few. You're free to tag along."

"Sounds fun, but I can't," she said, sipping her juice.

"Oh yeah, what are you up to?"

"So you weren't listening when I told you this the other day?" Sasha said, doing the eye roll/head shake combo.

"I'm sorry, baby, what did you tell me?"

"That I had to take my car to the dealership to get the oil changed and a brake lamp replaced."

"Oh."

"Yeah, just what I thought. I swear sometimes it's like talking to the wall with you."

"Man, you're in a funky mood this morning. Are you sick again like you were last weekend?"

"No," she sharply replied.

"Is it that time of the month?"

Sasha jerked. "Say what? Why does everything have to be about that? Why is it that I just can't be annoyed that you don't listen sometimes?"

"Well, if you stopped to think about it, you'd realize you're not looking at this from my perspective. You women ever stopped to think that you pick the wrong time to try to tell a man something? When he's engaged in a sporting event on TV or playing his PlayStation or has just walked through the door from work and just wants to chill, I'm sorry, baby, but that's just *not* the time to be trying to tell him something that you want him to hear or engage in serious conversation. By the way, what was I doing when you told me this?"

"Nevermind, this is pointless."

"Actually, it's not. This is interesting because I'd like an answer. What was I doing?"

"Okay, fine—you were on your PlayStation, I think."

"See what I'm saying, not a good time, baby. That's all I'm saying."

"Fine, you made your point, but you were still wrong for not listening."

Marti shook his head and began smirking. "You don't even believe that one, but I'll give it to you because I'm about to do some studio work and you women always want to be right."

"Whatever!" Sasha returned before making her exit, heading toward the upstairs bedroom. "I've got to get ready for my study date."

"Now, I *heard* that." *Study date. She's got jokes.*

Marti rolled up in front of the studio and glanced at the "Mo Musik Recording Studio" lettering on the glass entrance. Kirk, his music fraternity brother, was waiting for him inside. "Sup, frat?" Marti said, embracing his old college chum. "Glad you called. It's been way too long. What, two years...at that gig in Frisco?"

Kirk pulled away to take a good look at Marti. "Yeah, brotha, but you're looking good."

"Man, I have to do something to keep up with these young cats."

"I hear ya, I hear ya."

"So whatcha got for me?" said Marti anxiously.

"Well, let me introduce you to the crew. I've been telling them about you. They're a cool group of cats, even Alicia who's the lead singer. She's like a kid sister, man, and I swear we get into it like family, but you know how that is."

Marti and Kirk entered the commodious control room. There were about five guys lounging on sofas. And once she noticed them approach, Alicia stepped out from inside the vocal booth to join the rest of the band.

"Alright, gang, this is Marti." Marti extended his hand as Kirk ran off the introductions. Of course, there was Alicia, the youngest at twenty-eight, who, even though she stood only five foot three, apparently could belt out Jazz tunes like nobody's business. Kevin was on keyboard. Leonard was on guitar. Tiko played trumpet. Mike played trombone. Derrick played bongos. This was a fairly young band; they had only been together for five months, but Kirk had played with most of them at some point over the past few years. He met Alicia through Derrick, though. Derrick told Kirk that he knew this chick who could rival the best female vocalists out there, and he wasn't kidding. So Kirk decided to do his own thing. He had been talking about it for years. Played around on other people's stuff, but nothing ever panned out, and he took it as a sign for him to do his own thing. Of course, Marti knew all about that since he had put together his own band a year or so prior.

"Sometimes, we just need a push, man. That's why I decided to do my own thing. I got tired of gigging here and there for other people and not getting paid sometimes because something came up. And you know how folks can trip sometimes—not everybody wants to keep it drama-free. That stuff got tired real quickly. This is a good thing you're doing here. This Neo-Soul vibe is really picking up. You know

I'm still doing the Jazz thing; people feel us, man. It's cool because all I want to do is play—ya know, tell a story through the music."

"True that. But what's up with you and your band, man? y'all gigging around town?"

Marti shook his head. "Naw, we have this regular gig on Thursdays at that hotspot downtown, M's Cafe. Man, I love the music, but my day job keeps me busy and my moms, man, she just came back into my life. I've been trying to keep things straight with her and—"

Kirk interrupted, "And ya girl, gotta make time for ya girl," he said jokingly.

"Yeah, man. You know it. Honestly, I want to try to do more music, but with grad school and all, my plate's full."

"Brotha, you're all over the place."

"Tell me about it. So whatcha got for me?"

"Plenty, my brotha, plenty," Kirk replied to his long-time frat.

Three hours later Marti strolled through the front door of his townhouse to find Sasha cozy on the sofa with a bowl of popcorn watching television.

"Got enough for me?" he said, tossing his keys onto the coffee table before nestling up beside her.

Sasha handed over the bowl. "Sure."

"So we cool?"

"What do you mean?"

"You know...from this morning?"

"Yeah," she said, nodding. "We're cool."

Marti leaned in and kissed her on the cheek. "Good."

Chapter 17

Marti was pulling up to his townhouse when his cell phone went off. The urgency in Leslie's voice was clear indication that this was no social call. Apparently, her car had stalled on her on the highway.

"Okay, where on Highway 10 are you? What's the nearest exit you see? Can you even turn the car over? Just sit tight, I'll be there in fifteen minutes." He swung out of the parking lot like a bullet train, flicking on his hazards, as he raced down side streets, trying to get to Leslie. In the meantime, he contacted Nate, one of his boys from college, who worked at a body shop; he'd have him tow her car to the shop.

Marti inched his car up behind Leslie's stalled Camry then approached the passenger side of her car, where he found her head buried in a book. She hadn't even noticed he was there until he tapped on the window.

Marti opened the car door and hopped inside. "That must be some good book you're reading," he said, glancing at synopsis on the back jacket cover.

"It is. It's Black fiction, all the drama and angst and romance one could imagine."

"Well, listen, my buddy Nate is on his way with his tow truck; we'll just hang till he gets here."

"That's cool. I'm just glad I caught you. You're saving me lots of rigmarole."

Minutes later, a tow truck pulled in front of Leslie's car and backed up a few inches. Nate.

Marti took his exit to go reacquaint himself with his college friend.

"It's been awhile, man," said Nate, leaning into Marti for the "brotha shakedown."

"I know. It has been."

Nate began hitching Leslie's car to his tow truck. "That's one fine sista there. That's you?" he inquired of Marti about Leslie, who had checked out of her car and was now sitting in Marti's.

"Naw, man, it ain't like that. We're friends." Marti knew exactly where this was going.

"Yeah, okay...friends. So you won't mind if I holla at her?"

174

Marti was suddenly reminded why he and Nate never really hung out much. And there was no way he'd subject Leslie to a major playa like Nate. Nate was the kind of guy who wouldn't know how to treat a woman like she deserved, even if he had written instructions. Somehow, he always got the ladies. Marti just couldn't understand it. Nonetheless, Leslie would not become Nate's next conquest.

"Yeah, I mind," Marti said firmly. "Bra, you know how you are with the ladies. You got one on every block. Naw, man, you can hang that notion up."

"See, I knew you and her really had someth—"

Stopping Nate just short of making any assumptions, Marti quickly put his boy in check. "Hey, bra, just do your job, man. I already told you that Leslie's my friend. Just let it go, a'ight."

"It's cool. Whateva. But you know you're trippin', man." Marti could only shake his head in contempt. Some people would never change.

Nate finished his business, and Marti returned to his car.

"So what was that about?" asked Leslie. "You looked like you wanted to toss him into the river for a minute there."

"It was nothing, just Nate being Nate."

"And what does that mean?"

"Nate's still running the same games from college. You'd think that fool would have gotten his stuff straight by now."

"Hey, I know too many people like ya boy. I don't think they wanna evolve."

"Then that's sad," said Marti, starting the car then merging back into traffic behind Nate.

"Hey, let's just talk about something else. First, thanks again for doing this. I can always count you to have my back. Now, I need to know something."

"What's that?"

"How'd you do in your first summer session?"

"Oh, that. Yeah, I didn't do too badly. I got a B+."

Leslie mused, "Look at you getting your lesson."

"Shut up, Les," replied Marti, turning into the body shop lot. Nate wasn't exaggerating when he said his shop was just up the street. "Just sit tight, I'll take care of everything."

Marti left his car to go talk to Nate. Ten minutes later he returned. "Alright, here's the deal," he said to Leslie. "They think it may be your transmission, but they're gonna check it out tomorrow morning and give me a call with their assessment. I told him to contact me on this so you won't have to be bothered. I'll let you know what they say when they call in the morning. Is that cool with you?"

176

"You know you don't have to do this," she said. "I can take it from here, really."

"I want to do it. It's no problem, Les. Now how about something to eat?"

"Yeah, because a sista is famished. That's where I was headed before my car decided otherwise."

"Food, it is."

***

The remainder of Marti's summer was a bust. He'd spent much of it in class, and with only a couple weeks left before returning to work, he knew he'd better make the most of what was left of it. Sasha wasn't too thrilled about him being MIA, but tried to be understanding. To compensate for his absence, however, he promised he'd spend tonight satisfying her every whim.

With Luther Vandross serenading in the background and a full moon as their backdrop, slowly he unzipped her strapless dress, stopping midpoint to caress her shoulders gently as he followed with a trail of kisses along her neck, pausing only to trace the butterfly on her back with his finger. "When did you say you got this again?" Marti whispered into her ear then nibbled her lobe.

Sasha could hardly concentrate, scrambling for the words as her heart raced. "Uh…uh, back…" she managed, panting heavily before continuing, "back in…high…high school."

"I like it," said Marti, turning her to face him. He kissed her hard on the mouth, as if trying to make her face his last meal, and the passion grew even more intense when the image of *her* flashed behind his closed lids. *Whoa…* Suddenly, Marti broke from their embrace. *That wasn't right.*

"Something wrong?" asked Sasha, now confused by his actions. "You okay?"

"Yeah, yeah," he said, hoping to get back into the groove and please this woman as he'd promised. "It's cool." But it wasn't fine. Never had Leslie invaded his romantic interludes with other women, and now images of her taunted his very thoughts like shadows. He had to pull it together, focus only on the woman who was staring back at him, how beautiful and young and sexy and incredibly insatiable she was. She was everything, and she wanted him right now. She *wanted* him. More importantly, he wanted to be with her.

He began to think back to the day he first saw Sasha standing in the doorway of class, how incredibly sexy she looked—her caramel skin, dark eyes, gorgeous ebony locks, those long stems, and it was enough to erase any traces of Leslie from his mind. While his massive frame engulfed her, he was ever so gentle as he lifted her into his sculpted biceps—her heart, a beating drum against his chest—and carried her over to bed.

Soft moonlight escaping from the partially drawn curtains beamed down into Sasha's face as she lay on a velvet pallet covered with rose petals, waiting and wanting and desiring, making her even more beguiling and the seduction evermore titillating. She was quite the temptress, glaring up at him with that naughty smile, inviting him to ravish her. And ravish her, he would.

That night Marti gave Sasha everything she ever wanted in a lover—passion, romance, attention. He was her every desire, her every fantasy, and he would not stop there. He would make sure the mood was carried over into the morning. By the time Sasha opened her lids to a new day, he had drawn her a hot bubble bath and sprinkled lavender bath beads into the water. He placed her huge terrycloth robe on the hook at the back of the bathroom door and matching slippers on the bath floor facing the tub; everything was now set to perfection. He then approached her bedside to find Sasha looking completely dazed into his chocolate brown eyes, wondering perhaps how she had gotten so lucky. Marti lifted a willing Sasha out of bed, carried her into the bathroom, and proceeded to disrobe her before she slide her body underneath the thick blanket of soapy foam.

"Should I wash your back?" asked Marti, pouring body wash on a sponge.

"Please and don't stop there," she said, bringing her knees into her chest.

Marti gently ran the sponge along every inch of her petite body before tossing the sponge into the bath and rising from the edge of the tub. "Where are you going?" she asked, sounding a bit disappointed that the spa treatment was coming to an end.

"To fix your breakfast," he said.

"Don't go," she said in a soft tone. "Get in with me."

"Should we pick up where we left off last night?" he said, smiling.

"It had crossed my mind."

"You naughty, naughty woman," returned Marti, removing his clothing to join her.

Chapter 18

Marti returned to Baker High from summer break ready to tell Leslie about Sasha. They hadn't very many run-ins since he came to her aid when her car broke down several weeks prior. They'd played phone tag more often than not, and well, Marti realized it was no use trying to protect Leslie's feelings anymore when it was obvious she felt nothing romantic toward him.

"I have to talk to you," he said. Leslie was sitting on the couch in the teacher's lounge, as she always did during break time, but something was different. In her lap lay a book into which moments before all her attention was drawn. He knew this book and had tried on occasion to understand the complexity of the stories and lessons that unfolded throughout its crisp pages. Why was she reading it? Why was she reading the Bible?

"Yeah, so do I."

"What is it?" Marti returned with curiosity now tugging at his shirttail. He had a good idea what news she was about to break.

She began to smile. "I-uh-I did it," she said.

"Did what?"

"I got saved."

Suddenly, that great moment of silence invaded them. There they were staring at each other until Leslie gave up waiting for a response from him, any response, and resumed her reading. Marti continued to stand there trying to process what he'd just heard. He wondered why she was a believer now. What signs out there indicated that there even was a God? Clearly, there was an evil force present, something so diabolic that it could only be explained as a *devil*. But there had been no real signs of God in his life or the life of his family, only evil. Marti had never seen any signs of a Supreme Being who controlled everything and saw everything and knew everything. It was ridiculous, this notion that God existed. And the argument that the Bible was literary proof that God was real, Marti again thought ridiculous because there was no one who had outlived time to argue that any of those stories ever happened. Many had searched and attempted, but there was just no logical or scientific explanation. Yet she still believed. Millions of them believed. And Marti wondered why. Perhaps it could be explained as a human need to latch onto something far greater than they, or someone whose powers were so fantastic and terrible that not even the most feared superhero could match. This human tendency was manifested even in children whose need to believe in Santa Claus was so great that when parents revealed the truth their hearts were shattered. Yes, perhaps this was it.

Marti was certain he was on the right track about the existence of God because the world remained divided on the question whether or not there was one or many Supreme Beings, proving his theory that "God" was symbolic, a representation of a *good* far greater than the good capable of humanity, a *supernatural good* created by human imagination. To believe in God was to believe in a "perfected self," human good magnified a million times over. This explained why it had different names and different manifestations. What it symbolized or represented was relative to its creators. This explained why Muslims served Allah, why Native Americans worshipped the Sun and Moon and Stars and Nature, why many Asians worshipped Buddha, why the world at large believed in God.

Marti could now somewhat understand why Leslie needed to believe like so many others. The alternative was bleak—either be succumbed by that diabolical force or be rescued by a good capable of destroying all evil. For Marti, it read like a comic book—this good versus evil saga. Had the world really created its own superhero to combat evil, a hero whose existence could not be proven because that existence was only real to those who believed? Still, Marti thought that a bit ridiculous. Weren't people smarter than that? Surely, Leslie was. Didn't they realize that fantasy could never overtake reality? So this human-created entity could never overtake the forces of evil in the world unless...unless God was no figment of human imagination, unless God really did exist. Either way, Marti would have to give it more thought.

Marti turned to her after pondering. "First of all, why didn't you say anything that day your car broke down?" he asked.

"There was nothing to tell, this just happened a couple of weeks ago."

"Okay, but I still don't understand why you believe that God even exists," asserted Marti.

"See, I think you're looking for some huge billboard written by God himself saying: 'Yes, Marti, I really am up here.' I think that would satisfy your...whatever it is that keeps you tugging at the question of God's existence. You've spent your life approaching things from an empirical point of view, but on this one issue, it just seems to me that you're making excuses," she contended. "What could I possibly say to make you understand why I had to make this choice? But you remember that conversation we had awhile back when you talked about you feeling like something was missing from your life, like you felt empty?"

Marti nodded. "Yeah, I remember."

"Well," she said, "I understood what you were saying more than you'll ever know."

"Okay, Les, but what does God have to do with that?"

184

Leslie looked him squarely in the eyes and said, "God has everything to do with it. The thing is…I grew up in the church then when I got out on my own, somehow I lost my way. It's so easy to do—ya know, lose your way."

"What if you never knew that way, Les? What if God was never a part of your life or your upbringing, what then? Why should I believe in something that's not even real to me?"

"My belief in God, Marti, is based on faith," she continued. "I know that means nothing to you, but at some point I just came to realize that I didn't need proof to believe. Believing is something we all can do, but most times logic and reason stop us. Someday I believe we will learn everything we ever questioned. In the meantime, we just have to have faith in that and believe. And if you're still looking for something to chew on, chew on this: just ask yourself if you can really afford not to believe."

"Listen, Les, I've gotta run."

"One more thing…your mother's doctor…I think he was right. God brought her back to you," she said. "That's something He's done for you lately."

Marti just looked at her before turning away, heading back to his classroom. He began to think about his father, how his father taught him not to accept anything unless it could be explained or proven. But even his father had accepted that his own life couldn't get any better without sticking around long enough for proof of that. Why was he still subscribing to lessons given to him by a man who had proven that he didn't have all the answers; a man who made plenty of mistakes; a man who he thought was a coward?

Ascending the staircase, he continued to ponder why he felt so strongly about this. He began to think back on events from his childhood that were key in shaping his logic, things that ultimately led him to take this position? Fact is Marti could count on one hand the number of times he'd gone to church. While his father was living, church was never a big event in his family, although it might have been assumed that all black folks went to church—at least on Sundays. Marti adopted his father's notions about God and church early in life. His father insisted that church was full of hypocrites who were only out for your money. Though his mother felt differently, on a number of occasions defending the church, finally, she reasoned that she had an obligation to her husband and family life first, so they just didn't go. God was rarely mentioned in his family until his dad was gone. His mother began to attend church again, but Marti refused to go. He was a teenager, taller than she and stronger. There was little she could do physically to persuade him. She reasoned, but he ignored. Donald, on the other hand, was still young enough to remain obedient, so he went with her until he reached that age of rebellion.

It wasn't until he met Carolyn that he went to church for the first time. While they dated, she attended church off and on, and to please her, he went a few times with her. After they married, he went a few more times, thinking that would keep her content. His argument with Carolyn about this soon began to shape into the argument between his mother and father. As much as he grew tired of her nagging, she grew even wearier of trying to get him to go. Finally, the nagging stopped.

Marti had reached the door of his classroom when something struck him. The fact that his father argued against the church meant that, at some point in his life, he had gone to church. Wasn't it only fair that Marti investigate this more, this time attending church with an open mind, and drawing his own conclusion just as his father had done? At any rate, he'd have to revisit that later since the fourth period bell was now ringing.

Fourth period was a rowdy bunch of ninth graders, but Marti enjoyed this class the most. They would somehow take his mind off of the conversation he'd just had with Leslie whose classroom was only three doors down from his. Like clockwork, those who were always first in their seats like Amanda Snelling and LaShay Williams came coasting through the door ten seconds after the bell while others like Russell Baker and Michael Clark stammered through two seconds before the tardy bell rang.

One by one, Marti checked off the attendance list those present or absent. Only two of his twenty-four students were out. This was Myra's third day in a row missing his class, and she never missed school. Marti grew concerned and wondered if there was any news on her whereabouts, if she was ill. He'd have to ask around, starting with his students.

"Does anyone live near Myra or know if she's sick or not?"

"I do." Cynthia Smith was good friends with Myra.

"Yeah, well, what's going on with her? Is she sick or what?"

"Actually, I'm not sure, Mr. Johnson. She lives a block away from me, but I haven't seen her in the neighborhood lately."

"Well, aren't you two good friends? Haven't you tried to call her?"

"Yeah, but I haven't been able to get an answer, and I went over there yesterday and the day before to take her some notes from class, but nobody answered. Honesty, I'm a little worried myself." Now Marti really grew concerned.

"When class is over, I'll just have to check the front desk to see what they know. In the meantime, we should pick up where we left off yesterday: Why is geography important? Your homework was to write a one-page essay answering that question. Can I get a volunteer to come and read his or her essay?" Rachel, his brightest student, raised her hand.

"Very good, Rachel. Come on up," Marti instructed his star pupil who then rose from her seat, walked up to the front of the class, and stood behind the podium. Marti liked using the podium because it made him feel as if he were some college professor teaching in a lecture hall filled with students.

"Before I answer the question of why geography is important," said Rachel, "I first had to understand what geography was. The first person I asked was my dad because he was in the Navy and traveled quite a bit, saw lots of places. He would tell stories of how he'd go to a place where there was nothing, but countryside then be stationed somewhere else that was thriving with people and businesses. Somehow, from these stories, I came to understand how geography had an effect on culture. Geography can affect how people adapt to certain surroundings and dictate customs and ultimately impact language and communication. Geography can tell us about a certain people, like Asians or Africans or Native Americans. These people have distinct features, like darkened skin or slanted eyes or wide nostrils, and these features are the result of their adapting to their geographical location. Not only that, but geography can affect economic growth and commercial and residential development. You do not find many Metropolitan areas in the coldest places in Alaska and that affects the type of industry that will thrive there. In fact, commercial fishing and oil refinery are the leading economic activities in Alaska. Whereas, Hawaii, where the climate is always nice and warm and the place is absolutely gorgeous, pulls in a great deal of revenue from tourism. This is why I think geography is so important. Geography does not just tell us where we are from, but it has also impacted who we have become as a civilization. Thank you."

The class applauded as Rachel took her seat. "Very good, Rachel, that was a well-organized and insightful essay. You brought up some interesting points about geography. Most people look at geography as only studying locations and that *is* one aspect, but it is far more layered, and I'm glad to see that you have come to understand this. Will there be another volunteer?"

Kevin Wright raised his hand. He was a character in his own right, very intellectual, but a bit of a goof at times and was sure to introduce some bit of comedy into his reading. "Okay, Kevin, you're up."

Kevin made his way up to the front. "Let's see," he said, clearing his throat. "Well, I think geography is important because if nobody had even taken the time to distinguish between countries and states and cities and neighborhoods and streets, we'd all keep bumping into each other." The class burst into a loud rumble. Marti even let a smile slip. "Seriously, y'all," said Kevin, "think about it. We depend on maps and directions to navigate. Imagine this being a world where locations were not defined or named. Where would you say you were from—nowhere? Oh yeah, by the way, I'm from nowhere and I live on nobody street and so does everybody else in this world. So you see, geography is important because it is how we can tell one place from another, and also, like Rachel said earlier, it's how we can tell one race from another race. Tha-that, tha-that, tha-that's all folks," he

190

said, throwing up the peace sign then strutting to his seat as if he'd just given the Inaugural Address. The class again erupted.

"Well, Kevin, I'm sure that wasn't one page, more like two or three sentences, but you do make a good point. Geography does show us how to view the world in terms of zones or regions and lines of latitude and longitude and things of that nature. Thank you, Kevin. So you see, class, just from those two different points of view, how very important geography is to us. Why don't you all pass your homework up to the front? There's about ten minutes left of class. Use this time to review Chapter 14 in your textbook. There *will* be a test next Friday on the last three chapters we've covered. Okay, get cracking."

The wind was blowing particularly hard. Broken tree limbs were scattered about Sasha's walkway. Marti had an armful by the time he reached her door. It had been a usually long day, starting with the conversation with Leslie then him finding out some pretty upsetting news about one of his students. He just needed to see Sasha. He needed to bury himself in her couch that carried her scent, be surrounded by her things, see her face, hear her voice. Yes, that's what he needed.

On the second ring, Sasha answered the door. She was wearing a baseball cap and sweats. Marti thought she looked so sexy. "Hey, baby," he said, kissing her on the cheek as he entered the apartment. "Got a trash bag? That wind ain't playing out there."

"Yeah, under the kitchen sink." Sasha closed the front door and walked into the kitchen. "So, this is a surprise."

"I wanted to see you—that's all."

"You know I can't be much company because I got that paper to write."

"That's cool. I'll just go in the other room and watch some TV."

Marti was tying the bag of limbs when Sasha walked over, grabbed the bag, and tossed it on the floor then put her arms around his neck and kissed him. "I'm glad you're here."

A couple of hours later Sasha joined Marti on the couch. "Done?"

Sasha shook her head. "Taking a break."

"Here, lie back," said Marti, scooting himself further into the couch so she'd have room to lie next to him. He put his arms around her.

"You sure that's the only reason you came over?" asked Sasha. "You've never just wanted to come crash on my couch like that."

"Yeah, today wasn't a good day."

"What happened?"

"One of my students is in the hospital with pneumonia."

Sasha raised on the couch to face Marti. "Are you kidding me?"

"I wish I was. She's listed as critical up at Earl K. Long. I'm really worried about her, you know. She's a good kid."

"Thinking about going to see her?"

"I already have. I went straight over right after class today and talked to her folks. They told me to keep her in my prayers." Marti stopped to release a chuckle. "When they said that I thought to myself: 'How do you know I pray?'"

"Don't you?" she asked.

"Do you?"

Sasha shook her head and replied, "Not like I should, but I do."

"Well, I guess I'm still trying to work my way up to your level."

"What do you mean?"

"I don't even know if God exists," said Marti.

"Of course He does."

"How do you know?"

"I just know," Sasha confidently replied.

"Was it something your parents taught you? I mean, really—how do you know?"

Sasha shook her head and threw up her hands as if to gesture that she could not give him a practical answer that would satisfy him.

"Don't worry about it," Marti added.

"I'm sorry. I just—"

"Like I said, don't worry about it," Marti repeated. "This is not your issue to resolve, it's mine."

Chapter 19

Marti laid his keys in the basket, slid his card through the reader, and headed toward the treadmill for thirty minutes of cardio. For five-thirty in the morning, it was pretty crowded. He'd taken the last available machine. He recognized most of them as regulars, even spotted his free weights partner Douglas and gave him a nod. This was his daily routine: an hour and a half at the gym before work. A good workout mentally and physically prepared him for what would usually turn out to be a long day, and it seemed that the days had gotten longer ever since he and Leslie had the conversation about God.

He just couldn't talk to her anymore, not like he used to. Maybe he thought that she would change now that she had become a Christian, like she wouldn't be down anymore, like they wouldn't be able to hang out and shoot the breeze, or he'd have to watch what he said around her in fear that he'd offend her. He'd have to work too hard to maintain a friendship with her now. She was different somehow, but was it even fair for him to assume all this about her just because she had become a believer? Whatever. He'd come there to work out, not dwell on Leslie and that conversation.

After a ten-minute cool-down, Marti walked over to the free weights and stretched some more before beckoning Douglas to come over and spot him bench press.

"…Eight, nine, ten. A'ight."

Marti rose from the bench to switch with Douglas. Douglas completed in bodybuilding on the amateur level. He and Marti met last year when Marti joined the gym.

"So what's up with you and Sasha?"

Marti began to flex in the mirror behind him. "We're still kickin' it."

"What about Leslie?"

"I'm always thinking about Leslie." Marti turned away from the mirror and reverted to spotting his friend. "Ready?" he asked, changing the subject.

"Why don't you just talk to her?" said Douglas, getting back on the subject.

"You know she's a Christian now?"

"And what's your point, man? So am I."

"Point is I ain't."

"But you been thinking about it, haven't you?"

"Yeah, man. I've been giving God some thought."

"Listen, man, you're just thirty-five. You ain't got to make a decision about Sasha and Leslie today. But God, man, don't rule that out, just don't rule that out."

"Yeah, I hear ya."

Marti finished the rest of his workout thinking about what his friend said. Here was somebody else telling him to keep an open mind about God, which was proving difficult to do since he spent a good portion of his life trusting only those things that made sense. Leslie had once again pegged him to a tee. As much as Marti enjoyed a good debate, he just couldn't make an argument against her. The fact is he really was only open to those things that satisfied his logic. His first day on the job as a teacher one of his ninth graders asked if it would be okay for the class to say the Lord's Prayer during home room everyday, and he gave her a political response. He said that it might not be such a good idea to have prayer because there was a chance that not everyone shared the same faith or was a believer. He offered that she pray her own prayer to herself before class if she liked. The student, a bit disappointed with his response, then asked whether he prayed. He said nothing. With great sadness, she responded, "Now I understand."

He was feeling the same way around Leslie the way he felt that day around that female student—like he was a horrible person for choosing not to be a part of their exclusive club. Leslie made him question things about himself he wanted never to confront.

Marti had showered and gotten halfway dressed when Douglas walked into the locker room. "Hey, man, still here, huh?"

"Yeah, I decided to clean up here. Gotta pull an extra early one today. Gotta conference scheduled before class. This kid's mom finally decides to care now that her son is about to flunk. Man, it never ends."

"Tell me about it."

Marti walked over to the full-length mirror to give himself a once-over. "Hey, Doug, let me ask you something."

"What's that?"

"What made you become a Christian?"

"Actually, man, I grew up in the church, but you know how it is…That stuff was over my head and I didn't want to be there. Moms made me go. Most times I'd be sitting in the back with my boys and we'd be trippin' out. Man, I didn't pay any attention to that church stuff. It didn't make any sense."

"See, man, that's what I'm saying. It ain't adding up for me either."

"But it will just like it finally did for me."

"How?"

"Man, it took a car accident seven years ago to get me straight. You shouldn't even be talking to me right now, but I'm still here, and I thank God everyday for that."

"At least you've got a reason."

"Hey, I'ma tell ya something. If you're looking for some kinda sign that tells you this is the right thing to do, then this is it. You're asking questions, that's the first step. Tell ya what, come to Bible Study with me tomorrow night. Sounds like you need some answers and that's the best place to get them."

Marti hesitated to give it some thought. "I don't know, man—"

"Hey, it's just an invitation."

"Yeah, okay then." Marti replied, collecting his gym clothes before heading for the door. "Later."

Marti had anticipated as much from his parent. She threw a fit about her son being on the verge of flunking his class, but Marti's hands were tied. He'd been trying to get the boy's parent to take some interest in her child's status since the beginning of the term, and now that he was about to fail, she wanted to be all concerned, and not just that, but down right ugly and accusatory, blaming Marti for not keeping her informed. Well, that was a lie, and Marti had all the paperwork to prove that he had in fact attempted to keep her in the loop. He had kept a record of every note that he'd sent home or phone call he'd made to this woman about her son. Some parents just never learned.

Leslie ducked her head in his class. There was still about twenty minutes before the kids would be arriving for school that day. "Hey, you alright?" said Leslie, approaching Marti's desk. "I heard that woman screaming at you about her child. She had a lot of nerve saying that stuff to you. I hate when I get a parent like that, trying to make me feel like I've done something wrong."

"Yeah, I'm cool. I swear sometimes I wonder why I ever became a teacher when I have to put up with all the crap we face today—these unruly kids, the hostile parents, and all the bureaucracy. Teaching isn't about helping kids learn anymore, it's only about what kind of test scores you can produce. I'm telling ya, Les, I'm getting sick of it by the day. That's why I had to go back to get my Master's. Sometimes I just think I'll better serve teaching students on the college level."

"I know what you mean because it's certainly not the paycheck that keeps me coming back every morning, but there are those moments when I just know that I've made an impact, those tiny glimpses in the year when I know that something that I've said has stuck with my students and that's what motivates me to keep trying.

Otherwise, I'd not even bother to do this anymore. I'm still young. I can find something else to do. I bet you didn't even know that I used to want to be an anchorwoman."

"Get out of here!"

"It's true. I did. I used to sit there glued to the news after school and watch Jillian Anderson do her thing and want to be just like her. Sometimes I'd practice being her in my room in front of the mirror. I was good, too," said Leslie, laughing. "But that was eons ago. I sort of fell into English when I went off to college. When I took my first college English Literature course, I instantly took to it. I loved reading English novels and writing literary criticisms, and slowly my desire to be on the news faded and was replaced by wanting to be an English teacher. I think I just wanted to present to kids that world of literature that I'd been introduced to in college."

"I still can't believe you were almost the next Barbara Walters."

Leslie chuckled. "I wouldn't say all of that, but, yep, I was feeling the news thing for awhile."

"Just never know all there is to know about a person."

The look on Leslie's face was suspect. "Why do I feel like that was a loaded statement?"

"I don't know. I was only talking about you wanting to be on the news."

"Well, I think it's more to it than that, but we'll talk about this later because the kids are gonna be arriving soon. I've gotta get back to my classroom. This is not over. I want to know what that comment was really about. I think I know, but I need to hear it from you."

Before Marti could say anything or even attempt to argue his original point that he meant nothing more by his comment, Leslie had disappeared out into the hallway, headed toward her class. He could hear the clash of her heels against the floor that soon came to a stop. She was right, though. There was something more there. He was referring to her becoming a Christian when he made that comment. It was eating at him and he just didn't know why. Marti rationalized that maybe it was because it made him confront something that he was not yet ready to face. But he really could not shake the overwhelming feeling that this would change Leslie so much that their friendship would suffer, and he certainly did not want that.

Still, Marti found it hard to validate what he was feeling because what Leslie did with her life really had nothing to do with any decisions or choices he made for his own. It shouldn't have even mattered that she told him that she was now a believer. It was something good for her. It was something meaningful for her. How was he going to explain then that he was in some ways bothered that she was a Christian now? No, Marti wasn't exactly looking forward to continuing that conversation during break time.

Marti barged into the teacher's lounge, where he found Leslie standing at the vending machine. "Okay, let's go ahead and hash this out now," Marti said to her, plopping down on the pea green pleather couch.

"Will you at least let me grab my snack from the vendor?" Leslie put her money into the machine, made her selection, and grabbed the fallen potato chip bag from the vendor compartment.

"Whatever."

"Hey, you don't have to get an attitude with me," she said, opening the bag of Lays. "You made that questionable comment earlier, not me, and I just want to know what you meant by it."

"Earlier you said you knew what I meant, so go ahead and tell me what I meant by my own statement. You seem to know everything there is to know about me."

"Okay then, fine. I think you have a problem with me being a Christian. I really do. What I don't know or understand is why?"

"That's ridiculous, Leslie, and you know it."

"Is it?" asked Leslie.

"Okay, I'll admit, it took me by surprise, but what does that have to do with me, you becoming a Christian?"

"I just think it makes you question, even confront your own spirituality."

"What spirituality? I don't subscribe to any of that Bible stuff," he said firmly.

"Perhaps you should," urged Leslie.

"Well, I'm done talking about this."

"Sure you are," she said.

"What is that supposed to mean?"

"I just think you might be trying to leave this subject alone, but it's not leaving you alone."

Marti said nothing in return, only stared at the wall pensively, so Leslie took her cue and left him in deep thought. She'd obviously hit a nerve. But again, she was right; he couldn't shake the matter from his head.

Chapter 20

Marti entered the main sanctuary of Douglas' church taking in every detail. Stained glass windows surrounded the edifice. At the back of the church was a balcony. At the very front was a huge pulpit with organ and drum set on one side and baby grand piano on the other. The choir stand was directly behind the row of chairs placed on the pulpit for the ministers of the church. While the edifice could seat at least five hundred, not more than thirty or forty people were in attendance for Bible Study. Everyone had seated themselves on one side of the church, scattered among the first three or four rows. A podium had been placed at the front for the speaker. The entire sanctuary buzzed with low chatter.

After they took their seats, Marti grabbed a Bible from the back of the pew in front of him.

"We're going to be discussing Matthew, Chapter 24," disclosed Douglas.

They were early, and there was still about thirty-five minutes remaining before service started, so Marti began to read quietly to himself. He carefully read each verse, stopping at verse 5, which set something in motion in what Leslie was quick to label as his close-minded thinking. "For many shall come in my name, saying, I am Christ; and shall deceive many." Marti pondered that verse awhile, remembering his train of thought the other day during his conversation with Leslie. Could this be the reason the world was religiously divided? *Interesting*, he thought to himself, *interesting*. He read further and stopped again at verse 31. The word *elect* struck him. He had seen it in verses 22 and 24 and here again it was referenced. "And he shall send his angels with a great sound of a trumpet, and they shall gather together his elect from the four winds…"

Marti leaned over to Douglas. "Who are the elect?" he asked.

Douglas smiled. "The elect are all who are saved, all followers of Christ. They will spend eternal life with Christ in Heaven. That's why it is imperative that you really give God some thought. Believe me, you wouldn't want to be left behind when the end comes, man."

"So it's all about going to Heaven?" Marti concluded, still trying to put things in perspective, still trying to make things black and white. He didn't like gray areas. It was easier for people like Marti to accept something not so tangible if they could devise ways to make it logically concrete.

"Going to Heaven is the ultimate reward for choosing salvation. But choosing to live a life on earth that patterns the life of Christ is in itself its own reward."

"How's that?"

"I can honestly say that I like who I am now. I'm not out running the streets, making trouble like I used to. That's how I ended up totaling my car years ago. Back then my head was on backwards. I'd try anything once. Me and this other cat called ourselves dragging. The light caught both of us. He kept going. I tried to stop, lost control, and ended up flipping over my car. It seems stupid now. I should have just kept going like him. I was breaking the law anyway. I don't know what made me think that it wouldn't be so bad if at least I observed the traffic lights."

"That's messed up, man."

"Listen, Marti, I ain't gonna lie to you and say that instantly you stop having desires and thoughts you had before you got saved. Truth is, some days you might question your salvation when you're struggling the most with your old way of thinking. Temptation will always be something that we must overcome, but it's not impossible when God's gotcha back."

"If that's true then why would anybody want to get saved? If you're saying that I'm still gonna have struggles then what's the difference?"

"Hey, becoming a Christian doesn't make you perfect, and it certainly doesn't mean you're not susceptible to daily obstacles or spiritual trials. The difference is now when stuff bothers me I can pray about it. It's easier to give it over to God and believe than it is to try to work that stuff out myself. Ain't that what you've been doing?"

"Yeah."

"And how successful has it been doing it your way?"

"You already know the answer to that, man. That's why I'm even here."

"Remember when I said stuff in the Bible used to be over my head? Now since I've been a Christian, God has increased my spiritual insight. I have a greater understanding of the scripture. I'ma tell ya, man, reading the Bible has helped me figure out so much stuff about my life. Best thing I ever did."

Marti was formulating more questions to ask Douglas when a lady, who he later learned to be the pastor's wife, approached the podium in front. "Good evening everyone. Good to see all of you. In fact, I see a few new faces. Good to have you. Let's begin with prayer.

"Precious Father, we thank you for another opportunity to fellowship together. We thank you for life, health, and strength, for your tender mercy. As we embark upon another Bible Study, we ask that You help us prepare our hearts and minds to openly receive and give. We ask that You open up our understanding. Touch the speaker tonight, Lord. Touch each person seated here this evening. Help us to use wisdom in all that we say and do tonight. All these things we ask in your son Jesus' name. Amen."

"So you want to try this again?" asked Douglas, turning the pages in his Bible.

"I don't know man, I'll let you know." But Marti already knew the answer to that. He had no intention of stepping foot into that church or any other anytime soon. He just wasn't ready for that. Besides, he'd seen and known a lot of people who went to church and professed to be Christians whose lives didn't really reflect all things good and free of sin. He'd heard Christians curse and seen them drink and smoke and knew those who had one too many indiscretions. But Douglas was different. He seemed to live what he preached.

"Okay, said the pastor, "let's begin tonight's Bible Study. I thought, however, we'd change the order of things and have a sort of forum going here, where I'd pose a question or topic and we'd all discuss it. Tonight my question to you is this: How do you know that you need God in your life if you don't even know God?

The topic seemed to have been meant for Marti, tailored especially for his hearing. A member of the small congregation raised her hand.

Pastor acknowledged the volunteer, "Yes, Sister Bell, you have an answer for us tonight?"

Sister Bell, a rather tall, but stout elderly woman with streaked silver and black hair pulled back into a bun, nodded her head, as she rose from the pew. "I do, pastor. The Lord has a way of making Himself known to non-believers. After all, He works in mysterious ways. He sometimes works through the ordeals and obstacles that we face to get our attention. Because He loves us, He will seek us out when we don't know to seek Him out. There's a passage of scripture, Revelation 3:20," she continued, now peering down at the opened Bible she was holding, "that reads: 'Behold, I stand at the door, and knock: if any man hear my voice, and open the door, I will come in to him, and will sup with him, and he with me.'"

"Yes, Sister Bell, the Lord is merciful and righteous and wants for each of us to experience that perfect peace that can only be found through Him," agreed the pastor. "For the Bible tells us that Jesus is 'the way, the truth, and the light' and that 'no man cometh until the Father, but by Him.'"

Three in the morning, Marti stirred from his sleep, only to be conflicted by his inner demons. While Sasha lay beside him sleeping peacefully, he tussled with restlessness and intense feelings of uncertainty. How was it that a person could spend nearly thirty-six years on earth and feel so unsure about everything he once believed he knew? he wondered. Were there any absolutes? This he questioned; however, Marti's restlessness was punctuated still by something even more substantial than his wavering certainty. He had no peace.

As he lay there, peering over at Sasha, Marti's mind wondered back to Bible Study, which for the life of him felt as though it was meant especially for him. Peace, the pastor said while looking in Marti's direction in the congregation, was what you felt when you knew things were right between you and God, and joy was the manifestation of that peace through actions. Marti did not know such joy, but he certainly wanted to have it. Yet he continued to try to rationalize God while realizing more and more that perhaps the only way he could experience such joy was through knowing Christ. "In thy presence is fullness of joy." The scripture lingered on the cusp of Marti's thoughts as he dozed back off to sleep. How long could and would he evade what seemed so apparent to others, others like Douglas and the pastor and Sister Bell and now even Leslie?

When Marti woke around seven forty-five, Sasha was still sleeping. He left her in the bed undisturbed, slipped on his robe, and headed downstairs to the kitchen for a bowl of oatmeal. His heart was heavy for some reason; things were beginning to close in on him, apparently so much so that he woke Sasha with his grunting.

"Hey, baby, everything okay down there?" she said, her voice growing louder as she descended the stairs.

"I'm okay, couldn't sleep. I didn't mean to wake you."

"You didn't. I got up to use the bathroom and realized you weren't there. Why can't you sleep?" she asked, now standing face to face with him in the kitchen.

"Okay, you really want to know the truth? It was because of you. You know you snore."

"Quit playing," she said, rolling her eyes. "I do not."

"You do, too. I mean you were calling the cows home last night."

"Oh, my God, and I kept you up," said a stunned Sasha.

"Yep, so don't be mad at me if I buy you some of those breathe right strips."

"That's just mean, Marti. I can't believe this. I must have been really tired or something. I hadn't done that since I was a kid."

"What do you mean 'since you were a kid?' How do you know whether you snore or not? Do you record your nocturnal breathing patterns or something?"

Sasha shook her head in opposition to Marti's cynicism. "Okay, see, that's not funny," said Sasha, scowling.

Uncontrollable laughter erupted from his loins.

"Wait a minute," she said, realizing he was only teasing her. "See, I knew I didn't snore." It was much too important to Sasha not to have

clarity   on   this   one   issue.
After all, no woman wanted to find out that she snored, especially
from her lover.

"But I had you going, didn't I? Man, you should have seen the
look on your face when I said you were snoring. You were so hurt,
but you looked so adorable. I don't know how I stopped myself from
jumping you then and there, but I wouldn't have been able to pull this
off, and it was so worth it."

"Whatever," sassed Sasha. "You've had your fun at my expense. I
guess you're happy now."

"Oh, baby, don't be mad. Don't be mad," pleaded Marti, pulling
her to him in an embrace. "I'm sorry."

Sasha smiled reluctantly before pulling away to grab a
bowl from the cabinet. "So if I didn't wake you, why couldn't
you sleep?"

"Lots of stuff swimming through my head," he replied. "I spent the
better part of the night watching you while you slept and thinking
about what Doug's pastor said in Bible Study."

Sasha tilted the box of cereal and a mass of corn flakes trickled
into the stoneware. "And what was that?" she asked, retrieving the
milk from the fridge.

"Hey, you know you could have eaten the rest of that oatmeal."

"Naw," she said, "I don't feel much like the heavy stuff this morning."

"I guess I'll toss what's left then."

"You were saying about Bible Study?"

"Hey, baby, don't sweat that. Let's just talk about something else," Marti insisted.

"Okay then…so what's on the agenda for today," asked Sasha, loading her mouth with a spoonful of flakes. Marti stood over the kitchen sink rinsing out his dishes.

Turning around to face her, he said, "No plans, I think I'm just gonna chill. Have one of those weekends."

"You sure you're okay?"

Marti peered off into space before answering, "Yeah, I'm good. Don't sweat it. I'll figure this all out."

Chapter 21

S till recovering from sleep deprivation, Marti hoped he could rest more soundly tonight. He even persuaded Sasha to stay at her own place, wishing not to interrupt her sleep in case he had another narcoleptic episode. And as fate would have it, Marti battled yet another night of restlessness. He tossed and turned in bed until he was subdued by a burst of light, in which stood a figure, a figure not clear to him at first. Marti rose from his bed and cautiously drew within a few feet of the illuminated figure.

"Hi, son, it's me."

A bewildered Marti reached out to touch the figure, but drew only air. "This isn't real, it can't be. You're dead."

"It is, son. It's me."

"I don't believe this. Why are you here? I've got nothing to say to you."

"You'll figure it out," said the apparition before vanishing.

"Wait, what does that mean, 'I'll figure it out?' What does that mean!" shouted Marti.

Minutes later Marti opened his eyes and darted them around the room, not giving them time to adjust to the darkness. *It was just a dream*, he thought, *a really weird dream*. When he finally tired of surveying his room for what he knew was never there, he glanced over at the clock radio on his nightstand. Huge red digits read 4:35. Darnit, how was he going to get back to sleep now when still resonating in his mind was his father's voice? He'd figure it out, it said. Figure what out? What was there to figure out?

The bathroom mirror did not reflect anything conspicuous about Marti, no signs that he'd fallen out of bed during the night and hit his head on something blunt, causing him to hallucinate the paternal figure that seemed so real, though this would have been apparent hours ago if such a thing had really happened.

He ran cold water over his face then patted it dry with a face towel. Drawing closer to the mirror, Marti uttered to himself, "It was just a dream, man." Not quite convinced, however, Marti turned away from the mirror, thinking that if he stared at his reflection long enough his father might very well appear. One visit from the dead was enough for him, and he wondered if his mother or even Donald had ever been visited. What puzzled him more was that he didn't know what to make of his father's words. It was as if he spoke in some code, leaving Marti at a loss. The ghostly presence may as well have left an encrypted message on Marti's nightstand because he'd have faired no better with it. Even worse, he'd spend all day preoccupied with this, and his students just didn't deserve that. They commanded his full attention and required that on a daily basis.

Marti regrouped. He had to finish getting ready for work, but when he returned his attention to the mirror, his greatest fear was realized. There standing behind him in the looking glass was his father's mysterious presence, as eerie as last night's occurrence. Marti's racing pulse became less a concern when an acute pain exploded through his upper body, forcing him to grab his chest with one hand and clutch the side of the porcelain sink with the other to keep from falling uncontrollably to the cold bathroom tiles. As Marti turned around to investigate, he inhaled deeply to slow his rapid heartbeat, notwithstanding the pain throbbing in his chest region, which he had no way to abate. There was nothing there, no sign of the figure.

A hot shower was what he needed to put back on course this rather queer start. Marti scurried toward the shower area, reached inside, and turned on the water. A few moments later he had slipped inside. The warm water showered down over the top of Marti's head, sending a tranquil sensation over his entire body while inviting thoughts more of a mundane nature, like the fact that his birthday was in three days on the 21st of October. What an inauspicious way to lead into the day one was birth into the universe. There was something so ominous about it all.

At any rate, Marti would not further sabotage his shower time with such thinking, but he would call his mother later in the day, hoping she could shed some light on the unsettling apparition.

When Marti approached the school office door, Leslie had already made her morning round to the teacher's lounge and was heading toward her classroom.

"Running late today, aren't we?" she said, raising a brow.

"Don't ask," muttered Marti, pulling the office door toward him, "Rocky night and even rockier morning. I just need some coffee right now. I'll talk to you later, kay."

Leslie replied, perplexedly, "Yeah, sure."

Later during break time, Leslie approached Marti who was sitting at his desk. "So what was that about this morning? You practically dissed me like I was the Grinch who stole Christmas."

"Hey, I'm sorry about that. By the way, I'm not doing the lounge today. I've got to make a phone call to mama."

Leslie sat on the counter. "Everything okay with you? You look as though you've seen a ghost."

"Funny you should say that because that's exactly what's got me all uptight."

"What's that supposed to mean?"

"Last night, right, I'm trying to sleep and then I see my daddy's ghost and he doesn't say anything, right, except that I'll figure out why he appeared. So I'm freaking out about this and then this morning he shows up again in my bathroom mirror and just like that he's gone again. So now I'm about to call mama and see if she's ever seen him."

"Hey, I know you ain't trying to hear this," she said, empathetically, "but my mama said she used to see grandmama all the time...you know, while she'd be tending her garden or washing clothes or cooking. I asked her if she was ever spooked and she said that she wasn't because it was her mama."

"Well, father or not, I ain't trying to share my crib with a dead man."

"Hey, I hear ya. I'm gonna get out of your hair now and head down to the lounge so that you can call your mama. By the way," she continued while heading toward the door, "I haven't forgotten that you have a birthday soon. We'll have to do something."

"Yeah, okay," said Marti, waving her off.

Marti reached into his inside sports coat pocket and pulled his cell phone out, turned it on, and punched in his mother's digits. It rang twice before she picked up her receiver. "Hello," said the soft-spoken voice on the other end.

"Hi, mama, it's me."

"Everything okay, son? You don't sound right."

"Not exactly," he answered. "I've got something to ask you, but I'm not sure how to say this without spooking you."

"Just say it, son."

"I saw daddy last night and then again this morning and it's freaking me out and I'm not sure what I'm supposed to do with this, him just showing up like that and saying practically nothing."

"Well, what did he say?"

"Only that I'll figure it out, but you don't seem surprised."

A noticeable amount of time lapsed before she responded, and what felt like minutes to Marti could not have been anymore than a quarter of a minute. "Mama, you still there?"

"Yeah, son...I was just thinking back to the first time your daddy appeared to me."

Marti gasped. "Say what? When was this, mama?"

"Oh, it was back when you were just boys, and he was just too real to be a ghost. I put it out of mind because your daddy was dead and that was the end of it."

"What did he say, mama? What were you doing?"

"I was getting ready for bed after making sure you boys were settled and he appeared in my bedroom window. My heart leaped out of my chest at first, but his words calmed me. He said not to be scared, he wasn't there to hurt me, he was just sorry he did this to us and that was it. I guess that's why I was really able to go visit his grave all these years. I'd never seen your father that calming and reassuring before, not even when we first became an item."

"I wonder if Donald has ever seen him."

"Not sure, son, but maybe you should ask him."

"I think I will, mama, and thanks for telling me about this, but you said 'the first time.' There were others?"

"Oh yeah. It's been awhile, but he'd manage to pop up occasionally, not saying much, except that he missed me and was sorry he missed out on your lives."

"Thanks, mama."

"One more thing, son."

"Yes, ma'am."

"Why don't you invite your lady friend over next Tuesday? I'm whipping up a little birthday dinner for you and it would be nice if she'd come, too."

"Mama, you know you don't have to do that."

"Who said anything about having to do anything? I want to do this, son. Hadn't we missed enough birthdays together?"

"I suppose you're right."

"Course I am, I'm ya mama. I love you, son."

"You, too, mama, and I'll be in touch. Bye."

"Bye, son."

Marti restored the phone to his jacket pocket and took out his planner, flipped to the calendar section, and jotted in the October 21 slot, "Dinner at mama's with Sasha" and in the October 23 slot, "Go see Donald." Class would be reconvening in five minutes. It was time to expunge the supernatural from his thoughts, assume his game face, and teach some Geography.

Chapter 22

Marti entered the second bedroom converted into a home office, stealthily approaching a head-bobbing Sasha, who was apparently thoroughly enjoying the tunes blaring through the earphones of her mp3 player. The tap on her shoulder startled her so that a noise unrecognizable to the human ear escaped from her mouth. "Oh, my God, Marti, you should never do that to people, you know that! You scared me half to death. I have to remind myself that you have a key to my place. Still, you shouldn't walk up behind people like that."

Marti's empathy was temporarily put on hold by uncontrollable laughter. "I'm sorry," he said, coughing between fits of laughter. "I'm sorry, but...oh my goodness, woman, you didn't hear that squeal or whatever that was that I heard. I didn't realize you could produce such a sour note."

"Forget you, Marti."

The glint of contempt behind her eyes did not register as anything more than her disliking of practical jokes. "I'm sorry, baby, I am."

"Well, you shouldn't do that to people."

Finally collecting himself, Marti got around to his reason for being there. "So you ready to go? Mama's waiting for us. I know she's outdone herself with this birthday dinner. It's only gonna be the three of us, but watch, she'll have enough there to feed a small army of foot soldiers. Mark my words."

"Yes, I'm ready. Let me go grab my purse from the bedroom. And I'm serious, Marti, don't be trying that again on me, you got that!"

"Loud and clear, ma'am," he said, winking. Sasha was not amused.

Marti further attempted to pamper Sasha during the car ride to his mother's house for his little prank. "Hey, if it's any consolation, I'll treat you to a movie after we leave mama's. I'll do that for you on *my* birthday," he said, emphasizing the fact that this was supposed to be his day. "How's that sound?"

"Oh, and now I'm supposed to be grateful? You darn near give me a heart attack and now try to put a Band-Aid over my chest. Whatever, man. You can keep your movie."

"You're really upset by this, aren't you?" he asked, looking over to find her grimacing.

"I just don't like being in a state of alarm. I hate when people come up behind me like that."

"Yeah, okay, I get that, but I think it's more to it than that. Look how you're acting. Most people would just laugh it off after the initial shock, but you're really upset by this. Did something happen to you to make you so sensitive about this?" This casual conversation was taking a severe turn.

"I don't want to talk about it, Marti," she firmly stated. "Let's just get to your mama's house, eat some cake, and have some fun. Like you said, this is your day."

"If you say so, but you know you can tell me anything."

"Yeah, I know. It was a long time ago, but it'll forever be etched in my mind. And I'll leave it at that."

"Yeah, sure," replied Marti, wondering what cause had brought about this effect.

While driving the stretch of highway to his mother's house, he thought the most tragic of things. He wanted to know—badly. Finally, he broke the silence to dig further into the core. "Were you ever assaulted or something like that?" he asked, to which he got only silence in return.

Surely, she'd heard him because she'd shifted her eyes at him after the inquiry before returning her gaze to the miles of rural area.

"Sasha. Sasha. Sasha!" The third time, more penetrating than the first two tries, won him a response.

"What?"

"That was it, wasn't it? You were raped. Why didn't you ever tell me about this? I should know something like this."

"I understand that, but it's not something you just go around rehashing. And no, I was never sexually assaulted, but the bastard tried to hurt me."

On that, Marti pulled the car over to the shoulder of the road. This deserved his complete and utter attention. "What happened?"

Sasha shook her head repeatedly with her eyes closed, as if trying to lodge the scenes— frames of the episode—from her mental reel. "It was back in undergrad. I was coming from the library. It was late. I should have walked with somebody. I shouldn't have been walking alone at night like that, but I wasn't thinking. Besides, I could see my dorm from the library. You just don't think stuff like this could ever happen to you. I didn't. He...um...he," she stopped, lowered her head and tilted it away from Marti, not wanting him to see the tears stream her cheeks.

"It's okay," he said, gently stroking her hand. "It's okay, I'm here. What...what happened next?"

Sasha faced Marti again, her eyes still wet. "He came up from behind, cupped my mouth with his hand, and tussled me to the ground. My saving grace was the people who were leaving the library around the time he decided to make his move. Their screams startled him and he broke for cover."

An astonished Marti didn't know what do. He really didn't know what to say. "Well, did they ever catch this guy?"

"Yeah, but it wasn't from any description that I may have given the police because I didn't even get a look at the guy. Like I said, it was dark and it happened so quickly. The only thing I could see as he ran off and jumped into his car was that he was wearing dark clothes. That's it."

"So how did they get this punk?"

"About a week later, he attacked a female student from another nearby campus coming from the library just like me. She happened to be a student of Hapkido and disabled him long enough for help to come along. And after some severe interrogation, he admitted to attack on me."

"See, that's why they need to have police patrolling these campuses."

"Agreed. After my attack, they beefed up security."

"Yeah, but it shouldn't take someone nearly getting raped before universities take responsibility for their students' safety."

"I shouldn't have been walking alone."

"Stop that right now!" blasted Marti. "This is not your fault. That guy was sick, plain and simple, and he deserves never to see the light of day ever again."

"They gave him life. He was a convicted rapist, with a prior release for exceptional behavior. He won't be getting out this time."

"Good! Some people just can't be trusted with their own freedom because they'll do no good with it, only bring harm to others and wreak havoc."

"And your brother, is he one of those people?"

"My brother is eternally remorseful for his crimes. There's not a day that goes by that he doesn't wish he could reverse his actions, but that's not possible. If given a chance right now to reclaim his freedom, he would do right by others and himself. He would contribute to society and not take away from it. That I believe with my whole heart."

"Then I hope that for him when he does get out," she said.

Marti restarted the ignition. "We're not that far from mama's now. She's expecting us. She doesn't like it when I'm late, but she'll understand."

"You can't tell her about this," said Sasha, grabbing his arm. "You can't tell anybody."

"I wasn't going to. I would only say that something came up that I had to tend to, apologize for my tardiness, give her a kiss on the cheek, and that should do it. After all, it is my birthday. People are always forgiven stuff on their birthdays."

A semi smile broke from Sasha's face. "Lest we forget," she said. Just seeing any hint of humor come over her after what she'd just shared was enough for Marti.

***

On Leslie's suggestion that they have a late lunch during planning hour, the two of them were now seated comfortably at a booth in their favorite Italian restaurant. One of the finer things about teaching high school was that it lent its educators certain freedoms and privileges not always afforded on the lower educational level.

"Sorry, we didn't get together yesterday on your actual birthday," admonished Leslie.

"Don't sweat it. I went to mama's and had dinner there."

"Oh yeah, what'd she cook?"

Marti ran off the list of culinary delights: the succulent pineapple-glazed ham, the steamed squash and zucchini simmered in onions, the ever mouth-watering homemade garlic biscuits, for which she's prized, and the rich, incredibly savoring German chocolate cake.

Marti made it a point to spend more time talking about the cake, allowing Leslie to live her love for all things chocolate through him.

By the end of his recap, Leslie was surely licking her chops. "Man, I hate I wasn't there," she said.

"Speaking of which, mama told me to tell you hello. She still remembers you from the hospital visit."

"And how is she doing? Any other repercussions from the fall?"

"None. That old woman is fit as a fiddle."

"And she better not ever hear you call her old."

"Whatever, I ain't worried about mama."

"Yeah, right. She'll never know we had this conversation; that much I do know."

Marti t'ssed. "Have you decided what you want to eat?"

"Hey, you had better change the subject before you dig yourself further into that hole you're in."

"Well, let me change it once again. You do realize," said Marti, "that since we are having this birthday lunch for me, next month we're going to have to do the same for you. It is November 8th, right?"

"Don't remind me that it's so soon to come."

"Leslie, give it up, you'll only be turning thirty-four," said Marti, trying to make her feel better about grower older.

"Well, I would expect that statement coming from you, old man."

Marti snarled, "Old!"

"That's what I said. You will be turning thirty-six, after all."

"Wait a minute, did you not just two seconds ago give me some discourse about calling my mama old and now you turn around and call me the very thing? Furthermore," he asserted, "I've only got you by two years, so what does that make you?"

"That makes me finer with time, that's what," tooted Leslie.

"Whatever."

"Tell me something, though."

What's that?" said Marti.

"Why don't we do this more often?" asked Leslie. "We've been friends for what now—forever? It just seems that our lives are leading us in different directions, and I don't like it very much. I know you think I'm going to spend what time we do spend together sermonizing you, but you know me better than that, Marti. The only thing I can do is plant the seed. Ultimately, it's your choice whether you believe in God or not. I just th—"

"It's not like that, Leslie," interrupted Marti. "And you're right, I do know you. You've never cast judgments about the things I do or what I believe, that's why I come to you about stuff."

"Then if it's not that, what is it?" she inquired. "Why don't we hang like we used to?" There it was point blank, the questions of all questions. He didn't want to lie to her, but what exactly would be the truth? Marti pondered a moment for the right way to address this issue.

"Has it been that bad?" he asked her. Yes, that was the ticket; answer a question with a question and evade answering for as long as she'd allow him. But Leslie was a smart woman, very perceptive, and this tactic would not hold up for very long, if at all.

"That's not the point and you know it, Marti. Why don't you stop trying to jerk my chain and just tell me what's been going on with you that you have so little time for me anymore? Don't think I'm being insensitive here. I understand you have school. I really do, but you don't even call me that much anymore, and when I call you and leave a message, it takes you forever to return my calls, if you get around to doing it at all. You're slipping and I want to know why. Is there something going on that you're not telling me?" There it was again, the point blank question.

Okay, that was it, he had made up in his mind to tell her about Sasha. "Listen, I gue—" For the moment, Marti was spared by the waiter finally approaching.

"Hey, man, what took you so long to get to us? We've been sitting here nearly fifteen minutes," chided Marti. "We ain't got all day, ya know."

"I'm sorry, sir. I apologize. This is actually not my section. I was just informed that I had to cover this section because your original waiter had an emergency. Again, sir, I'm sorry for the delay. What can I get you two to drink?"

Marti railed, "Man, just bring us two teas and we're ready to order, so you can take that down, too."

"Yes, sir. For you, ma'am?"

Leslie proceeded to give her order followed by Marti with his. When the waiter dismissed himself from their table to place their orders, Leslie had a few words of her own for Marti for berating the young man, who, given the circumstance, held it together remarkably well. In his profession, he was certain to deal with disgruntled patrons quite often. "Don't you think you were a little harsh on him? It wasn't even ole dude's fault, and he did apology—twice," she pointed out.

"I know. You're right. When he comes back out, I'll square things with him. I guess it's from being all stressed out over school. I'm so close, Leslie, I can taste it."

"So school's really getting to you?"

"I'm just anxious," said Marti.

"And excited, of course, about walking?"

"You know it. You will be there, won't you?"

Leslie rolled her eyes then replied, "Now what kind of question is that? Only way I'm going to miss you walk is if I'm either in jail or in the ground. And I pray to God neither of those is the circumstance. Yeah, I'll be there, alright, with my make-shift pom-pom, football jersey, and foam Super Bowl hand."

"And they'll kick you right out of there, you nut," said Marti. They both laughed. "In all seriousness, I'm sorry I hadn't spent more time hanging out with you over the past few months. This thesis project really has been kicking my tail. I can't just kick it like I used to." Okay, so maybe that was just a version of the truth. He'd been splitting his time between his thesis and his girlfriend and giving Leslie the backseat and for good reason, he had decided.

"You know what, forget I even brought it up," said Leslie. "I'm so proud of you right now, it doesn't even matter. You're trying to get yours right now, and that's all that matters."

***

Marti was spending another one of his Saturdays at the prison. He didn't mind. He enjoyed his talks with Donald, and he figured it was one of the few bright spots in Donald's existence. He'd just filled his brother in on the ghostly encounters and was anxious to learn if Donald had, too, been visited.

"He's never appeared to me," said Donald, shaking his head.

"He must have figured you had enough to think about. Besides, I'm the one who's harbored so much hatred toward him. I think it may be a sign."

"What kind of sign?"

"I don't know. Maybe it's a sign that it's time for me to leave the past in the past and forgive him.

"Could be, I have."

"What do you mean 'you have?'"

"Yeah, man, I did that years ago when I first got locked up in this joint. I realized that we all make mistakes. Now some mistakes are worse than others. Mine...daddy's are about the worse you can get, but I'm no better than him. He took his own life and robbed himself and us. I took somebody's life, and I did the same thing to somebody's father and brother, husband and friend. Wrong is wrong, ya know, but I forgave daddy because who am I to judge? I leave that to God," surmised Donald, pointing upward with his index finger and eyes.

"God!" exclaimed Marti.

"Yeah, you *have* heard of Him?" teased Donald.

"Of course I've heard of Him.

"Listen, I'm just saying, it's out of my hands."

"Yeah, I suppose you're right," replied Marti incredulously, marveled by Donald's profundity, such wisdom he knew could only have derived from his brother's incarceration. And the irony was not lost on Marti. He loved Donald, but he was much too capricious for his own good, and now he sat across his older brother, nevertheless, not spewing folly, but imparting insight. "Okay, man," continued Marti, "I'm gonna get out of here. I've stayed long enough, even learned a little somethin', somethin'."

"Alright then," Donald replied while extending his hand. "I'll be here." They both smiled. "Tell mama I said hi."

"Will do."

"Wait a minute, man, before you go."

"Yeah," Marti said, turning back to Donald.

The corners of Donald's mouth turned up. "Happy Belated Birthday, man."

"Thanks," said Marti.

Chapter 23

"Guess what today is?" said Marti, cheesing with hands his behind his back, obviously holding something.

"It's Nov 1st," Sasha replied. "But what are you doing?"

"What?"

"Your hands, Marti—why are they behind your back?"

"Oh, that."

"Yeah, that," said Sasha.

"Well, today is the day for a little music," he said, revealing the new release of his fraternity brother's CD, which featured Marti on drums.

Sasha, who was lounging on the couch, jumped up in excitement. "What, already!" she said, grinning. "Let me see it."

Marti handed the album to Sasha, who eagerly opened the CD cover to retrieve the booklet from inside, wanting to see his name in lights, so to speak. "There it is," she said, "your name in print. This is too cool. Go put it on. I want to hear you."

Marti vanished momentarily into his home office to start the CD. Soon his townhouse filled with music. "Dance with me," said Marti, extending his hand.

Sasha peered up at her fine specimen of a man—hair freshly cut, mustached trimmed to perfection, biceps bulging, chocolate skin glistening—and smiled before taking his hand. Marti then pulled his adoring lovely from the couch into a tender embrace, and the two began to dance to the sublime pulses of Neo-Soul oozing from the other room. They were in heaven.

***

Nearly a week since the release of the album, Marti was still on an emotional high, and not even a defiant best friend could put a damper on things.

"Leslie, I'm not going to fight you on this. I told you when we had my birthday lunch that I was going to repay the favor. Tomorrow is your birthday and we're having lunch today to celebrate it early. I want to be the first to wish you a great day," Marti insisted.

Leslie was sitting at her desk rummaging through her top drawer. "Marti, I was hoping that you'd have forgotten about that. I've got too much to do right now," she complained.

"Well, aren't you the one always talking about how we don't go out anymore or spend enough time together? Now, let's go, woman!"

"Boy, if I didn't like you, I'd—"

"Watch yourself," Marti interrupted. "You've got religion now."

"Don't go there," she said, rolling her eyes. "I wasn't gonna say something profane."

"Just come on, Les, we're wasting time."

"Where are you taking me anyway?" she asked, grabbing her purse from out of her bottom desk drawer.

"Anywhere you want. Besides, I've got a surprise for you."

Suddenly, Leslie's interest was piqued. "Surprise? What kind of surprise?"

"You'll see. Now where do you want to eat?"

"I'm in the mood for some trout," she stated. "Let's go to Riley's Fish Market."

"Oh, man, I haven't been there in ages."

Ten minutes later Marti had pulled into Riley's parking lot and the lunch rush was apparent from all the parked cars. Once inside, they had a five-minute table wait, but the food at this eighteen-year-old dive was worth any delay. It was a wonder that they had not frequented Riley's more often.

At a booth facing traffic, the two were seated and placed their drink orders with their waitress, requiring a bit more time for their entrée selections. When the waitress returned with their beverages, they were ready to give their lunch orders. Marti ordered the lunch special of fried catfish nuggets, potato salad, slaw, and hush puppies. Leslie got the baked trout with green salad and fresh string beans. While waiting for their food, Marti and Leslie passed the time with idle chit-chat.

"So what's in the gift bag?" asked Leslie.

"It's your surprise," he said, grinning.

"Well, what is it?"

Marti passed the gift bag across the table to Leslie. "Take a look," he said. "I think you'll like it."

Leslie slowly removed the contents from the bag: a CD and a small black velvet box. "What's this she inquired of the CD?"

"Ya boy made an album," said Marti proudly.

"Get out! When did you do this?"

"About five months ago," answered Marti. "An old frat asked me to play drums for his project. Check it out, got my name in the booklet. A brotha's trying to do some things."

"I see. I'm impressed. I knew you were playing at the club on Thursdays, but now you're cutting albums and stuff. Scared of you," Leslie said, nodding her head in approval. "I can't wait to check this out when we get into the car. I've always loved what you could do on drums. You've got an amazing gift."

"Yeah, I'm pretty stoked. I hope it does well. I hope people can get into the music. Anyway, you still got another present there. Go ahead and open it."

"I will, but let's wait. She's headed our way with the food," said Leslie, acknowledging the return of their waitress.

"Okay, ma'am, here's the trout that you ordered. And for you, sir, we have the catfish. Is there anything else I can get you?" asked their server.

"No, I think we're fine," said Marti.

As soon as she left their table, Marti insisted Leslie open her last gift, the black box. And Leslie gasped when she saw what was inside. "Oh, my gosh! No, you didn't!" she said in disbelief. "This is just too much."

"It's the one you wanted, right?" confirmed Marti about the silver necklace with yellow topaz birthstone pendant.

"Yeah, this is the one I was looking at online. I can't believe you got it. You're gonna make me cry, and you know I don't do that," said Leslie.

"Whateva, Les."

"I'm serious, Marti. That was weeks ago when I mentioned that I wanted to get the necklace. And actually, it hadn't crossed my mind since then. I can't believe you did this," she repeated, shaking her head. "You're just too much."

"Okay, woman, that's enough praise for one day, let's eat," he said to his friend, smiling. "I'm starving."

Chapter 24

P alm trees swayed in the breeze as he sat, surrounded by powder white sand and miles of ocean, sipping on something cool and refreshing when suddenly she appeared from that crystal blue water, glistening in the sun, as insatiable as ever. He just lay there watching her towel off, running the strip of terrycloth over a two-piece bathing suit that hugged her every curve. She first blushed after noticing his gaze, but the smile that followed invited something more...

A beeping alarm clock abruptly woke Marti from his nap. He was only having a dream, yet this was no ordinary fantasy, but one foretelling of his upcoming holiday plans. Marti had surprised Sasha with news of taking her to Palm Beach for Thanksgiving so that the two of them could celebrate his graduation early. Ecstatic about the trip, Sasha started planning right away while Marti spent his time preparing to defend his thesis project, the last step in the process before graduating.

He had spent much of that Saturday doing just that, working on his thesis project, and hoped that a couple hours of shut-eye would fuel him for burning the late night oil. Yet Marti still felt tired after waking, and didn't hesitate to return to his dream of paradise.

Later that day, he gave Sasha a call.

"Hey, baby, got some news about the trip. There's been a change in plans. My band is going to be the featured gig at Snug Harbor in New Orleans on Thanksgiving. It's a real cool venue to play."

"You know me," she replied, "I love to hear you play." Marti could sense a bit of disappointment in her tone

"It's gonna be great, I promise."

***

The night scene. New Orleans was swarming with thrill-seekers looking for some action in neon-lit bars or variety shops on Bourbon Street, which could easily be renamed "the strip that never sleeps," save for the long departed souls in neighboring graveyards guarded by black rod iron fence to ward off the curious or outright weird cloaked in black garb. The "dead" were buried in tombs on top of the ground; it was a constant reminder that death was a part of life. Christians argued, however, that a cold block of cement was not the final resting place, only a place of rest—for the moment, in which case life was also a part of death, eternal life.

Tonight the air was particularly crisp and a light chill nipped at their coattails as they settled inside the Jazz club, where Marti would be playing in less than an hour. He was pleased to be sharing this moment with Sasha. After all, she was a music eclectic who favored the classics like Jazz and Blues over the new age sound, but who listened to it all. It could have been that she herself was somewhat of a songstress. Sasha loved to sing, and Marti, realizing this, had the idea that he'd surprise her by bringing her up on stage to perform a number, something Sasha had always wanted to do. The crowd of about fifty or so people was just enough to be respectable and not too intimidating, but would she do it, could she do it?

When Marti introduced Sasha as his girlfriend, she began to blush. *Stop it*, said her eyes as she dashed them up at Marti. *You're putting me on the spot.*

"I have one more surprise," added Marti from behind the drum set on stage. "See that beautiful woman right there? Well, she can *sang*, y'all. Give her a warm round of applause as she comes on stage to give us a sample."

Sasha's mouth dropped as she scanned the room only to notice all the expecting faces in a crowd whose non-stop clapping bounced off the acoustic walls. More and more they urged and whistled and clapped and clapped and whistled and urged until she slowly stood to her feet and made her way on stage and found her place behind the microphone. What would she sing? She hadn't done anything like this since she was in the church choir years ago when kids had no inhibitions and loved the spotlight and wanted nothing more than to be the next Whitney Houston or Luther Vandross. Yes, what would she sing?

He promised her that she'd have a great time, but this was over the top, she thought as she searched herself for the right song. Finally, it came to her, something her granddaddy loved to hear, "My Funny Valentine." Purple, blue, green, and yellow alternatively flashed the stage while she belted sultry lyrics as if a seasoned Jazz singer, the band now feeling her vibe joined in. It could not have been more perfect if it had been arranged or practiced. Sasha was a natural; everyone could see that, most especially Marti who, from behind his set of drums, watched the rhythmic twists and jolts of her body, the movement of her hands, the swaying of her hips, and the motion of her head as she sang. She was feeling every note she sang, expressing every lyric that parted her lips. She belonged on stage.

"That was Sasha Clayborne, everyone."

Sasha returned to her seat to the sound of more thunderous applause, giving her a feeling she hadn't felt in years. Her heart was still fluttering from being up on stage. Her head was swimming with thoughts. She could barely contain herself, not quite wanting to tame what she was feeling just yet anyway. She wanted somehow to frame the exhilaration for as long as she could, keep replaying her performance over in her head, losing nothing of the overwhelming rush it gave her each time she remembered back to the first moment.

Impossible it was to encapsulate what had just happened and bury it in the earth so one day, many years later, it could be dug up and found untouched, unblemished. Someday it would be just a memory then eventually something faded into oblivion. But too few people subscribed to the philosophy of *carpe diem*. Sasha, on the other hand, had just taken that first step. Marti had only hoped that, from this experience, she would continue to *seize the day* and keep creating new moments so she did not have to rely on yesterday's fading memories, but, more importantly, he hoped that she would not let something so wonderful happen to her only once.

He wanted to say something. Instead, Marti kept looking over at her in the car while she gleamed with satisfaction. Sasha had not yet come down from the high of singing on stage hours ago, and he certainly did not want to take that away from her. She deserved it. It was her moment, one that could very well decide her future, a future that may once have been marked by long hours of graduate work and a nine-to-fiver and a thirty-year mortgage and babies and a minivan, now held promise of a singing career and the life of a recording artist. Yes, she was just that good a singer.

"What are you thinking about?" asked Marti.

"Ever wondered what your life would be like if you just stopped caring?"

Marti pulled up to Sasha's apartment. The drive from New Orleans only took an hour and a half. It was about twelve-thirty in the morning and he was pretty tired, but, understandably, Sasha was wired and he felt obligated to indulge her. "What do you mean 'just stopped caring?'"

Sasha reclined the seat in Marti's car and begin peering at the stars through the sunroof. The moon was full, but in less than five hours it would begin a vanishing act to make way for the sun.

"I think most people are just too scared to do what they really want to do, what they were really meant to do," she said. "They hate their jobs, but fear of the unknown is what drags them out of bed every morning. Face it, we are afraid to walk away from our comfortable existence, our stable livelihood to pursue our true passions. Aren't you?"

"Maybe I'm just an exception to the rule, Sasha, because I love what I do."

"You mean to tell me that you never wonder about touring with your band, going places, seeing new faces and things, sharing your music with the world?" said Sasha incredulously. "That doesn't excite you?"

"Of course it does, and some day I'll be able to do those things, but you have to put things in perspective."

"How so?"

"Well, you have to realize that no matter how talented you are the world only makes room for so many artists and performers and actors and painters. Meanwhile, you had better find a niche that you can be comfortable with until it makes room for your passion. Don't get me wrong—I love playing the drums and gigging with my crew. It puts me on a natural high, and sometimes it's hard to come back down to reality, to all the crap and chaos, but teaching pays the bills, and I'm good at what I do and I like what I do because I'm good at it."

Marti waited for Sasha to respond only she seemed to be expecting him to say more. And now that their conversation had nudged the sleep from his eyes, Marti was eager to continue. "I wanted you to see that there was more to your life...more to you," he said. "I wanted you to seize your moment because I believe some day that will be your life. That's why I called you up on stage. And you're right—fear keeps too many people from trying new things. Why do you think you waited so long to do what you did tonight? You were afraid. Afraid of failing. Afraid of not hitting the right notes. Afraid of forgetting the words. Afraid of being rejected by those listening. Afraid that you weren't good enough, and you are. But no matter how good you are, none of us can afford to stop caring or stop being adult about our responsibilities. That's what makes everything we have possible."

"I guess I knew that. I just needed to hear it," she said, adjusting the seat to the upright position. "Everything you said is true. It's just that sometimes I wonder if it's all worth it. Going to school and paying all this tuition and being away from my family and my…" Sasha's voice trailed off. What? What was she going to say? Marti wanted to know.

"Being away from your what?" He didn't want to assume, but his mind certainty thought a couple of things in those few seconds of pause. Maybe she had a kid. Wouldn't that be ironic?

"My friends. Actually, just one friend—Daria. I hadn't spoken to her in months. It's a sad thing when you realize that not everybody is going to be happy for you when you try to be more and do more. Daria and I, we both had the same opportunities, but she chose to get married and raise a family and I'm here. Don't get me wrong, I think having a family is great. I want the husband and kids and all of that *American Pie* stuff some day…Like I said, not everybody will be in your corner, not even your friends."

"Why don't you just call her?"

"What?"

"Call her. I'm sure she'll be glad you did."

Sasha shook her head. "Naw, Naw, I don't think I'm ready to do that yet. She said some pretty nasty stuff to me the last time I spoke to her."

"Tell me about it," said Marti, remembering his fall out with his mother and things he had said to her. There was just no excuse for his behavior.

"She chose her life. I didn't choose it for her. I begged her to take college more seriously and stay focused. The girl was smart as a whip, blew through high school, got through two semesters of college and fell for some guy she met at a football game and got pregnant with their first kid. Now they've been married for six years and have three children. I guess I should have expected as much from her, though. She was always trying to compete with me on some level, if not with boyfriends then with school, if not with school then clothes. No, I'm not sure I want to talk to her. Maybe I'm better off with her out of my life. I only want to surround myself with positive people. Life's hard enough."

"I know what you mean," Marti said, agreeing.

"I figured you would."

Marti chuckled. "I have had my share of growing pains, that's no lie. And sometimes you just have to cut people off, especially when they start actin' up. I say cut them off, man, move on, find somebody else to occupy your time with."

Sasha smiled. Having cast in his words just a hint of subtlety for easy translation, she understood that that was Marti's way of setting his approval on her choice to take up with him.

"You may as well crash here tonight. You look tired."

"Naw, I'm cool. I've got enough juice to get me home. Besides, if I stay tonight, you'd only distract me," he said, smiling, "and I've really got to spend much of tomorrow working on that thesis."

"Sure?"

"Positive."

Sasha leaned in for a kiss then another. "Thanks for tonight, you know, letting me come up there with you. I still can't believe I did that. It was amazing, so amazing! Today was definitely a good day."

"Yeah, it was a pretty good Thanksgiving," he said, giving Sasha one last kiss before she got out of his car and slipped into her apartment.

By the time he made it to his townhouse, it was two o'clock in the morning. It was settled—he was sleeping in. No phone calls. No gym. Nothing. Just sleep. He'd reserve the afternoon for his school-related responsibilities: reading, researching, and typing.

***

When Marti woke up around nine o'clock, he found himself stretched across the bed still wearing last night's clothes. He had, however, managed to kick off his shoes. Marti raised himself up against the headboard and wiped the cuts of his eyes then leaned over to grab the remote from the nightstand beside the bed. He had flipped through the channels twice when the phone rang. Marti immediately recognized the voice.

"What's up, girl? How was your Turkey Day?" It was Leslie calling from her mom's house in Dallas.

"Over indulgent," she said. "They're gonna have to roll my fat tail out of bed. I can't believe I ate that much. Turkey and pecan pie and dressing and more pie and rolls—way too much food. It's a shame."

"That's alright. When you get back, I'm gonna work you like you're in boot camp. Yeah, I've got somethin' for ya," teased Marti.

"So, how was New Orleans?"

"New Orleans was good. Felton asked about you."

"Felton…he's the trumpet player, right?"

"The one and only. I think he's got a thing for you."

"What? Marti, please. I barely even know him."

"That doesn't mean a thing. Every time I see him, he's asking about you. I just don't have the heart to tell him that he ain't got a chance."

"You don't know that," said Leslie.

"Yes, I do. Nobody knows you like I do."

"Yeah, yeah, whatever. You just make sure you tell Felton that I said hello the next time you see him."

"Oh, now you're trying to play me. I ain't playing cupid so you can hook up with some other dude."

"Say what?"

"Yeah, you heard me, Les. You women do stuff like that. Y'all hook each other up and then when it doesn't work out, you're ready to cut ya sista down for trying to help, so leave me out of that."

"Fine, I'll tell him myself," Leslie insisted.

"Okay, that's it. I don't want to hear anymore."

A girlish laugh rumbled from the other end of the phone. "Why, you jealous?"

"Jealous of who—Felton? Please, you've got to come better than that."

"I thought Felton was your boy."

"Yeah, he can play that horn like it ain't even funny," said Marti, "but he's an even bigger playa. Everything he sees in a skirt, he tries to chase. He better watch his back before he messes with the wrong sista."

"Guess I just better hold what I got then."

"I'm tellin' ya, you're better off."

"Better off for whom?" asked Leslie.

"Just better off."

"Yeah, if you say so," she said.

"I do say so. I know can't just any brother try to holla at you. He has to come correct."

"You mean I need a brotha like you?"

Marti almost dropped the phone when Leslie said that. "Did I say that? Where did that come from, Les?"

"Listen, before we go somewhere with this conversation that we may not want to thread, I'm gonna get off this phone and finish helping my mama in the kitchen. Some of the family are coming over today to finish off the leftover turkey and dressing. I'll talk to you later."

Marti hung up the phone and nudged back down in his bed. He didn't feel much like watching television anymore, and soon he'd get started on his project. He lay there thinking about Leslie's last comment about wanting a brotha like him. Could it be possible that she had thought about them getting together? Had she come to realize that they made sense, that he could be her Mr. Right? It was true, he and Leslie made sense, but he and Sasha made sense, too. Eleven years his junior, Sasha helped Marti to reconnect with his youthful side, a part of himself that he never quite had a chance to experience fully. Still, Marti wondered if they really had a future together. Given their age difference, could they really build a lasting relationship and did he really want that with Sasha?

Chapter 25

It was Friday, December 19, 2003. Commencement day was finally here, but Marti spent the better part of the morning reflecting, looking back over all the obstacles and road blocks he'd faced just to get to this day: divorce, his brother's trial, estrangement from his mother, and of course, his present predicament—the fact that he wanted two women, but loved only one, the one he didn't and figured he probably couldn't have. What a mess. And what was even worse was the fact that this was also going to be the day that he introduced both women to each other. How that was going to turn out...well, Marti just didn't know. Leslie's inquiries about all his strange behavior would certainly be answered, but this had to be done. He was tired of keeping Sasha from Leslie and not talking to her about all the things that were going on in his life. Even though he saw her everyday at school, they hadn't talked much at all since Thanksgiving when she called.

Leslie was busy trying to renew her life, trying to get to know God and become a better Christian, almost always reading her Bible during break time or on her lunch hour. How was he supposed to strike up a casual conversation, you know, just shoot the breeze, when Leslie seemed so deeply involved in her daily readings? It made Marti feel a bit uncomfortable that he was not doing the same, not trying to get himself together like she was. Most times he'd just duck his head in the teacher's lounge and give her a nod and leave. This was what their relationship had become—little nods of acknowledgement, most times in passing.

Marti realized, however, that the biggest problem was not really that Leslie had now found religion, but that he could not tell her that he loved her because he was afraid she didn't love him back. He knew she loved him, but he didn't know if she was in love with him and was just too afraid to jeopardize their friendship by telling him. Truth is, their friendship was already compromised even with him keeping silent, and it concerned him a bit that introducing Sasha to Leslie at the graduation would somehow grow them further apart. He just knew that Leslie would sink further and further into her new spiritual quest and give him even more space, figuring that this would probably be best so Sasha would not feel threatened in any way. She never wanted to step on another woman's toes and give any of Marti's girlfriends any reason to feel jealous of her friendship with him.

That was just the type of woman Leslie was, but, mostly, it was one incident that happened about a year ago that forced her to rethink or re-evaluate how others, especially other women, perceived her friendship to Marti. If nothing else, other women could always pick up on chemistry between two people, and Cynthia was no exception. The minute she saw the two of them together, she grew suspicious, thinking that they had something going on behind her back. After she found Leslie's number in Marti's address book, Leslie started getting the phone calls or voice messages threatening her to back off. And no matter how much Leslie tried to convince Cynthia that she had nothing to worry about, that she and Marti were just real good friends, Marti eventually had to break it off with Cynthia because she grew harder and harder to deal with. It had gotten so that he stopped mentioning Leslie's name around Cynthia altogether.

In some ways, though, Leslie could understand where Cynthia was coming from, even though she would not have handled the situation the same. No woman wanted to hear her man talking about another woman all the time no matter how good of friends they were. Many relationships had ended in disaster over coed friendships. Neither Marti nor Leslie wanted to repeat that history. And perhaps that was another reason Marti had waited so long to decide to introduce Sasha to Leslie as his girlfriend and Leslie to Sasha as his best friend.

Marti stood in front of the full-length mirror admiring the man in the black cap and gown peering back. *You finally did it*, he thought to himself, *and in less than two hours from now, you'll be sharing this moment with three important women*. Marti couldn't have been more pleased that his mother would be there. After all, these were the moments—those special events in a person's life—that were to be shared and celebrated with family, with parents. Then, there was Leslie and Sasha. While Marti did harbor some ambivalence about having the two of them there since they would be meeting each other for the first time, he reminded himself that everything would be fine because they were all adults and neither of the two women was the jealous type—he didn't think, at least he hoped. But then he grew concerned again, thinking that if it were he standing in their shoes, he'd feel uncomfortable, and that it really didn't matter if he was the jealous type or not. And since Sasha was his girlfriend, he was certain, at least from her vantage point, there would to be tension in the air thick enough to cut with a knife.

He stood a few minutes more in front of the mirror before tossing his cap onto the bed and walking into his closet to retrieve a pair of slacks and a shirt. He still had to shower and change before heading to Sasha's apartment, his mother's, then to the campus for the graduate line-up. He had little time to waste since Sasha wanted him to get to her place in time enough to spend at least ten minutes there. Last night over the phone she said that she wanted to give him something, and she wanted him to have it before the ceremony. Maybe it was a graduation kiss or cologne or a new shirt, something he could wear under his gown. Whatever it was, Sasha certainly sounded excited over the phone.

By the time Marti arrived at Sasha's and got out of the car, she was standing in the front door with a huge grin on her face.

"You're going to love this," she said. Marti walked inside, taking a quick glance into the kitchen to see if it was a cake or something. He saw nothing.

"Well, you got me curious," Marti replied.

"Just go have a seat. It's in the bedroom. I'll go get it." Sasha had only been gone a split second when she returned carrying a small wrapped box. "Here it is," she said, handing it to him. "Go ahead, open it."

Marti tore off the wrapping as if he'd find a corvette inside. Close. She had managed to score tickets to all four days of the February 2004 Buick Invitational in La Jolla, California, and Tiger Woods was going to be in the field, defending 2003's win. "Oh, my God, how did you—"

"Let's just say, I know some friends who know some friends. So I take it that I did good?" "Better than that. Man, I'll have to be sure to get a sub for those days next year. I'm marking it on the calendar first thing. Why didn't you get tickets for yourself?"

"You know I'm not much into golf. I'm just glad you like your gift."

"Come here," he said, reaching out and pulling her closer. "Man, if I didn't have this graduation to go to…"

"Come on, lover boy, let's go. We don't want to be late."

"Yeah, you're right." He gave her a peck on the cheek. "Let's go. Besides, we still have to pick up my mama."

In the car on the way to his mother's house, Marti thought about the tickets. "I still can't believe you did this."

"You said that you always wanted to go to a PGA tournament."

"Yeah, but I really didn't think you were paying attention."

"Lucky for you, I was."

Marti glanced over at Sasha and smiled.

"What?" she said.

"You're something else. That's all I can say."

"Listen, I didn't forget what you did for me on Thanksgiving. If you hadn't called me on stage, I never would have known how good it felt to be up there. I had never experienced anything like that before, but now I have because of you. I had to do something to show you how much that day meant to me."

"Well, you've outdone yourself."

Once Marti had collected his mother and they arrived on the LSU campus, they found Leslie already standing in front of Peabody Hall. *Here goes nothing*, thought Marti. The three of them approached Leslie who, once she spotted Marti, began to smile. Marti gave Leslie a hug then reintroduced his mother to her. "Mama, you remember Leslie, my best friend?"

Before Marti could finish his introduction, his mother grabbed both of Leslie's hands, firmly holding them in her own. "I sure do," his mother said, smiling. "You're the lovely young lady who came to see me while I was in the hospital last March."

"Yes, ma'am, I did. I'm sorry I hadn't gotten a chance to see you since then." Frankly, Leslie wouldn't have been able to explain why that was the case. It seemed to her that she should have visited his mother at least a few times over the last several months since the hospital visit. Why hadn't she? Did she mean so little to Marti that he would not invite her to his mother's house; after all, she was his best friend?

"Well, I'm certainly glad to see you again," his mother added.

Not wanting to alienate Sasha, Marti interrupted the reunion between Leslie and his mother to introduce her to his best friend. "And Leslie, this is Sasha...my girlfriend." Oops, he paused too long. Sasha was going to grill him for that later on, he just knew it. The two ladies exchanged smiles and shook hands.

"So how long have you been waiting?" asked Marti.

"Not long, not long at all." This was awkward, very awkward. Besides the small talk, there was nothing to say. And neither of the two ladies was going to say out loud what she was thinking: *Who are you and when did you get into the picture?*

"I guess I better get inside. Will the three of you be alright?"

Sasha handed Marti his cap and gown. "Yeah, we'll be fine...you better get inside now."

"She's right, Marti" added Leslie. "We'll catch you inside. And congratulations."

Although there wasn't going to be a main ceremony and all diplomas were being conferred by the Dean of each college in various locations on campus, it did not seem to matter to Marti, who was just glad this day had arrived. Marti disappeared inside of Peabody Hall to find the other graduates. The three ladies went inside to find a seat. The auditorium was steadily filling, but there were still a few empty seats. The ceremony was scheduled to commence in twenty minutes.

Finally, the moment came for the graduates of the College of Education to enter and take their seats. The traditional "Pomp and Circumstance" lead the procession. Black robes ordained each graduate, but the Master's candidates also had the pleasure of wearing distinctive hoods while Doctoral candidates would be invested with their hoods at the same time they received their diplomas. Leslie was so proud of Marti. She knew what he had gone through to get to this point, and not many people would have gone back and finished, especially if four years had gone by.

From his seat on the third row of the auditorium, Marti turned back and looked up into the row of seats where the three ladies were seated; his mother was seated between Sasha and Leslie. They were engaged in conversation it seemed until Sasha looked down and noticed Marti gazing up at them. The smile that came over her face was followed by a wave. Marti returned the wave and smiled then turned his attention to Leslie. When his eyes met with her eyes, their silent conversation began—the story of their now four-year history together, something he and Sasha had not established; Leslie's affection for him and certainly his affection for her. Maybe it was the prospect of another woman moving in on unoccupied territory that she never really gave much attention, but was now interested in because she realized she could see herself living there, maybe that's what was going on inside Leslie's head when she peered back at Marti so intensely. At any rate, Sasha was completely tuned out by them. She, on the other hand, certainly saw what was going on between the two of them, but said nothing. It was neither the time nor the place.

At ten-thirty, the Dean of the College of Education began to call each graduate. Next, it would be the Graduate School, and Marti would have his moment to walk on stage and take his diploma in hand and finally say, "I did it." A modest level of applause was given to Marti as he crossed the stage and much of that he received from Leslie, Sasha, and his mother. The graduation ceremony lasted forty-five minutes. And as he suspected, a heated conversation sparked between him and Sasha right after, as the two of them were headed for the car. Marti was just glad that Leslie had already left. He certainly didn't want there to be a scene in front of her, especially if it was going to be about her. It was equally good that Marti had insisted that his mother wait out in front of Peabody Hall while he and Sasha went to get the car because he wouldn't have wanted her to witness him and Sasha arguing either.

"If she's your best friend, why haven't you ever mentioned her?" Sasha questioned.

"Hadn't I? I thought I had."

"No, Marti. Today was the first time I'd ever heard her name. Wait a minute…no, it's not. It was her name that you were saying in your sleep that night."

"Are you implying something because I don't like your tone?"

"My tone is fine," she said sternly. "It's you that I've got a problem with."

"Me!" interjected Marti.

"Yes, you. It doesn't make sense that you never said a word to me about her, and from the look on her face when we were introduced, you never said a word to her about me. What's with that?"

The two of them stood at the trunk of the car. "It sounds to me like you're accusing me of something, and I want to know what it is?" Marti insisted.

"I just think it's weird that you didn't tell me about her," she pointed out.

"And why should I? She's got nothing to do with us. I don't treat you bad. I respect you. I give you the attention you need, so why is this even an issue?"

"Just forget it, Marti. I don't want to talk about it anymore."

"Fine."

"Fine."

"Fine. Can we go now?" said Marti.

"You got the keys."

"Geez, you sure know how to ride a brotha."

"What!" exclaimed Sasha.

"Nothing."

This was one time that Marti was especially thankful for an understanding mother; otherwise, it would have been awkward for him to try to pretend that all was well in front of his mother had she invited them over to her house for dinner. Linda Johnson assumed Marti would want to spend some time with Sasha alone to celebrate, and insisted that he drop her home first. Besides, she was tired and wanted to get some rest, she told him. If she only knew what was really going on. Perhaps she had figured out from the silence during the car ride that there was some tension between her son and his girlfriend. Nonetheless, Marti did as his mother asked and dropped her off first.

The silence continued during the car ride to Sasha's apartment, and when Marti dropped Sasha off at her place, neither one of them exchanged a good-bye or anything remotely cordial to the other. He was not going to attempt to imagine what could be going through Leslie's head. What would ordinarily be a celebratory occasion was shaping up to be quite a disheartening experience for Marti. The Master's degree laying on the passenger's seat should have been enough to keep his spirits up. Instead, Marti spent the better part of his drive back to his place trying to overcome the pang brought on by what had just happened between him and Sasha after graduation since that's what men were supposed to do—shake stuff off, not let things like this get the best of them, or pretend they didn't have pain and hurt and feelings of depression. Men were supposed to have the prowess of Superman and, emotionally, the toughness of a Taurus. That could not have been further from the truth because, at that very moment, Marti felt like crawling under a rock and tarrying there for awhile.

Chapter 26

Now that Marti had handled his graduate school business, it was time to shift gears to what had once been his favorite holiday, Christmas, which was in four days. Although he and Sasha had been having their issues since graduation a couple of days ago when she found out about Leslie, she had still invited him to come home with her to Denver for the holiday. Sasha's hope of trying to get their relationship back on track was dashed when Marti told her that he would be spending Christmas with his mother this year.

Marti was happy he wouldn't have to repeat last year's lackluster episode of sitting in front of the television watching parades all morning—I mean, really, how many times could you find a sixty-foot-long Garfield balloon exciting? Even Leslie had gone home to Dallas to spend the holiday with her mom and had planned to do the same this year. Though this year's festivities would include sitting at his mother's table, he really missed that feeling he got when he was surrounded by friends and family, everybody sitting around trying to do a year's worth of catching up in a day. The men, of course, would all be in the back watching football and chowing down on Big

Mama's homemade dressing and giblet gravy in between shouts at the floor model television because the ball had been intercepted on the twenty yard line and ran back for sixty yards. Then there were all the kids running through the house, clenching onto toys that were still in the packaging, trying to get someone to tear off the hard plastic or the million strips of tape. And there was always, always the one or two inquisitive preteens hiding around the corner, trying to listen in on their mama's conversation, and her stopping long enough to give them a quick look that said, "Go back in the other room and play and stay out of grown folks' business!"

Even after his daddy was gone, they'd go over Big Mama's house for Thanksgiving and Christmas and Easter and Fourth of July. It was tradition. And Marti knew better than anyone why tradition was so important; how much these family gatherings had impacted his life; how very important they were in giving him a sense of belonging, especially after his father's suicide, which for the longest time made him feel rejected. Nonetheless, Marti was more than grateful for this year's plans that would spare him another insufferable year of watching a 450-pound, helium-filled cat float between two skyscrapers in ten-degree weather.

***

A ringing phone tore Marti away from contemplating what he should do about Sasha, and his heart skipped a beat at the sound of Leslie's voice on the other end of the phone. He hadn't spoken to her since graduation and he knew this conversation would have less to do with her wishing him a Merry Christmas as it would her wanting to know why he didn't tell her about Sasha along time ago.

"I guess you can't call anybody," said Leslie.

"What, no, 'Hey, how ya doing? How's your Christmas going?' What, I don't get any of that, Leslie?"

"Yeah, all of that, but you know why I called."

"No, but I'm sure you're gonna tell me," Marti cynically stated.

"Fine, I'll cut to the chase. Why didn't you tell me about Sasha? You kept your relationship with her from me for almost a year. Seriously, I don't *even know* how you managed to pull that off."

Marti laughed. "Tell you the truth I don't know how I did it either, especially since I had planned to tell you when we came back from summer vacation, but..." he said, pausing.

"But what? Why didn't you?" asked Leslie.

"I-uh-I got sidetracked by your news about being saved. After that, well, you know...like you said before, we did start growing apart. I guess it was just never the right time."

"Yeah, we don't talk like we used to, so I guess I can understand you not telling me about Sasha," reasoned Leslie. "But why didn't you tell her about me?"

Marti had suddenly made up in his mind that he would tell Leslie the truth about his feelings for her. He didn't want to go into the new year playing the "pretend game" anymore, pretending she meant only a friend to him. "There's something you should know," he said, getting ready to profess his love for her until he heard the phone beep. "Hold on Leslie, another call is coming in."

Marti clicked over to the voice of Sasha. He knew he'd better take it since he felt obligated to try to salvage what was left of their relationship or at least part on good terms if it came to that. Clicking back over, Marti said to Leslie, "I better take this, it's Sasha calling from her parents. I'll talk to you later. Have a good Christmas."

"Yeah, you, too."

Marti clicked back over to Sasha. "Hey."

"Hey. Listen, I'm sorry about before. I've been bugging every since I met Leslie at your ceremony, but I saw something there, Marti, and you can tell me that I'm just exaggerating, but I know there's something there."

"I'm not fooling around if that's what you think, Sasha. I haven't been with anybody, but you since we've been together."

"And I believe that, but I think you have feelings for that woman and you're just not willing to admit it to me, maybe not even to yourself. And if I'm right, then we don't have a future together," she said.

"But I'm with you, Sasha. That should tell you something."

"Before that day, it meant everything to me, and that was enough. I don't think it is anymore. I'm not secure enough in us for that because you've never looked at me the way you looked at her. I can't describe it, but it made me feel like I was intruding on something between the two of you."

"Do you really want to do this now?" asked Marti. "You're on holiday; you should be enjoying your family right now. We can talk about this when you get back, can't we? I really don't want you spoiling your Christmas thinking about such things."

Reluctantly, Sasha agreed. "Yeah, okay, when I get back, but I'm not letting this go."

"I know, I know. Just go eat some turkey and dressing or something. Enjoy your people. You don't know how long you'll have them around. Besides, I'm headed to mama's. She says she's done it up over there, and I can't wait to dig in."

"Yeah, you're right. By the way, I'm coming back in time for New Year's Eve. I thought we'd ring in 2004 together."

"Yeah, cool," said Marti, his response lacking in enthusiasm. "That'll be great. We'll go to a party or something. Now, go be with your people, okay."

"Okay," said Sasha.

Marti placed the receiver in the holder. Between Leslie and Sasha, he was emotionally spent. However, it wasn't anything that some of Linda Johnson's homemade peach cobbler couldn't cure.

Chapter 27

With the phone cradled between his shoulder and ear as he grabbed bottled water from the fridge, Marti formed his mouth to do the inevitable—end things with Sasha. "Sasha, this isn't gonna work," he said frankly into the receiver. "We've had the same argument four or five times over the past month since my graduation. We even talked about this after you came back from Christmas with your parents. Heck, it's what ruined our New Year's Eve."

"Well, you know why that went down," countered Sasha. "Things got heated the minute she showed up at that party."

"This isn't about Leslie. It's about you not trusting me. Like I told you that night, I haven't done anything…with anybody. And I've been in enough drama-filled relationships to know that they are not for me, so let's just squash it now."

Marti twisted the top off his water and took a sip before heading to the living room and crashing on his leather couch, propping his bare feet up on the coffee table, exposing his well-manicured toenails to the world.

"I just think there's something you're not telling me, Marti. Why can't you just be honest with me? Your whole demeanor changed the second you saw her at that party. You lit up like a Christmas tree. Was I even there anymore after she showed up?"

"Don't be ridiculous. I you told that there's nothing going on between me and Leslie—nothing. I promise you."

"Do you want to be with me?"

"Ye-yeah, of course I do."

"Then tell me the truth."

"This again? That's it, Sasha. I don't want to do this."

"Then don't, okay."

"I guess that's it then," said Marti.

"Yeah."

"Bye, Sasha."

Refusing to return the sentiment, Sasha hung up, leaving the dial tone buzzing in his ear. Marti hung up the cordless, grabbed his car keys, and headed out the door. He drove around the city for awhile before ending up at Leslie's townhouse. It was uncharacteristic of Marti to show up at Leslie's unannounced, but he had to see her.

Leslie opened her front door surprised to see Marti.

"Can I come in?"

"Yeah, but what are you doing here?" she asked.

"I just had to see you."

"Okay, but what are you doing here?" repeated Leslie.

"Me and Sasha just broke up," said Marti, closing the door behind him.

"So you rushed over here to dump all of this in my lap?"

"No, I went driving around first."

"That's not the point," said Leslie.

"Then, yes, that's why I came over. Does that answer your question?"

"Is that all I am to you?" she questioned.

Of course, that wasn't all she was to him. Hadn't she figured that out by now? He'd all, but written it across his forehead that he was in love with her, but now it was Marti's time to seize the moment and make his declaration aloud, in the open—this time without interruption. No confessions from Leslie or phone calls from Sasha would stop him.

Just say it, he kept telling himself. *Just tell her...right here...right now.* Unable to find the right words, Marti leaned in, while the two of them stood in her hallway, and kissed her... long...passionate...hot...sweet...felt right...felt good...he didn't want to stop. Reciprocating as though she wanted this to happen as

277

much as he did, Leslie embraced him tighter before abruptly pulling away.

"I'm sorry, I shouldn't have done that."

Leslie shook her head. "Where did that come from? You just broke up with Sasha."

"I know, you're right. I better go."

"Yeah, maybe you should. You're trippin' right now."

"Yeah, okay. Later," said Marti, wasting little time to exit the scene as if a crime had been committed.

He scurried to his car, jumped in, and sped off. He hadn't zipped out of her place like a mad man because he felt bad about the kiss. That kiss was great. Without a hesitation, he would kiss Leslie again if given the chance. No, what bothered him was the fact that he and Leslie were in different places in their lives. She was going to church and studying the Bible, things he had never considered much of his life. He was still looking for logic to show him the right thing to do— truth is, he already knew what that was. He needed to get some perspective. He had to make some changes, knowing full well that he wasn't going to resolve anything by sitting around thinking about it.

***

Their relationship had been over nearly five weeks, but the collection of golf ticket stubs he held in his hand as he sat on the plane headed back home from California reminded him of the eleven months that they had dated. He hated the way he and Sasha had broken up, but reasoned that eventually it would have happened anyway. Still, Marti was not content with the way his life had unraveled. There were too many unresolved issues.

Although he'd only spent three days away, Marti stood in his living room glad to be back home among his things. On impulse, he reached for the phone to give Leslie a call, but remembered—with some regret—that they weren't exactly on speaking terms, not since the kiss. "You're not ready for her yet," he mumbled. "Got to get your stuff together first." Toting only a garment bag and his shaving kit, Marti ascended the staircase to his bedroom, flipping on the light switch before tossing the baggage in the closet. Marti kicked off his shoes, grabbed a set of bath towels from the rack at the top of his closet, and headed for the bathroom. The image reflected from the mirror showed signs of a man who had been on a plane for four hours, a man whose face now bore a five o'clock shadow. *First, a shave then a long hot shower*, in that order he thought.

Until Marti had removed the last trace of stubble from his chin, the occasional faucet drip played second to the syncopated clicks of the Remington. Already he felt better. He was beginning to look like himself again—clean cut, polished. The shower, however, would prove most therapeutic. Fifteen minutes later, Marti was a new man. He toweled off, threw on a pair of silk pajama bottoms, gave his pearly whites a good cleaning and swig of mouthwash, then headed for his bed, which looked awfully inviting. Tired and restless, but not quite ready to call it a night, even though he had work in the morning, Marti clicked on the television hoping he'd find something interesting to watch at one o'clock in the morning.

The blare of the television and flashing images coming from it had become Marti's bedtime companion ever since he and Sasha split. The place seemed so empty at night now that the left side of the bed remained unoccupied by the warm body of a woman. Some nights as Sasha quietly slept he'd watch the rise of her breast; the steadiness of her breathing; how a wayward strand of hair graced the side of her face; how the sheet draped over the contour of her hip, taking on its form. Marti longed to have that again. It's what he missed most about being in a relationship. But he wanted something more than just being in a relationship, he wanted the security that came with being married. Although he and Carolyn didn't work, he still believed that marriage afforded him something—a type of security—that he'd never get as a bachelor. He needed Leslie in his life. He was no good without her.

Just when he thought he had run out of channels to search, Marti came across a pre-recorded segment about Mel Gibson's latest film, *The Passion of the Christ*. Private showings of the film had already evoked criticisms from the Jewish community. Given his recent wonderings about God, Marti was compelled to go check out what was all the controversy when the film premiered in two weeks on

February 26th. By one-thirty, he had dozed off to the lulls of a Bowflex infomercial.

***

For the next two weeks, Marti's routine was much the same: he avoided Leslie at work as much as possible, went to the gym afterward—at least three times a week, came home to an empty townhouse, flipped on the television, and randomly viewed stations until he found something worth watching. On Mondays, that was *Fear Factor*. Marti still couldn't understand why anybody would even attempt to eat worms the size of Twinkies or immerse themselves in a vat of foul-smelling fish guts only to walk away empty handed, which made it no less intriguing to watch every week. Thursdays, however, he had his music gig, and the weekends, he reserved for visiting family. And then, of course, there was today.

Marti had circled the cinema parking lot for about five minutes until forced to park in a remote lot and make the hike just like everybody else who thought that arriving an hour before the movie started would be enough time to get a good seat. Men, women, children, black, white were packing in by the droves and their chatter all buzzed of the movie. Some had already seen it the day before when it premiered and were back to see it again. The four ticket lines that were opened were forming so long that people were beginning to wrap around the building. And there was a kind of excitement and anticipation that filled the air.

While standing in line, Marti thought back a few years to the time when America was consumed with the "What Would Jesus Do?" buzz. Today was nothing like that. Today was not at all about what Jesus would do, it was about what Jesus had done. When he'd finally gotten his ticket and walked inside the theater, Marti was met by a throng of folks at the concession.

"Excuse me, you dropped your ticket," said Marti, reaching down to collect it from the ground then handing it to the woman who nearly lost her footing in the mob of pre-teens. "Church group?"

Slightly irritated, she responded, "Yes, I'm the designated chaperone." She took the ticket from him. "Thanks."

"Looks like you've got your hands full."

"Yes, they *are* a bit rambunctious."

"We were once like that, too," said, Marti, sympathizing.

The woman smiled. "I hope not."

"Well, enjoy the movie."

"Same to you."

Marti walked into a packed screening room finding only floor seats available. He hated sitting that low, but reminded himself that it was not about that either. The showing of the film was immediate, not introduced by previews of coming attractions. At first, Marti found himself invested only in the award-winning camera work, yet clearly if the somberness of the opening scene was any indication of gravity of entire the film, Marti was certainly in for an anticipated ride.

Scene by scene the vivid cinematography began to invoke in him empathy, yet it was not until he was confronted with the brutal and horrific account of the crucifixion that he was convicted. When the movie was over, he walked out speechless. Again, he saw the woman he'd helped earlier. Her obnoxious bunch had settled into understated melancholy; some of them were fighting back tears. "What did you think?"

"I think I'm going to be unable to sleep tonight," acknowledged Marti. "That was—"

"Life-altering," she interrupted.

"Yeah, exactly…exactly."

"Well, I must get my crew to their homes. You have a good night and God Bless."

"Same to you."

With the effects of the movie still lingering with him the next day, Marti opened his nightstand drawer and retrieved the Bible that was given to him the very first Bible study he attended with Douglas. The Concordance directed him to the passage of scripture of choice, and as he began to read the account of the Crucifixion as told by Matthew, the images from the movie were made even more vivid. Marti shuttered at the very thought that Christ had taken and suffered such undeserved punishment and brutality, where he was beaten so sadistically the flesh was ripped from his bones. Marti shut his eyes, yet behind closed lids he saw the flesh-piercing thorns as barbs in Christ's head. He opened and closed his eyes again, but heard the striking blows of spikes being driven first through Christ's hands then His feet.

As he read on, he began to ponder the question as to why anybody would sacrifice himself for people who ridiculed and cursed him, for people who would rather allow a convicted murderer go free than a man who was without crime. Yes, he pondered, yet logic and reason could not answer him this. What he did reason is that here was a man whose love for humanity transcended all other love, and that was huge.

As he began reading the next of the Four Gospels for its account, it became quite clear why he was so affected by all of this. Seeing that movie only confirmed what he was beginning to feel in his heart. This course had been set the moment he truly began to question and inquire about God. For the first time in his life, he had clarity about what it meant to be a "believer" because something inside knew that this was real. He realized that there was not a more urgent time than now that he change his spiritual course because he had been given

God's love, and since he was now accountable for that love, he should give something in return by choosing salvation.

Chapter 28

Marti had convinced himself that he would not set foot in any church again, yet today he found himself wanting to be in no other place. The first time he had ever stood in Douglas' church, it was nearly empty. Today the pews in the church were nearly filled. There was an organist hammering keys on the organ; a pianist accompanying on the baby grand; drummer foot-thumping the snare; choir belting melodic gospel from the choir stand; ministers sitting in the pulpit along with the senior pastor who was sitting behind the glass podium. Praise and Worship service was beginning. Marti had once before witnessed something like this when he went to church with Carolyn. For him, however, it was like experiencing it for the first time because he was now participating and understood why it was necessary for people to show so many emotions when they attended church. He found himself having the urge to lift his hands and join in with the congregation as it sang "I Surrender All."

I surrender all

Oh, I surrender all

All to Jesus, Precious Savior

I surrender all

Repeatedly, they sang:

I surrender all

Oh, I surrender all

All to Jesus, Precious Savior

I surrender all

Douglas, he learned, had seen the movie twice and was excited that it had such an effect on Marti. He added that the film was not only winning souls for Christ, but it was also reminding people that what Christ had done was nothing short of selfless because He had given His life in spite of men, to redeem mankind.

"Not just that, it was everything, man, everything," Marti also offered about what changed his heart.

"I know. I knew when you started asking questions months ago that God was dealing with you then. It was just a matter of time before you found your way, man. I wasn't worried. The Word says, 'Seek and ye shall find.' And you did just that."

"Now I just have to confess it with my mouth because I believe it in my heart," said Marti to his friend.

"That's right."

When the pastor made the petition out to the congregation for those to stand who were now ready to accept Christ into their lives as their personal Savior, Marti stood to his feet. He was one of a few others who stood.

"All who are standing, please come to the altar," said the pastor. Marti made his way up there. There were five of them standing side by side across the altar.

"Salvation is a matter of choice," the pastor added. "We are all God's children, but we must choose to accept God as our Father, as our Comforter, as our Spiritual Guide because He is all of these things to us…"

At his father's funeral, the minister, while giving the eulogy, had made similar remarks about George Johnson—that he was a son, a brother, a husband, a father, a friend. The one thing the minister never said about Marti's father was that he was a Christian man. If he had said it, it would not have been true. This was a reality about his father that Marti would have to live with, yet this was no longer true about his own life now that he had stood before God and man and professed his sins and accepted Christ.

***

What now? That was the new question Marti pondered while stopped at a traffic light, heading to work. He had accepted Christ into his life, but what did that mean exactly? How would his life change? Who would he become now as a Christian? What would happen if he stumbled along he way? Then he thought about Leslie, who would, rather than spend her time during break shooting the breeze, now quietly read and mediate on scripture. It then occurred to him that much of what he now questioned, he'd find the answers to in the passages of text that he kept tucked away in the nightstand beside his bed.

As he proceeded on to work, the thoughts continued to unravel in his head. Then something he recently heard pastor say in sermon came to mind: God convicted those who began to falter. Yes, it would be this conviction that he would use to serve as his guide, he would count on this. If nothing else, Marti knew that he could seek spiritual counsel from Douglas. He knew that this was the real reason that Douglas was in his life—God had designed it that way. It all began to make sense to him now. Everything that had happened was supposed to happen. Despite his resistance, his course was set all along. As Douglas once told him, God was always in the midst, yet sometimes people are so busy looking the other direction that they don't see Him.

Marti went straight to his classroom after signing in, bothering not to check his box and get his morning coffee. Even still, he would be expecting Leslie to pop her head into his classroom just to see if he was in, and sure enough she did just that.

"Knock, knock," she said, smiling before approaching his desk.

Marti tore himself away from reviewing his lesson plans. "Hey."

"You do realize we have to talk about what went down in my place a few weeks ago," said Leslie, leaning [propped] against the front of Marti's desk with raised brow and folded arms.

"I'm surprised you let me go this long without talking about it," he said to her.

"Truth is, I wasn't ready to go there with you. I told myself that you were just trippin' because you had just broken up with Sasha."

"Listen, Les, we should hook up this weekend because we really need to talk about what happened.

"Sounds good," she said, heading for the door then disappearing into the hallway seconds before the bell rang and Marti's students began to file in, no doubt anxious to take their end-of-the-chapter Geography test.

After taking attendance and beginning to administer the test, the unexpected happened. One of his students asked him if he liked Ms. Mitchell.

Marti immediately stopped what he was doing to address this. "Excuse me?" Suddenly, the room grew quiet. The attention of the other students was diverted from test-taking preparation to gathering innuendos about their teacher's love life.

"You know, are you trying to get with her?" asked the young man confidently.

"First of all, that is none of your business. Second, why would you ask this?"

The inquisitive student then stated his reason. "I saw you two heading home in the same car one time and y'all looked mighty friendly to me." The silence was broken by the collective "Ooooos."

"Ms. Mitchell is my co-worker and friend. And we'll leave it at that. If you spent as much time getting your lesson as you do worrying about my personal life, then we'd have skipped you to the next grade by now."

The kids began to laugh and tease their classmate. "Aw-huh, Rico, you got clowned," one of them blurted. Marti only shook his head and proceeded to pass out the remainder of the tests. Kids.

Chapter 29

Marti stood over the grass-covered burial plot, peering down at the cement tombstone. From the fresh boutique placed in front of the headstone, he knew that his mother had visited recently. In twenty-one years, however, this was only the second time he'd been here. The first was the funeral. While his mother tried to get him to visit his father's grave whenever she would, Marti always refused, always remembering the heaviness of that first visit. Somehow the hard lines of the headstone managed to transport him back there...to that gloomy day and what he would still recall as one of the longest car rides he had ever taken.

"Fix your tie, son," his mother instructed from the front seat of the black family car that was second behind the hearse in a long procession of cars headed to the burial site. Sitting on the backseat were Donald, who was still sore that he wouldn't be getting the brand new BMX bike that his father had promised him for his birthday, and Marti, whose fixation with the world on the other side of the tinted glass caused him to miss his mother's command.

"Marti, I said straighten your tie, we're almost there. I want you boys to look nice, no slouching and carrying on. All eyes will be on us."

"Yes, ma'am."

An inquisitive ten-year-old Donald, soon to be eleven, then asked, "Mama, where's daddy right now? Is he is heaven or hell?"

"Man, shut up. Don't be asking stuff like that," Marti replied, nudging his younger brother in the side.

"Alright, boys, that's enough. And Donald, I don't know where your daddy's soul is right now, but his body is in that coffin that we're about to stick in the ground."

"Will I ever see him again, mama, because on TV sometimes dead people come back and visit?"

"No, son, I don't believe so."

Marti grew even more irritated by his brother's rant and gave Donald the stern "evil" eye that warned him not to say another word or suffer the consequence later on when they were back in their room and not under the watchful eye of their mother. It was enough to hush Donald.

The past unleashed its hold on Marti and his present-day surroundings were again in focus. With his purpose returned to the forefront of his thoughts, Marti would confront his father to relinquish himself of a haunting past that recently sprung on him ghostly visits, which left him not only quasi-phobic of mirror-glaring, but also in want of explanation.

Having taken a deep breath, he preceded the exhale with a series of questions, all to which he realized he would get no answers. That was of little importance to Marti. He knew that his presence there at the site was giving him the closure he so desperately needed.

"I know I'm supposed to forgive you. I know that, it's the right thing to do. Still, I have to get some stuff off my chest first…stuff I've been asking myself for the past twenty years. Why'd you do it, man? I-I-I don't understand it. What would make you do it? It was a cop out and you know it. Don't you realize the mess you caused the family? Putting a bullet in your head didn't solve a thing for nobody—just made more problems.

"Until recently, mama and I weren't even speaking, and Donald, man, Donald's got twenty years in the pen. What was I supposed to tell folks when they asked about you: *Oh yeah, by the way, my daddy killed himself?* Most people idolize their old man. I've spent my life trying to be nothing like you, man. We placed you in ground, put dirt on top of you, and that was supposed to be it. You weren't supposed to keep popping in my head, in my marriage, in my life. You weren't supposed to keep telling me how to think, what to think. You gave up that right when you checked out on us. I didn't need you anymore, and you certainly didn't deserve to zip in and out of my world whenever you got the urge. I may have screwed things up with Carolyn because I couldn't see past all the experiences I had as the kid whose daddy killed himself, but you can hang it up if you think I'm gonna do that to Leslie. I love her too much. I need her too much. And one of these days I'm gonna man up and just tell her how I feel and stop putting it off like I did with you. What has it been—twenty-one years? That's a long time, man. That's how many years you missed. If only we could turn back the clock.

"Maybe I should have been more thoughtful and understanding of what you must have been going through. I guess I did what all kids do at that age and looked at you as superman, invincible and incapable of failure, but you made mistakes, lots of times, and the more you did, the less I saw you as a superhero. Maybe you knew this...felt it...saw it in my eyes...heard it in my voice, but all I could think about is how you let us down. I just don't understand how you could leave mama like that," he said, just then remembering what brought his parents together in the first place.

There was always a different, embellished version of how the two of his parents met. According to his father, they were high school sweethearts, but Marti's mom would always set the record straight that she hardly even knew George those first couple of years at Baker High School. When the truth finally came out, Marti learned that his father had been checking out his mom since tenth grade, but didn't muster the courage to approach her till his senior year and even then it took lots of coaxing to win her over because she was concentrated solely on her academics. Right after high school, they married and were expecting with Marti six months later.

Marti could certainly understand why his father had such a major crush on his mother Linda. She was a beautiful woman. She had long, jet black hair, a trait she'd inherited from her own mother who was part Cherokee, olive skin, and the most piercing brown eyes.

"After all that chasin', man, it seems like such a waste now. When I finally get Leslie, I'm never gonna let her go, and I'm certainly not gonna skip out on her like you did mama. You know she used to try to get me to come out here to see you? I never could understand why she even bothered. You left us, remember? But I ain't nearly as mad at you as I used to be. I hated you then. I don't anymore. I keep remembering back to those times when we used to play together. Maybe I am coming around. Maybe God is changing me—after all, I'm here, took me twenty-one years, but I'm here."

March winds tossed the last of winter's leaves about as Marti treaded toward his car. He had done what he had come to do. He had made an effort. Perhaps now he could move on and his dad's ghost would no longer haunt him or tease him like a thing of the past not quite ready to let go. Marti slipped comfortably behind the steering wheel, placing both hands on either side. "Where am I going now? I've got to talk to somebody." Only one person came to Marti's mind—Douglas. And he knew where he'd find his buddy, the same place he could always find him.

A half hour later, Marti was parked outside his fitness center, and just as he had suspected, his friend's car was in the lot. Having spotted Douglas doing a set of curls when he walked inside, Marti gave the "what's up, man?" nod and headed toward him.

"Hey, bra, I didn't think I'd see you again till tomorrow at church. You haven't been showing your face around here lately," said Douglas, placing the dumbbell on the floor before extending his power glove-covered hand.

"Yeah, man, I've been taking care of business." Marti took a seat on a workbench.

"Oh yeah?"

"I went and visited the gravesite this morning and said my piece."

"Did it do you any good?"

"Yeah, Douglas, man, it's kinda funny, but it did. I finally got a chance to tell him how I felt, how jive he was for bailing out on us like that. I still don't understand why he did it. You ever get that way, man?"

"Listen, my friend, I ain't gonna lie. Remember when I told you about my accident? Well, the doctors gave me a fifty percent chance of never walking again. And yeah, man, I wanted to die. What was I gonna do without my legs? But I thank God today that I didn't give in. I mean it took me six months of physiotherapy and occupational therapy to take my first couple of steps, but it happened. Now look at me."

"Now that's what I'm talking about—things always get better. They may look bleak at first, but you can't stay down forever."

"No, you can't," agreed Douglas.

"But you know what really bothers me?"

"What's that?"

"He missed out on so much," said Marti, pausing for a minute. "He took his own life, man. There's no honor in that. It's just wrong."

"I feel ya, bra. And what's worse is that when you commit suicide, man, that's it. There are no second chances."

"And in this world, we need all the chances we can get. We make too many mistakes before we finally get it right," Marti surmised.

"True that, true that. I've made my share of them."

"Yeah, and I'm still trying to fix mine."

"And you will, man, it takes time," replied Douglas while flexing in the wall of mirrors.

"Speaking of time, man, when is the next time you compete?"

"May 1ˢᵗ at the Canton Open Bodybuilding Championships in Ohio."

"You ready?"

"As ready as I'll ever be. I still have a solid month of training, but I feel good about my prospects."

"Yeah, Doug, you're looking good. I'm trying to be like you."

"Then I guess you better get off that bench and go grab one of them dumbbells over there."

"Forget you, man," Marti said, dismissing his friends. "I couldn't anyway. I've gotta get out of here. I'm meeting up with Leslie in a couple of hours. We gotta have that talk."

"Talk? What talk?"

"The one where I finally tell her how I feel about her."

Douglas put the dumbbell that he was curling down. "Whoa, that talk. Man, that's big. I know you've been feeling her for awhile."

"I know, right. Well, wish me luck."

"You won't need it," said Douglas. "I know you'll take care of business."

Marti started for the entrance of the gym. "Alright, man, I'm outta here."

Tonya Snow-Cook

Chapter 30

In less than an hour, Marti would be meeting Leslie for dinner to have the "us" talk. And the pile of clothing on his bed continued to grow as he tried to decide the best outfit (and women thought they were the only ones who did this). If he wore something dressy, that might make her nervous. Something dressy might signal aggression. That was no good. On the other hand, wearing something too casual might be interpreted as indifferent or fickle. That kiss certainly complicated things. He never had to worry with any of this before, at least not for these reasons.

When Leslie walked into J. Alexander's, Marti had just been seated at a booth. Throwing up his hand, he beckoned her and she approached.

"Nice jacket," she said, sliding into the booth.

"Well, you look absolutely gorgeous as always. You did something different with your hair?"

"Kinda, I decided to moose it back. You know, give it a different edge. Do you like it?"

"Oh yeah, I think you should keep it like that."

"I may," she said, glancing over the menu. Marti began to glance over his as well. The waiter approached about a minute later.

"Hello, my name is David, and I'm going to be your waiter today. Here are some complimentary bread and butter. Now what can I get you two to drink?"

"I'll have tea," answered Leslie.

"And you, sir?"

"The same." Marti returned.

"That's two teas," confirmed the waiter. "Do you still need a few minutes to decide on what you are having this afternoon?"

Marti nodded. "Sure, man, give us another minute or so."

"Very well, I'll be right back with your teas."

"So what are you having?" Leslie asked Marti. "Everything looks so good. I better not get too crazy. I'm just now recovering from last Thanksgiving."

"Woman, please. You are one of the finest women I know. Splurge a little because the food is all that. I'm telling you, this place has the best prime rib of beef and baby back ribs."

"Splurge a little, huh? Is that what you were doing that day, splurging?"

He couldn't hide his embarrassment, so he released a boyish laugh. "You mean the kiss, right?"

"Yes."

"No, that's not what I was doing. I wasn't just testing out my options. I'm in love with you," he said with a seriousness in his eyes that Leslie had never quite seen in them before. "Do you hear me? I'm in love with you, and I have been for awhile."

"Then why didn't you—" The waiter returning with their teas forced their conversation on hold.

"So are we ready to order, folks?"

"I believe so," answered Marti, glancing over at Leslie to see if she needed more time. Apparently, she had decided.

"So what can I get you, ma'am?"

"I'll have the lime chicken, a toss salad with extra ranch dressing, and I believe that's it."

"And for you, sir?"

"Let's see. Let me get the filet mignon, well-done, with the loaded baked potato, and let me get the toss salad as well, ranch dressing."

"Thank you. I'll get those orders out to you as soon as possible," he said, retrieving their menus then leaving.

"Why didn't you tell me how you felt?"

"C'mon, Leslie, you never sent out any signals other than the one that said that we'd be friends for the rest of our lives. You know I can't take rejection, especially not from you."

"You know when I saw Sasha there at your graduation and realized that she was there for you, I felt jealous, I think. The truth is, I didn't like it. You could have told me about her, you know. You always told me before."

"That's before I realized how much I cared about you. And no, I didn't use Sasha to try to get over you."

"I'm sure she didn't see it that way," Leslie presumed.

"She didn't. She felt used, and I'm sorry she felt that way because that's not what I was trying to do all."

"Doesn't matter, Marti. I can only imagine that what's replaying over in her mind is the fact that you couldn't commit completely to her because you were in love with someone else—me."

"I really did care about her," returned Marti.

"I'm sure you did, but that doesn't lessen the hurt any."

"Yeah, I know. I should have just been upfront with you about the way I felt and never dragged Sasha into it. And listen, while I'm trying to start a clean slate here, I want apologize about New Year's Eve. I didn't expect to see you at that party. I really didn't. I didn't even know you knew about it."

"I wasn't even gonna go," said Leslie. "A girlfriend of mine told me about it and convinced me to go. Imagine my surprise when I walked in and saw you and Sasha. And Sasha didn't at all look happy to see me."

"She wasn't," Marti replied. "She suspected something was up."

"So how long have you felt this way?"

"Since December 2002."

Leslie's mouth dropped. "What!" she exclaimed.

"Yep, remember when you got sick and I came over and took care of you?" said Marti.

"I wondered why you kept stopping by. It was just a really bad cold."

Marti took a sip of his tea. "Didn't matter. I would have thought of any excuse to see you."

"So what now?" she asked.

"Well, how do you feel about me?"

Leslie started smiling. "Remember last summer, yes, that dreadful summer that we hardly spent anytime together?"

Marti nodded. "Yeah, the summer you got saved."

"Well," said Leslie, "most of the time, I thought about you. I was so ready for school to start again. God has a way of showing us things even when we think we aren't ready to see them, and he kept showing me you."

Their waiter finally returned with their food. "Is there anything else I can get you, more tea perhaps?"

"We're fine, thank you."

"Well, enjoy your meals."

The two of them began to sample their entrees. Leslie seemed a bit dissatisfied that her chicken was still much too hot to enjoy. She was hungry. "I want to be with you, Leslie, that's the bottom line," Marti asserted. "I know that you are a Christian now, and that was another reason I couldn't tell you. You didn't deserve a man who wasn't. It was that conversation we had that I just couldn't forget. Remember, you said that you couldn't afford not to believe?"

"Yeah, I remember."

"Well, you forced me to ask myself that same question. Believe me, I tried to forget that conversation. I tried, I really did, but I couldn't forget. And after that night when I ran out of your place, I was really forced to confront my own spirituality."

"You mean, after we—"

"Yeah."

"I'm glad," she said.

"You're glad?"

"Yeah, glad that you kissed me," she said, cutting off a cube of chicken with her knife. "I'd had thoughts about it, what it would be like. At the same time, I immersed myself in the church, so I wouldn't lose focus. Getting myself right with God had to come first. It just had to. None of this would work [between me and you] if I kept running from God, and believe me, I was tired of running, tired of feeling empty, but I'm glad it happened. I love the way you touch me."

"Me, too."

Before sampling her entrée, she asked, "So what's with that intense look then?"

"Just thinking," he said.

"About the kiss?"

"Yeah," replied Marti, "that and about how I now understand why you made that decision."

"Decision, what decision?" she asked.

"You know, to focus on God. Something in you changes, it just changes. It makes you want to do better, be better. That's all we can do, and I knew I couldn't come at you until I was a better man and that meant confronting my own demons. You know how hard that is? No man wants to confront himself or get in touch with his feelings. It's too subjective. We always have to be strong and in charge; there's no room for emotions, not the kind that women experience. But I know differently now. I realize that that's the only way to become a better man. You have to be willing to look at yourself and admit that you need things or that you don't have all the answers or that you can't fix everything with an equation or logic or reason. I suppose," Marti surmised, "that that's what really turned me to God. I finally realized that there had to be somebody out there who did know all the answers, and I'd rather have Him on my side then anybody else in this world."

The waiter approached again. "Is everything okay? Oh, you're running low on tea, sir. Let me get you some more." He quickly returned with a filled glass. "Just let me know if you need anything else."

As soon as the waiter disappeared, Leslie leaned forward and beckoned Marti to do the same then she planted a nice, long, soft kiss on his lips.

"What was that for?" said Marti with a smile.

"I've been wanting to do that for weeks now...ever since the first time. And I know I gave you grief about it, but that kiss stirred up something in me."

"Did it?" said Marti.

"Yeah, something I think I have been longing since..." Leslie's words faltered as it became clear to Marti that she was thinking about something.

"What is it, Les? Finish your thought," he urged.

"Remember when I cut my hair way back when?" she said.

Marti nodded.

"I want to tell you about that—you know...why I did it."

Leslie went on to explain to Marti that she cut her hair because she had just gotten out of a four-year relationship and needed a change and that's why she was in no rush to start something new with anyone, but Marti broke through and opened her heart to the possibility and that's when she had to admit to herself that she was falling for him. She admitted to being scared and not wanting to be vulnerable to someone else. She needed to be in control and was quick to throw up her wall when she felt that she might be losing that control. She had to protect herself, had to protect her heart because the last guy, her fiancé, had broken it. He called off their engagement. She later learned why. He had met another woman, an older woman, someone he'd been chatting with over the internet. Leslie admitted to being clueless about any of it. She trusted him. She wanted to be with this man so much she had agreed to marry him when he proposed to her on Christmas day in front of her family then popped open the ring box with the one and a half carat diamond solitaire. She was speechless, couldn't believe he was doing this, right then, right there, in front of everybody. Then her thoughts started rushing, but her answer was "yes." She was convinced that he was the man that she wanted to spend the rest of her life with.

"Things don't always turn out the way we think they should," added Leslie. "I would have sworn at that moment when Keith proposed to me that that was it, that was going to be the start of my new life. I loved him, first time I'd ever loved someone like that. It's hard to get over something like that, you know?"

Marti reached across the table to grab Leslie's hand. "Hey, hey, he was stupid. Why he would let you go is beyond my comprehension. All I know is that I'm not letting you go. You hear me—I'm not letting you go."

"I hope not."

"Naw, you're it for me." Marti paused a few seconds. "You're all I ever wanted."

"I've got something important to ask you, though," said Leslie. "What are you expecting to happen between us?"

"I'm just trying to do the right thing by you, but not just that, you know. I'm trying to do the right thing by God, and I don't think we should build this relationship on sex. Not that I don't want to be with you in that way because I do think about it. I just think that for this to work between us we have to put things in perspective."

"Yeah, I agree, our commitment to God comes first," said Leslie, nodding her head.

"That's the way it should be."

Leslie nodded again. "Yeah—but that doesn't mean this is going to be easy. I'm attracted to you, you're attracted to me. We're bound to want to go there."

"Like I said, I do think about it, being with you."

"Me, too," she admitted. "We just have to...have to take this slow and not flirt with danger."

Marti agreed then beckoned the waiter for the check. "Hey, let's get out of here. I want to take you somewhere."

"Where and what about my car, I met you here, remember?"

"You can trail me. Now, grab your purse and let's get out of here. You're going to love this place."

Marti and Leslie pulled into the parking lot at the levee. There was a huge out-of-commission Navy ship at dock, maybe docked there as a tourist attraction. A light breeze bounced off the Mississippi as the barges passed by. Ever now and then headlights of the cars crossing over the bridge could be seen, but a second bridge about twenty miles away was nearly engulfed in the night. Marti and Leslie were in good company with other couples who were hand-holding or snuggled up, walking about. The two of them sat on a bench and watched the barges and just talked and kissed and talked some more. They were an official couple now, and Marti loved every minute of it.

Chapter 31

S asha's call came as a surprise. She wanted to meet, to talk is all
she said. Talk. What was there left to say that they hadn't already
said the night they broke up? Granted, he was never in love with
Sasha, but he did care about her and tried to make a go of it despite
what he had felt for Leslie. Now, she wanted to see him...to talk.

This situation took him right back to college, just after he met
Carolyn, his ex-wife. Before her, he was in a two-year relationship
with Dana. Dana. Dana. Dana. She was a female version of him. They
were just too much alike, and neither was willing to change. They
were in constant debate about this and that, and oddly enough, he
found that so attractive about her. Finally, he had met a woman who
had an opinion. He liked that about her. By the same token, her
assertive personality often clashed with his aggressive nature, which
led to their many break ups over the course of their two-year drama,
but they'd wind up back together after the dust settled. Then, when he
met and started dating Carolyn, Dana, who he hadn't spoken to in
about a year, called. She wanted to give it another go, thought that
they could make it work. Said that she still loved him even after all

that time, but Marti had moved on. He knew it could never work with Dana. There was no use wasting anymore time trying. Besides, he was with Carolyn now. He liked Carolyn. She was sweet and didn't debate him about every little thing. Of course, it wasn't until later, after they'd married, that he realized that Carolyn wasn't compatible with him either, but that was beside the point. The point was that he just didn't want Dana anymore.

So maybe that was it. Maybe Sasha wanted to date again. He'd prepare himself for that conversation just in case. He was trying to sort things out with Leslie, and he wasn't about to screw that up, especially since he had admitted his feelings to her. How would that look, him trying to mess around with two women? He was a grown man, better than that. He had seen enough brothas trying to have their go at five or six women at a time, and the outcome was always the same. If ever there existed a handbook about the ten thousand reasons why a man shouldn't date more than one woman at a time, these brothas would be the first to get a copy.

Marti felt better about meeting Sasha after he talked to Leslie. He told her about the call and said that he had a pretty good feeling why she wanted to see him. Marti reassured Leslie that it was over, that he didn't want Sasha; he wanted to be with her. Leslie said very little their entire conversation, just listened mostly. She said she was glad that Marti told her about his plans to meet Sasha because he was more or less giving her an opportunity to object. He was making a conscious effort to establish complete trust in what was blossoming into a relationship between two friends, the best of friends. And Leslie needed that. She needed to know that taking their friendship to the next step was not a mistake.

Sasha was already seated at a table when Marti walked into the coffee shop. He approached her and took a seat. He didn't even bother to exchange pleasantries. Satisfying his curiosity came first. "Okay, Sasha, you got me here. What's this about?"

Marti listened as she began to explain her irrational behavior toward the end of their relationship. Sasha started by first admitting that she took a huge emotional gamble to be with him, having experienced a series of not-so-good relationships. She was cautious when they first met in class, careful not to send out any signals, that's why she wasn't very talkative. He was persistent, she said, laughing, persistent, but pleasant. So when he asked her out a month later, she decided that she'd confront the challenge of dating again. She'd lay to rest her fears about what he might do; she'd stop second-guessing her decisions, which she, while dating him, made more from her heart than from her head. He had a kindness about him that she found both refreshing and familiar, she said. Many of her ex-boyfriends had a similar kindness about them. Yet, as the relationship wore on and they grew used to her, the kindnesses would stop. He was never like that. In fact, she admitted that it was she who had sabotaged their relationship with her insecurities. She had made a mistake not trusting him, and she realized that after assessing everything. She said that she honestly believed that she let the perfect man for her slip away and that motivated her to give him a call.

Sasha took a sip of her espresso. "Remember the trip?"

"Yeah."

"God, I was so excited when you asked me to come with you to New Orleans. I thought it was all too good to be true. And all those times we spent together. Remember the time you stayed over and just slept on the couch? God, I was so upset about my pops. You knew I needed you there, so you stayed. Somewhere in all that, I fell in love with you, Marti. And I know I never told you before. I don't know…maybe I didn't want to put any pressure on our relationship, on you, but it's important that I tell you this now. I need you to know that I screwed things up, not you."

Marti felt guilty that Sasha had put more emotionally into their relationship than he had. He didn't want to admit it, but yes, he had used Sasha to get over his feelings for Leslie. He wasn't completely innocent in all this, and he couldn't let her think he had been, especially now that he knew about her past relationships. At least he wanted to walk away from her with her knowing everything and still feeling that she could trust men no matter how foolish they sometimes were, himself included.

"Sasha, I have to tell you something," he said with a bit of hesitance in his voice.

"What is it?"

"Before I-uh…before I met you, I was in love with someone, and—"

"Leslie," interrupted Sasha.

"Yeah, but it's like I told you before, we were just friends, and I never told her. Then I met you, and I looked forward to class because I knew you would be there—"

Again, she interjected. "Still, you were in love with her. I knew it…I knew it. I could tell."

"Believe me I tried to shake my feelings for her. I wanted things to work between you and me."

"No, you wanted me to rescue you; that's what you wanted. You couldn't have the woman of your dreams, so you used me."

"Sasha, that wasn't my intention. I never pretended when I was with you, and I meant everything I said to you, but I couldn't lie to you and tell you that I loved you when I was still feeling those things for Leslie."

"True, you never did say that you loved me. I think that's why all those insecurities started rising in me. Then when I saw the two of you together at your graduation, looking at each other like you were, I

319

just knew, so I kept pushing to make you admit something. I don't know, maybe I just wanted you to admit that you loved her. And then on New Year's Eve, seeing her at the party…well, deep down I knew I really couldn't compete. Still, this doesn't change what I feel for you. And I understand that you are in love with her. At least now you know that I am in love with you."

"You know you're really making this hard for me," said Marti.

"How? Listen, I don't regret anything, not the time we spent together, not the trip, none of it…She's a lucky woman."

"I'm sorry, Sasha. I wish—"

"No, you don't, and you shouldn't. You're with the woman that you love, and that's how it should be, so please don't apologize for that. I just hope that I find someone who'll someday feel the same for me what you feel for her." Sasha rose from the table and stood there a second before leaning over to give Marti one last kiss on the cheek. "Good-bye."

Marti followed her with his eyes until she disappeared out the entrance of the café. He knew that that was his last time seeing her. He then scanned the café. Everyone seemed engaged in conversation. Then there was him, sitting there alone. He realized he hadn't spent enough time with Leslie. He wanted to be with her. He wanted to see her face. Marti took out his cell phone.

"Hey, it's me. Can you meet me at…?"

He sat there for another twenty minutes before Leslie appeared in front of the coffee house. He watched as she entered the café then raised his hand. When her eyes met with his, she let slip from her face a huge smile that sent his heart racing. He knew he loved this woman. The closer she drew the faster his heart sprinted.

"Hey."

"Hey." Marti began to stare.

"You're staring," said Leslie.

"Yes, I am."

"Why?"

"Because even when we're not together, I want always to remember your face," he said.

Leslie laughed. "Now you're making me blush. Is this the face you want to remember, me flushed?"

"Yeah, I want to remember all your faces, all your expressions, everything about you."

It was true. If a man loved a woman, he'd use his mind like a camera and photograph her every characteristic. Marti had certainly spent a great deal of time mentally photographing Leslie.

Suddenly, it began to rain, a crazy kind of rain. It came down violently as if taking vengeance on the earth and all its inhabitants. And, naturally, there were those fighting to escape it, scurrying about,

321

but Leslie and Marti were safely inside, watching this unexpected downpour through the huge glass windows of the small café.

"Lucky for you, you didn't get caught in that," said Marti.

"Yeah, looks like I just missed it."

Marti and Leslie's talk of weather was soon lost in the chatter of fellow coffee drinkers. Several conversations were now brewing about what was happening outside.

"It's obvious we don't get this much," Leslie remarked, scanning the café. "Everybody's talking about the rain like it's the World Series or something."

"I know. So what do you think it means? It *is* coming down pretty hard out there."

Leslie sipped her cappuccino. "Maybe it's God's way of washing off some of the stench of this city. People have gotten so beside themselves. One of my kid's parents was arrested the other day for selling pornography. Can you believe that? And a couple of weeks ago there was the grocery store shooting, remember? More and more folks are turning away from God."

"Yeah, but you and I found Him. That's got to count for something, right?" offered Marti.

"Sometimes I wonder why it took me so long to stop running," she said.

"What do you mean?"

"I used to be like so many people. I ignored what was right to satisfy what I wanted. Sometimes I even think that's less forgivable, but I was running from something."

"What?"

Leslie looked Marti in the eyes. "The same thing you were running from, the kind of life I thought would inhibit me in someway. It's ironic because I'm more content now than I've ever been. Things just seem to keep falling into place, you know what I mean?"

Marti nodded. "Thank God for second chances."

"I think most of us go through life thinking we have it all figured out," she offered, "until one day we realize we don't. Then it hits us just how alone and miserable we really are. It's at this point—at least it was for me—that God becomes more a part of our consciousness and less an afterthought." Leslie paused to organize her thoughts before continuing. "I have no regrets about choosing salvation that's why I sometimes wonder why I ran for so long. I sometimes sit and watch people say and do crazy things because deep down they are unhappy with their lives. They've pretended for so long that they've convinced themselves that the torment they are in really isn't so bad. And it's funny how I could never see that before."

"Like I said, thank God for second chances."

Chapter 32

It was Saturday and Marti was on his way to see his brother Donald. The thirty-minute drive to the prison always seemed much longer with only an occasional farmhouse or duck pond as scenery. Sometimes he would take his eyes off the road long enough to glance at the grazing cattle. The drive against this pastoral backdrop, one not eclipsed by distracting skylines, glitz and glimmer, did, however, give Marti a chance to think, to reflect. It seemed he was doing that a lot lately.

Fifteen minutes into his trip, Marti's road trip was brought to a halt. There was a massive car wreck ahead, looked to be at least four cars involved. One car had completely flipped over in the median, and the driver of that car was being strapped to a gurney. Two other cars, with extensive damage to both the front and back ends, were blocking the two ongoing highway lanes, preventing anyone from proceeding. A forth vehicle, a minivan, was already being hooked to a tow truck; damage to it wasn't nearly as severe as it was to the other cars involved. The scene was crawling with flashing sirens and ambulances and people, some merely spectators. Marti wondered what might have been the cause, maybe a wild animal or recklessness or maybe someone fell asleep at the wheel. It was a wonder no other cars were involved. Then he saw, being pulled from one of the cars, a child, at least nine or ten years old. Was she still…? Marti couldn't bring himself to finish the thought. Though he'd always thought he was incapable of such feelings, his heart burned with sorrow as if she were his own daughter. It was then that he began to rethink his position on having kids. Perhaps he had been selfish before, using his father as an excuse. Perhaps he did have something to pass on to his own child, that piece of himself, which had come from his dad, that was good—music, his appreciation for melody and lyrics and passion for creating something from abstract notes and making it tangible, making it real, making it his own. Music could be his legacy.

An hour had passed before the wreckage was cleared enough to make the roads passable. As Marti drove past the scene of the accident, he thought about the little girl and hoped that she was okay. He even found himself saying a small prayer for her, nothing out loud. No, he simply thought the words. *Let her be okay*, he said in his mind. *Just let her be okay*. While all this was still very new to him, he felt better having interceded on the little girl's behalf.

It had never taken Marti that long to get to the prison, and he was exhausted. He wouldn't stay the full time allotted today. He'd see his brother, explain the delay, exchange some small talk, and leave, maybe go and see Leslie. Yes, he wanted to see her face.

326

Marti sat at the table only a few minutes before his brother, escorted by a prison guard, appeared. The guard removed Donald's manacles and he took a seat across from Marti. Marti hardly paid his brother any attention, still thinking about the accident and the girl.

"What's on your mind, man?" asked Donald.

"Nothing you would understand."

"There you go again with that *nothing talk*. What's on your mind, man?"

"There was an accident on my way to see you. It's kinda got me thinking about some things—that's all," said Marti.

"Thinking about what?"

"A little girl was hurt," Marti said sadly. "It's crazy, man, because I kept thinking that she could have been my—Like I said, man, it's crazy and you wouldn't understand."

"Why, you think I don't think about that kind of stuff sitting up in here? Sometimes I do wish I had a wife and some kids, but then I'm glad I don't. I don't want no son of mine seeing me like this. What kind of man would he grow up to be? The cycle would just keep going."

"Cycle?"

"Yeah, man," said Donald. "Face it, we had a lousy old man. He bailed on us. Now, I'm here and you—"

327

"I'm what?" interrupted Marti.

"You tell me," said Donald.

"I'm trying to get my act together—finally."

"And here I was thinking that you already had your stuff together."

Marti chuckled. "So did I."

"So how's mama?"

Marti smiled. "Mama's good, real good. She wants to see you."

"Oh yeah," replied Donald, who then stood up and walked over to the window. "Sure is a pretty day out. Man, I miss it out there."

"What about the world being too big a place for you?"

"Yeah, but prison is too small a place. I realize now that I'd rather be out there than in here."

"No arguments from me, bra," agreed Marti. "So what about getting out on good behavior?"

"Yeah, but I may not be eligible for that for another five or six years."

"Shoot, anything's better than serving the whole twenty."

"Yeah," said Donald, returning to his seat across from Marti. "So what's up with your lady friend?"

"Sasha? Oh, we broke up. I'm seeing Leslie now."

Donald grinned. "Finally, my man's got the woman he wanted. It's about time. I thought I was gonna have to pull some strings from the inside and send her a singing telegram on your behalf. Life's too short, man. You've gotta be with the people who make you happy. Do the things that make you happy. Live a life that makes you happy. Can't be settling for second choice. Can't be doing that."

"I hear ya."

"Hope so," replied Donald.

"Yeah, man. I think I'm gonna rent a movie or something and go over to her place after I leave here."

"Marti, man, I just can't believe you finally told her how you felt. I'm happy for you, man. I know how much you were digging her. I guess she must have been digging you, too. Hey, maybe you could bring her up here some time. I'd like to see the woman who stole my brother's heart."

"C'mon, man, don't go gettin' all sappy on me. But, yeah, I'll bring her up here one day. That's cool. Anyway, look, man, I'd better be getting out of here."

Marti and Donald both stood up then Marti walked over and gave his brother a hug. "Alright, man, later."

"Later," Donald returned. "And, hey, tell mama I asked about her."

"Will do," said Marti as he disappeared through the door.

On his way back to the city, Marti decided he wouldn't go straight over to Leslie's house. He drove to the gym instead, hoping he'd run into his buddy Douglas. He always kept his gym bag in his car. This afternoon he wanted to talk to Douglas more so than pump iron. As he'd hoped, there was his friend across the gym lifting weights.

Marti approached Douglas. "Man, am I glad that you're here," said Marti.

Douglas chuckled. "When am I not here? I feel like this place is my second home, but I love it."

"Listen, man, can I talk to you for a second?"

"Sure," said Douglas, putting down the free weight then taking a seat on a nearby workbench. "What's up?"

"You got a kid, right?"

"Actually, I've got two of them," said Douglas.

"How did you know you were ready to be a father?"

"Well, man, both of my kids came as a surprise, especially Doug Jr., my oldest. Man, I was scared to death when his mama told me she was pregnant. I didn't know the first thing about being a daddy, but when you see your kid for the first time, man, I don't know what it is, but something in you just makes you love them and want to give them everything you can. It's gonna be the same way with you."

"You think so?" asked Marti.

"I know so. You can't be no teacher and not want to be the best father you can be. Man, you have a gift of being able to relate to kids, so when you have your own, you're gonna be just as good at being able to relate to your own kids."

"I appreciate this, man. That's just what I needed to hear," Marti said, standing. He then reached out to give Douglas a friendly grip.

Douglas gripped his friend's hand. "Anytime. So you're out?"

"Yeah, got go see my lady."

"I hear that."

Marti left Gold's Gym headed over to see Leslie, grabbing a couple of DVDs on the way. Even though they were now dating and showing up unannounced could be expected and accepted, he called her up on his cell phone to let her know that he was coming. He had made the mistake only once of showing up on a whim and did not want to take anything for granted, at least not anymore. She wasn't doing much anyway for a Saturday, she told him over the phone, just lounging around after having done a little house cleaning earlier. In fact, she was still wearing an old pair of sweat pants and her Spelman College t-shirt. Marti could only imagine what her years at Spelman might have been. He knew that she attended school there, but she never really told him about her experiences. After over five years of friendship, there were still all these things about Leslie he didn't know. In some ways, that's what made their relationship even more exciting. It was like getting to know her all over again.

There was no question that he knew enough about who she was as a person to fall madly in love, but there were pieces of her life that were obscure to him. In fact, now that he thought about, he had shared with her more things about himself than she had ever divulged to him. It all made sense now…that day he came over after breaking up with Sasha when she made what he thought at the time to be a snide remark about her being only a sounding board for him. Perhaps it was only her sarcasm talking, but Marti figured there to be some truth in her comment.

Leslie met Marti with a kiss when she opened the door, wearing a pair of house slippers to finish off her college look. In his mind, it didn't matter what she wore. She could have had a rag over her head and had been wearing a shirt and pants that were riddles with holes, and he would still think she was beautiful and desirable. Sometimes a women's sex appeal was greater when it was understated—at least he had found that to be the case.

"Looking good, looking good," returned Marti, handing her the DVDs. "I got you *Something's Gotta Give*. I know how much you enjoyed seeing it at the theater."

"Sweet. Hey, I'm gonna grab a soda from out of the fridge. You want one?"

"Yeah," Marti replied before making a pit stop at the bathroom. Leslie had already put the DVD in the player and was watching the previews when he joined her on the sofa. With her body at an angle, Marti noticed the lettering on the back of her t-shirt.

"What's 'Short and Sweet?'" he asked while fingering the last few ironed-on letters.

"That was my line name."

"Let me guess—you pledged Delta?"

"Yeah, how'd you know?"

"You have the sorority attitude."

Leslie paused the DVD and faced him. "How do you mean?"

"Nothing bad. I just know that Deltas don't take no stuff off nobody."

"Sounds personal."

"It is. Dana, the first girl I dated in college, pledged Delta her sophomore year and her attitude changed. She was already an aggressive person, but after she crossed over and officially claimed those bold red and white colors, man, she was nothing to play around with. Finally, I had to cut her loose."

"You know that's a loaded bunch of crapola, don'tcha?"

"See what I mean—attitude?"

"No, I'm serious. Tell me you're not trying to lump all Deltas in that category simply because you dated *one* soror with an attitude?" contested Leslie, rolling her eyes.

"Really, I didn't mean anything by it," he said.

Leslie hit the Play button on the remote. "Just watch the movie, negro."

"Hold on. Pause that again for a second."

"What?"

"How come you never told me anything about what it was like at Spelman or pledging? How come I'm just now hearing this stuff? I thought I knew you."

"It never came up—that's all."

"I don't buy that for a second. It just doesn't make sense that I'd know you this long and not know something like this. Did something happen at Spelman that you wanted to forget?"

"No, Spelman was great. Besides, it was a long time ago…I'm not even active. I just wear these old things around the house." Leslie scratched the back of her head. "I don't know why I put my line name on the back of my Spelman shirt. I guess I was just excited about crossing."

"Whatever. I told you stuff about me, a whole bunch of stuff."

"Yeah, which meant there was little time left during break time at work to fill you in on my emotional sagas and college experiences."

"Was I that bad?"

"Listen, you had just gotten divorced and you needed someone to talk to. I understood that. Really, I was glad I could be there for you."

"What about you? You must have been hurting and needed consolation, too, since you had just broken off your engagement."

"Correction, he broke it off with me," Leslie asserted.

"That's what I meant. Anyway, I wish you would have told me more about what was going on with you then. You have to tell me things. I don't want this to be a one-sided relationship where you do all the listening and giving and I do all the talking and taking," said Marti.

"I will tell you things. Things are different between us now. I'm in love with you," she said to Marti, causing him to do a double take. It was the first time he'd ever heard her say the words so openly, without being prompted. And while it felt good hearing her say them, Marti made light of it because he didn't want to make her uncomfortable. After all, she was once again putting herself emotionally out there.

"Well, I hope you're in love with me because I'm good for you, and I treat you right. I don't want to be with a woman who's just sticking round because nobody else has made an offer," said Marti jokingly.

Leslie wasn't laughing. "First of all, you know me better than that. And secondly, I'm with you because I want to be with you. We have a great thing here."

"I'm just making sure because I'll get up and walk out, and you'll never see me again. Then you'll be crying and carrying on, sounding like Florida Evans from *Good Times* after James bit the dust."

"See, why are you dead set on messing with me right now?" said Leslie, giving him a school girl tug. Feeling playful, Marti grabbed one of the decorative sofa pillows and went for the prize-winning blow across the side of her head. That was it. The pillow fight commenced with Leslie running upstairs to her bedroom to get reinforcement—a king-sized pillow from off of her bed. Marti was little match for the huge downy-filled cushion aimed for the back of his head. She had set her target in sight and made good contact. Bull's-eye!

"Oh, that's it!" he exclaimed. "That was a lucky shot. Next time you ain't gonna be so lucky. You see these muscles here, I'm about to put these *thangs* on you and, man, do they sting." Marti wrestled Leslie to the floor and pinned her there. She could do nothing, but resort to using her feminine persuasion to distract him.

"Wouldn't you rather be making out than playing this silly little game?" she said, smiling.

He thought about that prospect for a second. Of course he did. He was no fool—miss out on an opportunity to mess around, never.

Marti loosened his hold on Leslie and began to plant warm kisses on her neck. She ran her hands under his shirt up his back, penetrating his skin with her nails. He slowly made his way to her soft cheek then her mouth, finding her lips hot and moist. Leslie crossed her legs over his lower back, locking the two of their bodies so close that they were nearly meshed into one. Marti then put his left arm tightly around her waist and, using his right arm to lift and balance him as he planted one foot at a time, carefully lifted their entangled bodies off the floor and moved them over to the sofa.

He hadn't felt this much passion for anyone in a long time, but they had vowed not to cross that line. They were not going to flirt around with sex, they told each other. What then was this that they were doing now? It was sexual suicide to start something as romantically intense as they had and just stop. Most people couldn't stop. Most people probably wouldn't stop, but Marti and Leslie were not most people. They were trying to live according to Christian principles now.

They had fooled around on the couch for not more than ten minutes when Marti's better judgment kicked into overdrive and subdued his sex drive. "I think we should stop before we do something crazy here," he said.

Leslie, raising herself up on the couch, agreed. "When I initially made the offer, I didn't mean for it to get this intense," she said, fingering her hair back in place. "Celibacy is new to me, too, you know."

"I know we're gonna get these urges again," Marti added. "We can't control that, but we had better stick to the type of fooling around where we don't end up on the floor. And when it looks like it's about to get too heated, we should just stop ourselves right then and not try to flirt around with the idea. That stuff hardly ever works."

"You still want to watch the movie? Maybe it's too awkward."

"I don't think it is," replied Marti. "We didn't do anything. Listen, at least now we both know that there's great chemistry between us, lots of chemistry. That's important to know, right?"

Leslie seemed a bit taken aback by Marti's casualness. "So that's it? We just go about our business like nothing just happened?"

"Unless there's something you want to talk about, I say yeah."

"Okay, then. By the way, you are a phenomenal kisser," she said.

"Why, thank you. I was inspired."

"Just shut up and watch the movie."

"I will just as soon as you start it back up."

"Oh, hush!"

"Hey, woman, you want my submission hold again?" returned Marti, using his arms to gesture a submission hold. "You'd better be nice to me."

"Like I said, shut up and watch the movie."

"You're hopeless."

"Then love me anyway," replied Leslie, smiling.

Marti flashed his kilowatt smile in return. "Count on it."

Chapter 33

Marti was at the car wash giving his Honda Accord a final rinse when his cell phone rang. It was Leslie wanting him to come over to her place in about an hour. From her tone, he knew something was wrong or something had happened, but she didn't want to get into it over the phone.

Marti finished wiping down his car then rushed to his place for a quick shower and change. On the way to Leslie's place, he thought about his brief conversation with her earlier, how differently she sounded. Marti made it to Leslie's in about ten minutes and found a parking space right in front of her place. He turned off his car engine, got out, walked up the cobblestone walkway, approached the front door to Leslie's townhouse then stood there for a minute, contemplating how he should address Leslie when she answered her door. He then decided just to work off of her vibe, let her set the tone and control the conversation because the thing he knew for sure was that she was upset about something, and he didn't want to make things worse by offering any premature suggestions, especially if all she needed and wanted was just somebody to listen.

It only took her a half a second to open the door, and Marti walked into nothing, but disorder. There were boxes and clothing all over the place and that was just downstairs. He didn't know what the condition was upstairs, but just imagined its state being worse. At first, he thought that maybe her place had been burglarized, but then he noticed the black magic marker labeling on the boxes.

"What's all this?" inquired Marti, as he cleared a space on the sofa for him to sit.

"I've got to get some more boxes. This won't be enough, had more stuff than I realized."

Marti tried again. "Moving to a new spot?"

"You can say that," returned Leslie from the hallway. "I'm moving back to Dallas."

Marti got up and walked into the hallway where she was. "Dallas!"

"Yeah, I've gotta go take care of my mama. She's all the family I've got."

"What's wrong with her?"

"She's a diabetic, been one for years, but now it's gotten so bad that she's lost her eyesight and she can't get around and she doesn't want a nurse taking care of her and there isn't anybody else." She paused a moment. "I wish she wouldn't try to spare my feelings. Anytime I asked about her health, she always gave me a good report. I had to hear it from her doctor this morning that she had missed her last two appointments, and he was growing concerned because last time he saw her, which was about three months ago, her eyesight was failing then."

"Well…I mean, can't you just…just move her here with you?"

"I'll pretend you didn't even say that, Marti."

"Why?"

"Because I'm not about to uproot my mama like that, take her away from the only home she's ever known, especially how sick she is, just so I won't be inconvenienced."

"That's not what I meant, Leslie. I just don't want to lose you."

"I don't want to lose you either, but I can't think about that right now."

"I can't believe this is happening. I just got you in my life."

"Is that all you can think about?" asked Leslie. "My mama is sick and all you can talk about is what this will do to us."

Marti walked over to Leslie and embraced her. "Listen, Les, I'm sorry. You're right. It's just happening so fast. I haven't even had time to process any of this…knee-jerk reaction, I guess."

"I know this is hard, Marti. And I really can't consider your feelings right now because this is my mama we're talking about."

"Yeah, I know. So when are you leaving?"

"As soon as the term ends in a couple of weeks."

"Who's seeing about her now?"

"A neighbor's been checking in on her, making sure she gets her medicine and food. You've got to understand—my mama is very independent and this is hard for her. She likes doing for herself. I wanted to go back home a few years ago, but she insisted I live my life, but now it's time, Marti."

"So that's it?"

"Yeah."

"Guess I may as well make myself useful then." Marti went into the kitchen and began to clear out the cabinets and drawers. "Got another big box for these pots and pans?"

"Yeah, here." Leslie tossed the box down the hallway, and it landed at the entryway of the kitchen.

"Thanks, baby," said Marti.

"So I'm still you're baby?"

"Listen, you can move to Uganda, and you'd still be my baby."

"You really love me, don't you?"

Marti stuck his head out into the hallway. "Yes, I do."

"Then I guess I love you, too."

344

"You guess?"

"Yeah, you're a keeper."

"Whatever," Marti cynically replied as he ducked back into the kitchen.

Now back at his place after three grueling hours of packing over at Leslie's, Marti sat on the couch and stared at the blank television screen. It seemed a complete waste to have washed his car earlier since the rain was beginning to pour down as bold rods of lightening flashed across the night's sky. *She's leaving*, he thought to himself while thunder now boomed in the backdrop. Before he left, he assured Leslie that he really understood why she had to leave, but if she really wanted to know his true feelings, then they were these: he didn't want her to go; he didn't want to have to start all over again, hoping that the next one could measure up to her, because he knew that the long distance thing would never work; he wanted to make her stay, say something to convince her to stay; bottom line—he didn't want her to go. Having only mended the relationship with his own mother last year, Marti reasoned with himself that she had to go. You only have one mother, and Leslie's was sick, very sick.

The lights in the apartment began to flicker as Marti got up and walked over to the refrigerator. "Not this again. Give me a break, already," he grumbled to himself. The last thing he needed or wanted was another power outage after having one just last month that lasted nearly four hours because a nearby power line had been blown down (Baton Rouge was prone to hurricane weather). Marti grabbed the bottled water and turkey, cheese, and mayo from the refrigerator. Thinking, while fixing his sandwich, that he needed a change. He was sick of living the single life, in his bachelor pad. He was ready to settle down again, find a nice house somewhere, and plant some roots with her.

Marti cleaned up in the kitchen before returning to the living room. He sat on the couch again, set the partially eaten sandwich down on the coffee table then picked up the Bible, flipped to the Concordance, and skimmed through it till he came to what he was looking for: *WIFE.*

Marti then turned to the Proverbs 18:22 and read to himself: "Whoso findeth a wife findeth a good thing, and obtaineth favor of the Lord."

This was exactly how he felt about Leslie. She *was* a good thing, a *real* good thing. It then hit him—while sitting there in his empty apartment, the lights flickering every now and then, the rain pounding the pavement and beating against the glass patio door, the lightening and thundering evermore the backdrop of his existence—what he must do.

Chapter 34

How ironic was it for Marti, having finally gotten his mother back in his life after nearly eight years of estrangement, through unfortunate circumstances nonetheless, to have to break the news to her that he was now leaving? Wanting to prolong the wait no longer, Marti pulled into his mother's driveway earlier than his mother was expecting him. His heart pounded as he walked the cement pathway leading to the front door. Having taken a deep breath to calm himself, Marti rang the doorbell. The door slowly crept open, revealing, on the other side of it, the petite, middle-aged woman of fair complexion. Her long, black hair, speckled with touches of silver, was pinned up with two wooden hair sticks crisscrossed at the back. Marti lunged forward, with the top of her head falling just under his chin, to embrace his mother long and hard. He didn't want to say anything just yet, only hold her and remember what that felt like.

"You okay, son? What's the matter?" his mother asked after pulling from the embrace to close the front door.

"Yes ma'am. I'm just fine, mama."

"Well, come on here into the kitchen. I'm frying up some chicken. I wasn't expecting you for another hour."

"Yes, ma'am I know, but—"

"You ain't got to explain, I'm glad to see you, too. Go head on, son, and grab you a seat at the table over there. This should be ready in a minute or two. I hope you've worked up an appetite for some fried chicken and collard greens and sweet fried cornbread and sweet potato pie? From the looks of you, I think you may have traded in this here good ole Southern cookin' for, what is it now that they call those things, protein bars?"

"Naw, mama, I can't wait to dig in." That was an understatement. Truth is, his workout regimen and subsequent diet had restricted his intake of those kinds of foods, the kinds of fatty, greasy, artery-clogging foods that led to an ever increasing number of hypertension cases among black folks. But just this once he could and would make an exception, he'd always make an exception when it came to his mother's cooking. "Smells good, mama."

"Yeah, son, I was up early this morning hand-washing them greens. Have a look out back at my garden there. I've got all kinds of good vegetables growing back there. I want you to take something back with you. They can go with a meal for you and your lady friend. By the way, how is Leslie?"

Pretending he never heard his mother's question, Marti then got up and walked over to the back door to have a peak at his mother's garden from the window. "Oh yeah, mama, that's a big garden."

"I told you. Listen, son, grab me a couple of them plates out the cabinet over there," she said, pointing the huge wooden spoon she was using to stir the pot of greens in the direction of the cabinet.

"Sure, mama."

"And I'm still waiting to hear about that lady friend of yours." At only fifty-four, her memory was still sharp as ever, and she wasn't leaving this conversation alone.

"Leslie's just fine, mama. She wanted to come up, but she, uh, she…"

"Well, spit it out, son. She what?" Marti just wasn't ready to get into that with his mother yet. He at least wanted to eat first before breaking the news. It was almost as if she had some type of radar or intuitively knew that there was something more to his story.

"It's just that she had to take care of some important work-related stuff and couldn't come, mama—that's all." Linda approached the table with two steaming plates of her good ole home cooking and joined him at the opposite end.

"Well, eat up, son. Don't hurt my feelings." God, that was the last thing Marti wanted to do, considering.

Blowing the loaded fork of greens to an edible temperature, Marti took in a mouthful. "Mmm-umm, mama, this is good. You don't know how much I've missed your cooking."

"Well, doesn't Leslie cook for you?"

"Naw, mama, not really, we eat out a lot. People hardly sit down at the dinner table anymore and have family dinner like we did back in the day. This fast-paced world we're living in slows down for no one. Most times, we're good if we grab anything to eat at all."

His mama shook her head at the very notion. "Oh, son, don't say that."

"It's true. I don't even expect the women I date to cook for me—some do, some don't. You got more women out there pulling long hours like men, and when they come home, they just want to relax. Since Leslie's a schoolteacher like me, I'd just assume cook for her because she works just as hard as I do."

"Sounds like you love this girl."

"Yeah, mama, that's what I wanted to tell you. I do love her and I'm gonna move to Dallas with her when the school term ends next month."

"Dallas? Why are y'all goin' to Dallas?"

"Her mama is real sick with diabetes and has gone blind, and Leslie doesn't want to uproot her from her familiar surroundings, especially now that she's lost her eyesight."

"Yeah, yeah, that's right, I understand. Sounds like you have a good woman there, son. She loves her mama. And I see that you love her."

"Yes, ma'am, I do, but I love you, too, and I didn't want you to think I was abandoning you...you know, since we just—"

"Not another word about that, Marti. I'll be here. I'm not going anywhere, but I'ma tell ya something, son. If you find somebody special like I think you have, you better do everything you can to make it work. Do everything you can to cherish it. You need to be with the woman you love, and that's all to it, son. That's why they have telephones and postcards and envelops and stamps. When you think about your ol' mama, all you got to do is call. When you feel like jumping on a plane to this side of the world, that front door will be open. You just remember that."

"Yes, ma'am."

"Are you about ready for some of that sweet potato pie?"

"Oh, yes, ma'am!"

"Well, you ain't a guest. Go cut you a slice. Take as much as you like; otherwise, I'm gonna end up giving it all to my neighbors. Get a piece for Leslie and wrap it up with that foil paper on the counter there. And you make sure you bring my future daughter-in-law by before y'all go off to Dallas."

"Daughter-in-law? I never said anything about marrying her."

"Listen, son, I've been around long enough to know when a man has that look in his eyes, and you got that look."

"I guess I can't keep anything from you."

"Of course you can't. I'm your mama," she said, smiling.

Marti spent all of three hours over his mama's house, thinking as he made the hour trek back to Baker how good a visit it was and how much he'd miss her not being in the same city as he. All things considered, she had taken the news fairly well, yet he could hear the sadness in her tone as she hugged and kissed him good-bye. It was a sad moment for them, but he knew she understood and that gave him some consolation.

Marti put the two plates of food that his mother had wrapped for him and Leslie in the refrigerator then walked into the second bedroom that he had converted into a home office. He sat down at the computer and clicked on the Power button. Taking only a minute to boot up, Marti clicked the blue Internet Explorer icon on his computer desktop and typed the web address for Monster.com in the browser.

This was not something he could dawdle about; he had to find a school in Dallas that he could call home. While it was exciting to be moving away to a new city with the woman he loved, Marti had to be practical. It would do neither one of them any good if he didn't have a job, and they surely couldn't survive on Leslie's salary alone. Besides, he wasn't the type to live off a woman. If anything, he'd make it possible for her to leave her job. Marti would never be able sit home in peace knowing that it was her—and not him—out busting her hump to make ends meet. At least he could credit his father with instilling that in him.

His job query turned up sixty records, any one of them a prospect. That was the advantage of living in a big city, the opportunities seemed endless. Both enthusiastic and hopeful, Marti began to sort through the records, bookmarking those that might be a match for his experience and expertise; after all, he did now hold a Master's degree in Education. The sorting process yielded at least seven job leads, but only one really stood out in Marti's mind. Carter High School was looking for a Geography teacher to start next term. It sounded promising.

Marti spent the next thirty minutes updating his resumé, highlighting all his responsibilities at Baker High. Too bad those things didn't allow for personal experience; otherwise, he'd have lots more to tell, starting with the day he first met Leslie. And it seemed his life was full of irony. Nearly six years ago, he had transferred to another school to get away from a woman, now he was transferring to yet another school to be with a woman. This only confirmed for Marti what he already knew—that things always got better.

Marti then replied to each of the seven job leads with a cover letter and resumé, believing that something would turn up soon, a call, an email, something. It was just a waiting game now.

***

Sporting a short sleeve canary polo, a pair of khakis, his FootJoy golf shoes, and Nike sun visor, Marti was all set to make his tee time with some of his buddies from work when the phone rang. Maybe it was Leslie. He wouldn't hesitate to make time for her.

Setting his Callaway golf bag next to the phone, Marti picked up the receiver. "Hello."

"Yes, may I speak to Marti Johnson?"

"This is he." He didn't recognize the male voice on the other end.

"Yes, I'm sorry to be calling on a Saturday, but we were hoping to get a live voice and not a recording. Anyway, I'm Jeremy Townsend, the principal at D. W. Carter High School in Dallas. We were impressed with your resume, and I had hoped that if you had a minute, we could have a phone interview right now.

"Yes, that would be fine," said Marti, sitting down on his couch.

"I understand that you are looking to transfer from Baker High School, where you have been teaching Geography for the past five years. May I ask why the transfer?"

"Certainly. I like it at Baker, but I'm getting married and my fiancée's mother lives in Dallas, but she's very ill. We'll be moving there to help take care of her." His *fiancée*, that was a bit presumptuous, especially since he hadn't even popped the question yet.

"I see. So, Mr. Johnson, tell me a little bit more about why you enjoy teaching."

"I think most people view teaching as a way to instruct young people, help them to develop intellectually, and this is true of teaching, but I also see teaching as an exchange. I have found that I've learn as much from my pupils as they have learned from me. Honestly, I think kids need to know that they have a voice and that someone is listening to what they have to say. As teachers, we are not only there to help mold our students academically, but we are also there to help them become adults, and in order to do that, we have to be willing to learn from them who they are. Otherwise, it is difficult to direct them on any level."

"If possible, Mr. Johnson, I'd like to schedule for you to come to Dallas for a second interview. This would also give you a chance to tour the school and see what we are all about here at Carter. The bottom line is that we are looking for good teachers. With the demand for teachers steadily increasing, it has occurred to those of us who are in charge of placing the right teachers in our schools that we had better snatch up those dedicated to educating our young people when we can. Would next Friday be something that you could work with, say around ten o'clock?"

"That shouldn't be a problem, sir."

"Very well then, I will see you next Friday at Carter High. Simply come to the school office, tell the secretary who you are, and she will direct you from there."

"Thank you, Mr. Townsend."

***

With a six-and-half-hour drive ahead of him, Marti left Baton Rouge headed for Dallas around two o'clock in the morning. And while it was not much to the ride—he'd take I-49 North to I-20 West (four hours) through Shreveport then another 178 miles to Dallas (two and a half hours)—he gave himself more than enough time to get there. By the time Marti entered Dallas city limits, it was nine o'clock. He killed some time by stopping at a McDonald's for a big breakfast then made a quick change in a hotel bathroom before heading to the school. When he saw the South Polk Street exit, he made a right on South Polk, came to the first light, and made a left on

West Wheatland Road. D.W. Carter High School was sitting on the right.

As Mr. Townsend had stated during the phone interview, he had only to state his name when he walked into the main office. The secretary announced his arrival then he was directed to the principal's office.

When Marti walked into Mr. Townsend's office, the distinguished gentleman stood up to greet Marti with a firm handshake.

"Glad you could make it," he said. "Have a seat." Mr. Townsend, who stood at least as tall as Marti, maybe taller, must have been in his mid to late forties; he was graying around the temple, but in good shape, no less. Marti scanned his office for mementos and found that his wall was decorated with degrees, and Kappa Alpha Psi fraternity paraphernalia was scattered about his bookcase. "How was the trip?"

"Not bad."

"What's that, about a five-, six-hour drive?"

"About six and a half."

"Well, the reason I wanted you here for the second interview is so that we could meet in person and talk some more about the position and then I'd like to show you around the school. Let me just be frank with you, if we weren't interested in you or your credentials, you wouldn't be here right now. I'd hope that from this meeting today you'd find that Carter is somewhere you can see yourself teaching.

After an hour of interviewing and touring the school, the two of them were back in Mr. Townsend's office.

"I understand that you have some decisions to make, but I would like to offer you the position. We've interviewed several other teachers, and you seem to be the best choice for the job. And let me also add that we've already done a thorough background check on you and you have a stellar record, the highest remarks were given about you. If you need more time to mull it over, please take it, but let me know something at least by next Tuesday."

"Thank you, sir, but if it's all the same to you, I'd like to accept now."

Mr. Townsend extended his hand. "Well, that's wonderful," he said, smiling. "I'm certainly happy to have you aboard. We'll just need to take care of the transfer paperwork and I'll be in contact about the teacher's orientation for the next school term. Again, welcome aboard."

"There's just one more thing, sir."

"What's that?"

"Well, I'm going to be here until Sunday morning, and I've been to Dallas only a few times when I was in college, but not enough to know my way around the city. Can you recommend any good restaurants and sites to see?"

"You bet. You should try Pappadeaux Seafood Kitchen. What you want to do is get back on I-20 here, heading West until you come to exit 464A, taking that exit puts you on US-67 North. You are going to ride US-67 North out until you are ready to merge onto I-35 East. From I-35 East, you are going to take exit 430A, that's the Oak Lawn Avenue exit. Turn right on Oak Lawn Avenue and ride that out till you come to the spot. You can even see Pappadeaux from I-35 because there's a big waterfall that sets off the place. You might also want to check out Texas Stadium…"

Mr. Townsend proceeded to run down a list of places for Marti, but Pappadeaux was probably where he would eat tonight. He just wished Leslie was with him. He didn't particularly like telling her that he was riding to Ohio with Douglas to support his friend during his bodybuilding competition, especially since that wasn't until the 1st of May, the following Saturday, but to pull off his surprise proposal, he had to fudge just this once.

"Thanks a lot, Mr. Townsend," said Marti, extending his hand. "I look forward to getting started next term."

"Like I said, we'll be in touch to get you all set up for the new term."

Marti exited Mr. Townsend with a smirk on his face while his insides turned flips—he had landed himself a job in Big D. Everything was falling into place. Everything.

Later that evening, when he knew Leslie would be home, he called her from his hotel room. He missed her too much not to hear her voice.

On the fifth ring, she picked up the phone. "He-hello."

"Hey, baby, it's me."

"Marti?"

"Yeah, who else? Hey, baby, you okay?"

"Not really, I was sleep. I left school early today. I wasn't feeling well."

"What's wrong, Les?"

"I was running a slight fever and I couldn't keep anything down."

"Well, did you see a doctor?"

Marti could hear Leslie's grumbles. She hated hospitals and clinics or any place where they had needles. "Naw, I didn't go to the doctor, I came straight home."

"Well, maybe you don't need to be around there with a fever and not doing something for it. You need me to come back tonight?"

"What about Douglas?"

"Man, I ain't worried about Douglas. I want to make sure you're okay."

"Naw, baby, I'll be fine."

"You sure, Leslie, you really don't sound good?"

"I'm sure, I feel a lot better than I did a few hours ago."

"At least promise me that you'll call me on my cell if you get to feeling worse. Will you do that?"

"Yeah, I promise."

"Okay, baby, well, I'm gonna let you get some rest. I'll call and check up on you in the morning."

"Okay," she said lowly into the phone.

"I love you."

"I love you, too."

Marti didn't like leaving her to her own devices. He knew she'd lay there and suffer all night and never call him once. He found her in a similar state a few years back when she tried to pass off bronchitis for a really bad cold. He was glad he had stopped by when he found her hyperventilating in the bathroom because the congestion in her chest was restricting her breathing. What might have been only a panic attack was one of the scariest moments she'd ever had. Through the tears, she tried to explain to him that she felt like she was dying, like she wouldn't be able to take her next breath. The next few days were equally as terrifying when she'd wake in the middle of the night with spells of shortness of breath. Finally, Marti convinced her to go see the doctor, where she learned that she had upper bronchial infection and was prescribed medication that cleared up her infection within days. So what might seem trivial to Leslie, in Marti's mind, could very well be something worth checking out. He'd see in the morning.

***

When Marti called her early Saturday morning, Leslie certainly sounded better when she answered the phone. "Well, you sound a little bit like your old self again. How are you feeling?"

"Much better, my fever broke and now I'm just hungry, but I feel a little weak."

"Then you need to eat somethin'. You should have some chicken noodle soup in your pantry. Eat some of that and drink plenty of fluids, water is best."

"I wish you were here," she said, yawning. Oh, that was it. That was all Marti needed to hear.

"Me, too, baby."

"I'm gonna go get something to eat now. I'll see you tomorrow."

"Okay, baby. Bye."

Marti hung up the phone with Leslie, checked out of the hotel, filled up his tank, and started his nearly seven-hour drive back to Baton Rouge. Forgoing any misfortune, he should be back in his baby's arm no later than two o'clock that evening. Perfect. There was certainly no way he could enjoy Dallas knowing she was home sick, and while she would never ask him to change his plans, he knew she wanted him back home, and he wanted to be back there.

Marti

Chapter 35

Leslie massaged her fingers along Marti's collar area, pressing in ever so mechanically to remove the unwanted stress and tension knots. "You sure you can't come today?"

"I wish I could, sweetie, but I promised Theresa I'd help her paint her crib today."

"Who's Theresa?"

"You know from school. She teaches sophomore literature."

"Oh, okay. Still, I wish you could come. Donald's been buggin' me about meeting you."

"You tell your brother that I hate I missed him, but to save a seat for me the next time."

"Oh yeah, that feels good, baby. Don't stop. Yeah, right there." Leslie's hands had found their way down Marti's back near the lumbar region as he lay prostrate on her couch. "Maybe you can take this up in your spare time. You've got a knack for this. Second thought, can that idea. I don't want some other brotha gettin' in on my good thing."

Leslie snickered before returning, "You men are all alike. You brag about what you got at home, but if some other guy looks like he's about to get hungry for what you got, you're ready to whoop up on him.

"Hey, that's just how it is."

"Well, I won't quit my day job, thank you very much."

"How about we switch?"

"What, first you compliment my fancy finger work now you're trying to get rid of me?"

"See, it's not even like that. I'm just tryin' to repay the favor. That's what a good man does," said Marti, tooting his own horn. He had grown accustomed to striking up his own opus just to see her reaction. It was one of those perpetual habits that he wouldn't break unless she read more into it than simply what it was.

"Whatever."

"So?"

"Naw, I'm straight, but I'll tell ya what you can do for me before you go."

"Yeah, what?"

"Help me break down my bed." That was a consummate reminder that she would be moving soon.

"Then where are you gonna sleep?"

"On this here couch that you're sprawled across." It was certainly comfortable enough. Marti could attest to that. "I want to try to sell this thing to somebody at work if I can. I plan to get all new bedroom furniture when I get to Dallas. I've had that white wicker set long enough."

"You think somebody's gonna want to buy it?"

"I don't know. I might try to push it off on Theresa since I'm gonna be up to my eyeballs in Sherman Williams in an hour. I swear I don't know how I let that girl talk me into strapping on a pair of overalls when she knows that I ain't never rolled a strip of paint in my life, and, to top that, she wants to do some type of sponge treatment. It should be interesting—that's all I can say."

"What in the world is she trying to do around there?"

"I *do not* know, but much can be said about what boredom will compel a person to do."

"Alright, well, let's get to it."

The two of them headed upstairs to Leslie's bedroom, Marti tagging behind with his finger clasping one of her overall back pockets.

"You got any tools? An Allen wrench or something?"

"Yeah, yeah, that's what I forget. Hold on, it's down in the kitchen drawer." He could hear the descent of her brisk, heavy steps. A minute later she returned with a wrench and screw driver.

"What's that for?"

"I thought we might need it."

"I doubt it. The wrench should do."

"Well, I didn't know, and I wanted to save myself another trip down those stairs."

Marti shook his head, "Just get over here woman and give me a hand."

"I'll call you later after I get back," Marti said to Leslie before taking off, headed for his mother's place. He knew Donald wouldn't be expecting his mother to walk through that steel prison door. They hadn't seen each other since he'd been inside, and he could just imagine his brother's bewilderment. After all, Donald had no way of learning of his mother's status except through Marti's monthly updates, which had amounted to very little over the last seven years.

With his CD player pumping out the funky composition of J. J. Johnson, Marti inched down the winding street leading to his mother's house, just as anxious about picking her up as he was about seeing the look on Donald's face. Over the phone, his mother's tone revealed that she was just as eager and nervous about the reunion.

"Hey mama," said Marti, leaning over to hug her. Estēe Lauder still lingered in the imported fibers of Marti's black Dolce & Gabbana dress shirt after he pulled away. She had been wearing the same perfume for years now.

"Hi, son, where's that lady friend of yours, Leslie?"

"Oh, she couldn't make it. So you ready?"

"Yeah, baby, let me just grab my purse."

On the drive there neither had much to say. Linda stared out the window while Marti made quick glances over at her every now and then. She must have been thinking about her other son, the one she believed turned out the way he did because he hadn't a father figure in his life as long as Marti did. She did the best she could with what she had.

"Mama, you can roll that window down some more if you like."

"Naw, son, this is just fine. I'm glad you've been going to see your brother the whole while. It's good that he at least had somebody to check in on him"

"Yes, ma'am, and every time he'd asked about you, too. I was always sorry I couldn't tell him much."

She smiled, a light reflected from her sunken eyes. "Well, we're about to fix that."

"Yes, ma'am, we are."

Once they arrived at the prison, the two of them signed the check-in log and headed for the visitor's quarter. When Marti opened the door, his brother looked up expectantly, unaware of the surprise that awaited him.

"Hey, bra, I've got a treat for you today."

"Don't tell me I'm gonna finally meet the woman who stole my brother's heart?"

"Better than that," he said, turning back to open the door for their mother. "C'mon, mama."

With his eyes as round as half dollars and mouth agape, Donald jumped up and rushed over to his mother with open arms almost knocking her down with his enthusiasm. "Mama, I can't believe you're here," he said, squeezing her ever so tightly. Oh, mama, I've missed you."

Feeling the lump forming in his throat and the tear ducts wanting to release something, Marti fought back the emotions as he watched the two reunite. This was a long time coming for all of them. With the exception of his father, he had his family back.

"C'mon, mama, come sit down so that we can talk." Donald grabbed his mother's hand and led her to the chair. He sat across from the two of them. "You look real good, mama. Life's been treatin' you just fine, I see."

"I manage. My work keeps me alert, and the Lord's just been plain ol' good to me."

"Yeah, Marti told me you been tending to folks at a nursing home."

"Um-hum, been there almost three years now."

"Mama, tell him about Sharon," said Marti.

"Who?"

"Sharon, your girl from high school," Marti replied to his brother.

"What about her?"

"She called mama up the other day trying to catch up with you. Maybe she's trying to make a love connection again," said Marti, teasing his brother. "You must have laid some of that Johnson charm on her back in school."

"What did she say, mama?"

"She wanted to know where you were and how'd you been. Said she'd been thinking about you and wondered whatever happened to you."

"What did you tell her?"

"That you had gotten into some trouble awhile back and were doing time."

Donald said nothing in return. The starkness of his mother's words resonated in his head. It was the truth, and there was no getting around that reality.

Taking that transitory break in conversation as her cue, their mother reached into her purse and pulled out a tattered letter; it had been folded in three places, with each of its four corners dog-eared. "They found this in your father's office the day he killed himself. It's about time you boys know the whole story."

Marti took the letter—a suicide note, he presumed—from his mother and proceeded to read it aloud:

Dear Linda,

In all the years we been married, I ain't never had a hard time telling you how I felt, but today I can't seem to find the right words. I haven't been honest with you and now it has caught up with me. I'm in a lot of trouble with some people I borrowed money from to get the business started. I ain't got any other way out, but this. All I ever wanted was to give y'all the things I never had—a good home and a good life. I tried to make it work. You know I did, but that recession hurt us more than you'll ever know, Linda. Tell the boys I love them and I'm sorry. I wish, Lord, Linda, I wish I didn't have to do this, but if a man can't take care of his family he just ain't no good and before they catch up with me and try to hurt any of you I'm gonna finish the job before they get a chance. Remember, I love you, Linda. I may not have always told you or showed you, but I do. I always have. I always will.

George

"So that's why," said Donald. "That's why he did it. Why didn't he just tell somebody?"

"Because you're father was dealing with the kind of people who were ruthless, and he didn't want to put us in any danger."

Marti interrupted, "He knew they'd kill him, and if he tried to run, they'd come after one of us just as long as somebody paid."

"Yeah, son."

"He should have gone to the police," said Marti.

"And tell them what?" Donald said bitterly. "What could they do? Nothin'. He had proof of nothin'. Those kind of *lenders* always covered their tracks. They'll take you out just like that, and nobody would ever find out who was responsible. Pop knew that."

"And all this time I thought he was just a coward because he didn't have the guts to stick it out and see things through. In his mind, he was protecting us."

"Yes, he thought he was, but that doesn't make it right, son. No matter what the problem is, suicide is never the way out."

"Yeah, mama, I know. At least now I have some answers. At least now I know why he did it. Not knowing had been eating at me for years." It also answered the question of how Linda Johnson was able to forgive her husband, why the love she had for him never faltered.

Eager to disclose the outcome of his visit, Marti phoned Leslie as soon as he got home. He had much to tell.

"So was Donald surprised?"

"Yeah, but not half as surprised as we both were to learn the real reason my father killed himself."

"What!" exclaimed Leslie into the phone.

"Yeah, I know. My moms had been holding on to that suicide note for over twenty years."

"So why'd he do it?" inquired Leslie, whose ear he could only imagine was pressed ever so snugly up to the receiver, ensuring that she missed not even a pause.

He would give her the abridged version nonetheless. "Turns out he got mixed up with some loan sharks. When he couldn't pay up, they had it out for him."

"You're kidding!"

"Baby, I wish I were, but that's the whole story."

Leslie grunted on the other end. "You just never know what's really going on. I'm just glad you finally got some closure."

"Yeah, then why does it feel like this news introduced a whole new set of questions?"

"Maybe you should just leave it in the past, baby."

"Maybe."

***

He made no promises to her, knowing he was not yet ready to let the matter go. The past had once again resurfaced perhaps wanting Marti to probe the unanswered questions. Who were these "lenders," taking the words of his younger brother? Not in the business of settling old scores, Marti wrenched the malicious thoughts from his mind. Leslie was right, all the sorted details of George Johnson's dubious business affairs were buried with his father, and his death had obviously settled his debt. There was nothing more to—

Marti's doorbell rang. *Who could that be?* he thought as he went to answer. Through the peephole, Marti eyed a young brother wearing a

375

pair of brown shorts and matching shirt with the gold UPS emblem stitched on the front. He wasn't expecting any packages. Opening the door, he said tersely, "Yeah?"

With a clipboard in one hand and medium-sized parcel propped under his other arm, the UPS driver replied, "Yeah, man, I have a package for a Mr. Marti Johnson from Linda Johnson."

"That's me. I'm Marti Johnson."

"Let me get you to sign here, man, and you're all set."

Marti signed the sheet and took the package, the contents of which he would soon learn. He didn't wait to get into the living room before striping the package free of its Scotch tape. Inside were documents that appeared to be the financial papers from his father's business. In the margin of one such document, his father had scribbled the words: J. T. Smith, 180 days. On another, he had written the words: Preacha Goodlow, 90 days. The third name was one in which he could not make out from his father's penmanship, it having been smeared it seemed. Marti suspected that these three were his father's collectors, the very ones who threatened his entire existence over a few thousand dollars.

A few minutes later, he punched in his mother's digits. "Hey, mama, it's me. I got your package."

"Oh, that's good."

"Did you ever look through this stuff?"

"Yeah, but it didn't mean anything to me. It was just financial statements from the business. I figured you could do more with it."

"I found some names and dates handwritten on some of them. I think these were the people daddy owed. I don't know what to do now."

"Maybe we should just let it be, son."

"Then why did you send me this stuff?" Marti brusquely replied.

"It was a mistake, son. We should just leave the past in the past."

"Now you sound like Leslie."

"You've got a smart woman there, Marti. Concentrate on your life with her now. Your father's mistakes finally caught up with him. I don't want you to get all entangled in the web George spawned years ago. Go and marry that beautiful girl of yours."

"You sure about this, mama, because I can do some digging—"

"Yes, I'm sure. I want you to burn those things. They are ashes to us now."

Marti reluctantly complied, "Okay, mama, if that's what you want, then I'll let it go."

"Yeah, baby, I think that's best…for all of us. You'll see."

He would honor his mother's request and maintain Leslie as his focus. After all, she was leaving in a few weeks, and he still had some personal matters to handle, the most important of which was going ring shopping and finding the perfect diamond-studded testament of their love.

Chapter 36

Divided between the marquise and the princess, Marti had stood over the glass counter more than twenty minutes trying to figure out the best cut for Leslie's finger. The carat size he knew—definitely. One carat diamond solitaire for sure, he wouldn't dare give her anything less, especially since she had once already been given a one and a half carat by that Keith dude. What a schmuck? Still, he was undecided about that last detail and was glad when the sales clerk had finished with the other couple because he really needed her assistance.

"Can I help you, sir?"

Marti smiled. "Yes, you can. I'm trying to decide which of these rings to get."

"Well, sir, can you tell me something about her personality that could help us narrow down the selection? And what about her hand, does she have long fingers? If so, then the marquise would be a good choice. By the way, congratulations."

"Thanks. Let's see, Leslie is very independent and smart and witty. She's not much into frills. She's pretty conservative. Don't get me wrong—she's gorgeous, but she doesn't worry with stuff like makeup."

"Okay, sir—"

"It's Marti."

"Well, Marti, do you know the size?"

"Yeah, she wears a seven."

"Well, just from what you described of her, I think she'd like the marquise or the classic princess cut. Both of these are favorites."

"Yeah, that's what I was thinking. What would be your pick?"

"I like them both, but the marquise looks better on my hand because I have long fingers?"

"The marquise, huh? Let's go with that."

"Let me ask you this. Do you think she might like a platinum band? We have these here in platinum."

"Yeah, she does like to wear silver jewelry. In fact, that's all I've ever known her to wear. The platinum will go good with her silver jewelry."

"Okay, Marti, so we're going with the platinum 1.55 carat, marquise-cut diamond solitaire? That's a gorgeous ring, by the way. I think she's going to love that. And let me also add that all of our engagement rings are certified, and each comes with its own diamond certificate. Let's have a look at the certificate for this one you've just selected."

The sales clerk retrieved a binder from the counter behind her and opened it to the appropriate page. "As you can see, the certificate states the diamond's color, clarity, cut, and carat weight. It describes the diamond's shape, measurements, table, and depth percentages. It also grades the polish and symmetry. And you can see that there are also additional comments about any other noteworthy gemological characteristics, such as fluorescence, graining, etc."

"Sounds good. Let's wrap it up," he said, smiling.

"We do offer our own in-house financing. We would just have to run your credit and get you approved, or will you be purchasing the ring by some other method?"

"No, I'd like to finance it."

She began to walk toward the back of the store where the register was. "If you'd follow me, we can start the process. It shouldn't take long." She handed him a credit form. "I'll just need you to fill this out, and I'll need to see your driver's license."

Having just pulled into his barber shop parking lot, Marti wondered what "shop talk" would be circulating through that place today. Inside were men of all ages talking about every topic under the sun: politics, sports, work, weekend plans, women, weather. Marti took a seat in a chair. It would be at least twenty minutes before Ralph, his barber, could get to him. He would only go to Ralph. He didn't trust anybody else in his head. Ralph knew what he liked and gave the best clean shave he'd ever had. Larry, in the booth next to Ralph, started joking with Clinton, a regular who worked for the electric company, about the prospect of the electric company cutting everybody some slack on charges for running their central air units because May was turning out to be too hot for anybody's own good.

"C'mon, man, just don't write down everything you see on the meter."

"How many times have I got to tell you that I don't have anything to do with that?" Clinton countered. The fellas in the shop, including Marti, laughed. "That's why they don't trust us around that equipment; otherwise, they'd be losing money by the minute."

"You better know it," Marvin agreed. Marvin was the oldest barber there at forty-six. He owned the place, and Ralph was his son. "Man, it was so hot the other day that the heat came through the sidewalk into the soles of my shoes."

"C'mon, man, quit lying." Larry and Marvin always disagreed about even the smallest thing. If Larry said yellow, Marvin said blue.

"I don't have to lie—it's true."

"Whatever."

"Yeah, you just shut up and cut Clinton's head before you mess up."

Clinton interrupted. "If he messes up, I'll have to put these *bees* on him." The shop erupted.

"Alright, Marti, you're next," said Ralph. Ralph was only twenty-three, but already married with a two-year-old son who, from time to time, would hang out with his daddy at the shop.

Marti came and sat in Ralph's chair. "Just a trim today, man."

"I gotcha covered."

"You know I'm getting married, right?"

"Yeah?"

"Bought the ring today."

"When, man?"

"Don't know yet. I've got to ask her first."

"What? I thought you said you were getting married."

"She ain't gonna turn me down."

"Well, congratulations, man. So when are you gonna pop the question?"

"Next Friday."

"Hope it works out. I love my woman. She's the best thing that's ever happened to me."

"So is mine, man, so is mine."

***

The last week of school fatigue and indifference had permeated Baker High. Marti's students were particularly restless and ready for summer vacation. By Wednesday, his fourth period class had gotten their own ideas about how class was to be conducted that day. Kevin Wright slide into class with a boom box pressed up to his ear like a break dancer from the eighties. Myra, who recovered from pneumonia a week later, blew threw the door with chips and dip. LeRoy thought he'd treat everyone to a batch of chocolate chip cookies he'd made earlier in Home Economics and got ribbed for it. The spread also included cake and punch and sandwiches. His class had obviously planned this little surprise behind his back.

"Come on, Mr. Johnson, lighten up. Elvis has left the building."

"Come again?"

"In other words," explained Kevin, "school is out. You ain't gotta teach no more."

"That's 'anymore' and I'll decide what I have to do or not do." I mean, really, what was he going to do—tell them to put everything away and take out their Geography books? Of course not. "Alright,

384

just keep it at a minimum. The last thing we need is Principal Bell walking through the door because of noise complaints."

"Why are you so agitated, Mr. Johnson?" asked Rachel.

He was nervous about the proposal. Sure he had talked a big game in the barbershop last Saturday, but he had no idea what Leslie was going to say. He only hoped it was going to be "yes."

"Do I seem agitated?"

"Yes."

"Maybe I am," he said.

"About what?"

"I'm going to ask Ms. Mitchell to marry me on Friday, but you guys have to promise not to say a word to anybody about this." Phew, he got out. His students, on the other hand, were shocked at the news.

"For real?" asked Cynthia. "Mr. Johnson's gettin' married. Mr. Johnson's gettin' married." The class giggled.

"Okay, knock it off. Remember, not a word of this to anybody." They all agreed. "Now one of you fix me a plate; you're not going to sit up in my face and eat without me."

***

May 14th had finally arrived. Consequently, this was the last day Leslie would ever spend at Baker High School. She was packing up her things, stuff she'd collected over the last seven years, some of which she had been given by her many students and parents, when Marti walked in to offer his help.

"Thanks, I could use some," returned Leslie.

Marti scanned Leslie's classroom. "This place is sure gonna miss you."

"Not half as much as I'll miss being here. It's going to be hard to say good-bye."

"Then don't," said Marti.

"C'mon, Marti, we've talked about this. I have to go."

"No, you don't. You can move her here."

"I have to go, Marti. You know that."

"Yeah, I know. I just felt like being selfish for what it's worth."

"And I love you for it, but—"

"You have to go," interrupted Marti, packing the last of her things into a box.

"I can't believe this is it," she said sadly. "Seven years worth of stuff."

"Well," said Marti, "now it's my turn. Could you come over and give me a hand?"

Leslie bucked in surprise. What was he talking about, his turn? His turn for what?

"C'mon, now," issued Marti. "I know you've been here longer, but I bet I have just as much stuff as you."

Leslie got serious. "Wait. What's going on?"

Marti reached for Leslie's hand and gently pulled her into a warm embrace then gave her a long, but sweet kiss.

"What was that for?" she said, smiling.

"This."

What?

"This," repeated Marti, pulling the box from his pant pocket and opening it. "So?" he said with great expectancy.

A half smirk sort of settled across her face as she looked down at the ring then back up at him, but she replied as only she would by taking the ring from the box and slipping it on her ring finger. "Is that the answer you were looking for?" replied Leslie.

"What do you think?"

"Thought so," she said, leaning in for another kiss. "Can I get another one of these now?"

Marti kissed her lips softly. "As many as you like."

Chapter 37

When the alarm clock sounded off at eight-fifteen, Marti turned over in the bed and hit the snooze button, raising slightly up against the headboard before wiping his eyes free of sleep. His black tuxedo hung from his closet door with his shoes positioned on the floor right underneath. Although he would greet today as any other—shave, shower, and dress—it was no ordinary day. He had once before done this, but never with Leslie. To think that two hours from now he would be married to her. However bemused he had once been that his first marriage did not last, he certainly had no last minute trepidation about marrying Leslie, no uncertainty about the future, only the hope in the possibility of greater things in store.

Marti ran his head under the shower, letting the warm water from the huge gold-plated showerhead penetrate his pores, sending a tingling sensation down his spine that reminded him of Leslie's touch, her delicate hands moving down his back. He couldn't wait to be with her, and just the thought of her lying next to him in bed excited him. They had done well to wait. Their night of passion and love would be that much more special.

Taking a final glance at himself in the full-length mirror, he admired the perfect fit of his non-traditional tux: a classic three-button black suit with point collar shirt, black Herringbone fullback vest, and solid four-in-hand tie. He could only imagine what she was wearing— a woman who he believed could make a potato sack look good. With one last smooth-over of his trimmed head and thin mustache, Marti grabbed his keys and headed out the door for Richardson Chapel and his date with destiny.

With Leslie's younger sister Lisa standing in as her maid of honor and Douglas standing in as the best man, Marti's mother and a few of their closest and dearest friends rounded off their intimate ceremony of fifty guests. And to those in attendance, Leslie could not have been more stunning as she sashayed down the aisle in a white silk satin A-line gown with strapless bodice, exquisitely embellished with dazzling beadwork in a floral motif to the sultry piano version of the ballad, *Sweet November*—clearly not suggestive of their May wedding, but fitting in every other respect. Marti's face grew more animated with expressions of glee the closer his bride-to-be drew until she stood next to him and clasped his hand, cementing their union.

Pastor Hershey—who had given them counsel just a week prior— stood before them cloaked in a finely pressed robe and Bible in hand. "It has taken you two nearly five years to get here," he said. "Through trials and tribulations, periods of loss and spiritual gain, you have found your way to each other. So it is with great joy that we are all gathered here today to witness the holy union of these two people, for love between a man and a woman can withstand all obstacles, all boundaries, all loss, and all pain if it be true and ordained by God. If, for any reason, these two should not be joined in holy matrimony, speak now or forever hold your peace," he said, scanning for any objection among the privileged few. "Very well, let us pray.

"Lord, we thank you for this precious hour, an hour ordained by You that we may bear witness to the joining of these two people. We pray, Lord God, that You protect them with Your covering and guide them with Your precious spirit. We pray, God, that it is You that they seek in good times and in bad, that they may find themselves never out of Your reach. We ask, God, this day that You grant them favor and bless their comings and goings. We ask all these things in Your precious holy name Jesus. Amen.

"Marti, please face your bride. Do you, Marti Lumbard Johnson, take Leslie Marie Mitchell to be your lawfully wedded wife for better or for worse, for richer or for poorer, in sickness and in health from this day forth till death do you part?"

Marti, whose insides were turning cartwheels, smiled and said, "I do."

"Very well. Now Leslie, I'll ask of you the same. Do you, Leslie Marie Mitchell, take Marti Lumbard Johnson to be your lawfully wedded husband for better or for worse, for richer or for poorer, in sickness and in health from this day forth till death do you part?"

Without hesitation, she uttered, "I do."

"The rings, please. These rings," he said, palming them in his hand, "are representations of your love for one another, symbolizing not only completion, but continuation." Handing each the other's ring, he continued, "Marti, I ask now that you repeat after me as you slip the ring on Leslie's finger, and Leslie I ask of you the same as you slip the ring on Marti's finger. With this ring, I thee wed."

In unison, they repeated. "By the power vested in me and the state of Louisiana on this day, May 28, 2004, I pronounce you man and wife. You may kiss your bride, son."

After Marti and Leslie kissed for the first time as man and wife, Pastor Hershey solidified their union with a final proclamation, "Ladies and gentlemen, I present to you, Mr. & Mrs. Marti Lumbard Johnson."

Where they had gone conservative on the wedding, they spared little expense on their catered reception in the Blue Diamond Room at the Hilton Inn, a room whose enormous crystal chandeliers and intricate crown molding and marble statues set the tone of the elegant affair. A string quartet kept the room flowing with soft ballads and childhood favorites. Each of the intimate table settings was garnished with honeydew melon-scent voltage candles, a fresh pale pink rose bouquet center-piece, linen napkins, silver dinnerware, and imported china. To wet the palette, guests were served chilled ginger ale in crystal champagne goblets. Topping off the professionally-prepared menu, which was sure to delight their palettes, was sautéed chicken breast and salmon filet topped with pineapple relish, Caribbean chicken skewers, shrimp cocktail with sauce, bowtie antipasto pasta salad, spinach stuffed mushroom caps, bacon wrapped scallops, petite chicken salad sandwiches, baked spinach and artichoke dip served with tortilla chips, vegetable and cheese platter, melon salad, and assorted petit fours.

The wedding party, along with Marti's mom, was seated at a long table facing the guests. Tapping his champagne glass to garner everyone's attention, Douglas stood to toast the bride and groom. "I was honored when my man Marti asked me to be his best man. I know he would have liked to have had his brother carry out the task, so it meant a lot that he would choose me. During the two years that I known Marti, I've come to think of him as a brother, someone I could pass on advice and talk to and learn from, someone I could trust. One of the most important things I remember telling Marti was that if he didn't do anything else, he should give God a try. Well, folks, it seems that once he heeded that piece of advice, everything else in his life began to fall into place, including winning over that fine woman he's got sitting next to him. And so without further ado, please raise your glasses with me. Marti, Leslie, we love ya both. God be with you. To Marti and Leslie."

When the catered affair concluded around seven-thirty, they dismissed their guests and retreated to their honeymoon digs, a commodious one bedroom suite at the hotel, lavishly furnished with plush carpet, fine drapery, and a king-size bed embellished by a velvet duvet and assorted decorative bed pillows. Marti now had her all to himself, and if she wanted him as much as he wanted her, it would be a night never to forget.

Leslie slipped into the bathroom taking with her a negligee that she would not reveal until the perfect time, which left Marti desiring her all the more. "I'll be out in a minute," she said, turning on the faucet.

Marti slowly removed his tuxedo and slipped on the silk boxers that Leslie had given him a few days ago. He imagined that the soft, slinky fabric against his skin was her warm body against his. Marti ordered up strawberries and whipped crème before slipping under the cool satin covers to wait for his bride who, just minutes later, made her grand reveal. Bedazzled at the sight of the short, black teddy hugging every curl and curve of Leslie's figure, Marti smiled as he pulled back the covers, and she nestled beside him. "Here, try one of these," he said, dipping the large berry in the crème then feeding her. Her second bite he followed with a kiss, finding pleasure in the sweet taste of the berry juices on her mouth. It was enough to set their passion ablaze, and the two made love to the romantic ambiance of aromatic candles and soft jazz.

"Thank you," he said, holding her in his arms, their hearts still racing.

"For what?"

"For marrying me and for right now. Baby, I've waited a long time for this. I just can't believe it's happened."

"I know, it's pretty amazing."

"No, you were pretty amazing," Marti playfully added.

"Now you see why it was good that we waited? I don't think it could have been more special than that," she said.

Marti ran his hand down her cheek. "What's that look on your face?"

"I don't know...I just feel so alive right now, like I've been waiting for this all my life."

"Maybe you have. Maybe we both have and just didn't know it. Maybe that's why it feels so right."

"So what now?" asked Leslie, as she turned over to glance at the clock radio on her side of the bed. "It's nine-thirty. How about some room service? I'm starving," added Leslie before heading to the bathroom.

Marti grinned. "I see somebody's worked up an appetite."

Leslie poked her head out the bathroom door. "Oh, you think that's funny, don'tcha? Well, don't go getting your manhood all puffed up. I hardly ate anything at the reception—that's all."

"I should have known that you wouldn't even give me that. That's one thing I can say about you—you ain't never stroked my ego," said Marti.

"Well, I will say this—you have some real fine talents, Mr. Johnson, real fine."

Marti perused the menu. "Hey, baby, what do you want? They've got everything you can imagine. I think I'm gonna have some breakfast."

Leslie re-entered the huge bedroom and sat down at the foot of the bed with one leg folded and the other dangling off the side. "Breakfast?"

"Yeah, I could really stand some pancakes, sausage, and eggs," he answered before taking his turn in the bathroom to clean up. "Decide what you want and I'll order it when I get out."

"Okay, baby."

"And hey, besides breakfast, is there anything else I can get for you, Mrs. Johnson?"

Leslie, devilishly raising her brow, replied, "I'm sure I can think of something or another."

"I'm sure you will."

Marti

Chapter 38

"You'll never guess who that was on the phone."

"Who, Sasha?"

"Naw, Carolyn, my ex. Mama must have given her this number. She always had a soft spot for that woman."

"What did she want?"

"She said she needed to talk to me about somethin'. She's in town for some conference for the next few days, and she wants me to meet her at the Sheridan in an hour."

Marti was sitting on the edge of the bed when Leslie walked over, sat down beside him, and put her arms around his neck before kissing his cheek. "You going?" she asked.

"I don't know. That's the last thing I need, to be drudging up the past."

"Just see what she has to say, baby. I'm sure it's nothing. She probably just wants to try to reconcile. Y'all didn't exactly leave on amicable terms, you know."

"Yeah, you're probably right."

Marti peered down at his watch as he walked into the lobby of the Sheridan Hotel, where Carolyn was staying for the duration of the conference. It was three-thirty on the dot. Some five minutes later Carolyn emerged from the elevator, not knowing what to do with her hands—whether to shake his hand or hug him—once she had come face-to-face with her former husband. Decidedly, they exchanged neither and simply walked into the hotel bar and found seats at one of the booths.

"I don't know what it is about you women that make you keep poppin' up in my life after the fact," Marti asserted.

Carolyn did a double take before replying, "Excuse me?"

"Never mind. So what's this about?"

"I see you haven't changed much," she said cynically.

"On the contrary, I just have better things to do than sit here rehashing the past," he countered.

"That's not why I'm here."

"Then why *are* you here?"

"After you left, I started writing a book—"

"What, writing sonnets wasn't enough for you anymore?" interrupted Marti, to whom Carolyn then responded with a sharp cut of the eyes. "I'm sorry, I'm being spiteful. Go ahead, what's the book about?"

Carolyn continued. "Well, it's a non-fiction piece about our marriage entitled: *Why You Have to be Careful You're Marrying the Man and Not His Past: Dr. Carolyn St. James' Real Life Story of Marriage, Betrayal and Divorce.*

"So you made it official, huh?"

"Yeah, I went back and did my clinical and became a certified therapist. Now I have a private practice," gushed Carolyn, proud of her achievements.

"Well, I'm glad for you, but I don't know about this book. Sounds like you're going to be incriminating me."

"I can't release anything until you sign this document granting me the right to disclose details of our marriage that specifically pertain to you and your involvement," she said, sliding the papers across the table in his direction. "If you sign, you will be agreeing to allow me to use your name and release any detail about you and your past history that may have impacted or affected our marriage or had a hand in our divorce."

"And you actually expect me to agree to this? Naw, Naw," said Marti, shaking his head and thinking about what he had at stake. "You don't understand. I just got married. I'm happy. I can't be having you drudge that stuff up again."

"Marti, I'm not trying to complicate your life. The truth is, I need you to do this."

"You need me to do it? What's that about?"

"You have absolutely no idea the number of people I counsel who are on the verge of divorce because they're trying to compete with the past, which can take on the form of yet another personality or persona, for their spouse's affection. For those who are caught in this triangle, it's a never-ending battle."

"Okay, cut the psycho babble," demanded Marti. "I hated that even when we were married."

"Listen, people are affected by the choices they make in a partner, and it is that much harder to cope if that partner is still living in the past. Look what happened to our marriage. You, my friend, couldn't see past your father's mistakes and that inhibited you, even in your notions about having kids. George was always there, telling you what to do, what to think and dictating what you did, what you thought, how you responded, how you reacted. How could I compete with that?"

"But that was then, Carolyn. I've made my peace with the past. You just can't show up after five years and ask me to sign some papers so you can tell everybody about my life."

"Well, will you at least consider all the men and women this could help? This isn't about me trying to complicate your life. I'm glad things are going well for you," she said. "I just want to try to prevent others from spending the next ten years of their lives trying to make a marriage work that probably never should have been."

"Just let me think about it, alright?"

"Listen, I'm leaving town the day after tomorrow. Think it over; discuss it with your wife. I hope to hear something from you before I leave."

"Yeah, sure, I'll think about it," he said, rising from the booth.

Leslie was gone when Marti got back to the townhouse. She had left a note on the coffee table that she'd just run to the grocery store. Marti plopped on the sofa, tossing the document Carolyn had given him on the coffee table. She was asking a lot of him, but if it could help others, it might be worth what reservations he was now having and might still have when the book initially hit the bookstores and into the homes of thousands of strangers. Knowing that his story, their story had helped one of them would give him satisfaction. He then remembered once telling Sasha that she had to put things in perspective. For him, at that very moment, that meant also looking at things from a different perspective. Their divorce didn't have to be a negative in his life anymore. He had the opportunity now to change that. Something positive could come from his experiences, those he wanted so desperately to forget.

Marti heard the squeal of the front door as it opened. "Need some help, baby?" he uttered from the living room.

"Naw, I'm cool. I didn't get much, just a few things to tide us over for the next few days. So how was…you know?"

"Come in here when you finish. I'll tell you about it."

Leslie entered the living room with two plums in her hand, handing Marti one of them, as she joined him on the sofa. After noticing the document on the coffee table, she asked, "What's that?"

"That's what I wanted to talk to you about. Carolyn wrote a book about our marriage."

"You're kidding!"

"Nope. Those papers grant her the right to disclose things about me and my past—stuff about my father's suicide, about what went down between me and mama, about Donald, all of that. She said she wrote it to help people, to keep them from making the same mistakes we did."

"What's it called?"

Marti retrieved the papers from the table and read the title to her: *Why You Have to be Careful You're Marrying the Man and Not His Past.*

"Are you going to sign it?"

"I'm thinking about it. What if what I went through could help somebody? That's a good thing, right?" he asked her.

"Of course, it is. Well, whatever you decide, I support you, okay."

"Thanks, baby."

***

The next day Marti met Carolyn again; this time she was already seated at the same booth. Before he handed over the signed papers, Marti made his final attempt to assure himself that he was doing the right, "And you're sure you're not doing this to try to get back at me or something?"

Giving him one of her familiar looks, she answered, "Now, come on, we were married for eight years, you know me better than that. I don't regret our marriage. If anything, I'm a little contrite that it didn't work between us. You're a good man, Marti. You just came with a lot of baggage, and I tried to handle it from the viewpoint of a professional. I guess I should have been more of a wife to you. Anyway, thanks for this," she said, getting up from the table. "I'll send you a few autographed copies after publication. It's scheduled for release sometime in September."

Carolyn's vanishing act from the bar sealed the deal. He'd probably never see her again face-to-face. Before leaving, Marti walked up to the bar counter and took a seat. The bartender had his back turned when Marti got his attention and ordered a club soda with lime.

"Lady friend of yours?" asked the bartender while preparing Marti's order.

"Not quite. She was my ex."

"You look kinda down, pawtna. Wanna talk about it?" said the bartender, sliding Marti his drink then wiping down the counter.

"Let me ask you somethin', man."

"Yeah, shoot."

"You ever get the feeling that we aren't in control of anything, like we make decisions, but it's really not up to us to decide?" Marti stopped to sip his beverage.

The bartender nodded. "Sometimes I feel that way, but what's this really all about?"

"Man, all I wanted to do is start my life over," said Marti. "I just got remarried. I'm gonna be moving to a new city soon and starting a great new job. The life I once knew was dead to me. Then she pops up telling me that she's written some book about all the stuff I've been trying to forget for the past twenty years. See what I mean? Just when I think I've got a handle on things, something else takes over."

"Yeah, man, God works like that."

"I figured as much. I just wish He'd let a brotha know His plans ahead of time. Give a cat time to prepare, you know."

The bartender said, laughing, "Everything'll work out, man, you'll see." Those were words with which Marti had been all too familiar.

Marti then tilted his glass toward the bartender. "Cheers, man. Thanks for the talk," he said before heading home. After all, he had a beautiful new wife waiting for him there.

Marti

Epilogue

Having postponed the honeymoon till later, the newlyweds spent their second week parting with old friends and bidding adieu to loved ones they were leaving behind. The first on their agenda was a visit to East Baton Rouge Parish Prison to say their good-byes to Donald.

Giving his brother a final embrace before venturing off into unchartered territory with his new bride, Marti said into his younger brother's ear, "Alright, man, you take care and keep the faith. I have a feeling you're gonna be out of this joint a lot sooner than you think."

"I hope so, man."

"It's gonna happen, mark my words."

With their cars loaded with as much stuff as they could possibly carry and a moving truck trailing them, Marti and Leslie were off to Dallas, Texas, hoping to add to their already blessed lives as much bliss as any two people could possibly have.

The two settled into a three bedroom apartment in DeSoto, just outside of Dallas, but close to Leslie's mother. Finding it stir crazy at first, the two soon adjusted to the bumper-to-bumper chaos of early morning traffic. Everybody was either coming or going, including the two of them. Twenty to eight, Marti headed in the opposite direction to Carter High to teach Geography II to tenth graders while Leslie had a forty-minute commute, which usually included a hot cup of coffee, to downtown Dallas to teach accelerated English at Townview.

Things had certainly come together, and it was a wonder why they had ever waited so long to start their life together. When they joined The Potter's House under the leadership of T. D. Jakes, soon even that question was answered. On one of the couple's cruises, which Marti and Leslie took also as their honeymoon trip, they learned that sometimes it was all about timing—God's timing, confirming for them what they already believed about the history of their relationship.

A month after Carolyn's book released in September, it made *The New York Times* Best Seller List. Marti was contacted for an interview, but refused. The fact that the book was about their marriage was enough involvement for him.

For Leslie's thirty-fifth birthday on November 8th, Marti presented his wife with yet another little black box, this time inside was a key.

"What's this?"

"Guess."

"Don't tell me it's the key to your heart?"

"Naw, quit playing. This is serious."

"I don't know what it could be to, Marti. Just tell me."

"Look out the window."

"What's out the window?"

"Just look."

Leslie hurried to the window to find parked out in the driveway a brand spanking new silver 2005 Toyota Camry. "She looked back at Marti as if hoping he'd offer some explanation. She just couldn't believe it was sitting out there."

"It was time, baby—that's all, and I wanted you to have a sweet new ride for work. All I have to go is up the street, but you have to tackle that bumper-to-bumper traffic heading into downtown. So you like it?"

All bubbly like a school girl, Leslie lunged toward Marti and threw her arms around his neck. "I love it!" she said between kisses. "I love it! I love it! I love it!"

"Happy Birthday, baby."

The couple celebrated their one-year anniversary in style at SoHo Food and Jazz in Addison, Texas. Raising his glass of club soda, Marti toasted the two of them. "Here's to one year and many, many, many more," he said, leaning over to kiss his wife's soft lips before making his way up on stage. As a surprise, he had arranged to have his Jazz ensemble serenade the lovely Leslie with a piece that he had written entitled "Her Many Faces." That night, however, Leslie wore only one face, the face of a woman in love with her husband, as apparent from the glimmer of her deep brown eyes and those three words she mouthed to him from her seat: "I love you."

Later that year, Marti went into the studio to record "Her Many Faces" as his first single, and as a further tribute to his wife, included a black and white photo spread of Leslie and her many expressions on the inside of the fold-out jacket cover. Yes, *life was good* and there was *nothing* wrong with that.

Also by Tonya Snow-Cook

NOVELS

Marti

POETRY

Wandering Places

SHORT STORIES

Perfect Timing

TOY OBSESSION SERIES

Cynthia Kessler (Book 1)

Amanda Reynolds (Book 2)

Asher Kessler (Book 3)

Marti

Tonya Snow-Cook

www.ingramcontent.com/pod-product-compliance
Lightning Source LLC
Chambersburg PA
CBHW030030030726
47500CB00001B/34